THE INVISIBLE
CITY

ALMA BOOKS LTD
London House
243–253 Lower Mortlake Road
Richmond
Surrey TW9 2LL
United Kingdom
www.almabooks.com

The Invisible City first published in Catalan as *La ciutat invisible* in 2005
First published in English by Alma Books Ltd by in 2009

Reprinted 2011

Copyright © Emili Rosales, 2005
English translation © Martha Tennent, 2009

The translation of this work was supported by a grant from the
Institut Ramon Llull

Emili Rosales asserts his moral right to be identified as the author of this work in
accordance with the Copyright, Designs and Patents Act 1988

Printed in Great Britain by CPI Antony Rowe, Chippenham, Wiltshire

ISBN: 978-1-84688-090-2

THE INVISIBLE CITY

EMILI ROSALES

Translated by Martha Tennent

ALMA BOOKS

1

I hadn't given another thought to the Invisible City. Or perhaps I had in my dreams.

But then, a few weeks ago, I received an envelope with no return address containing a lengthy manuscript written in an elegant script of sinuous letters, a succession of staffs and loops. It immediately drew my attention. I am not accustomed to reading calligraphy, but after a first, slow perusal of the document I discovered that it was a journal by an eighteenth-century architect, someone by the name of Andrea Roselli. It was written in Italian and began with the heading: *Memoirs of the Invisible City*. I couldn't be certain that the title was written by the same hand as the text. Good Lord, the Invisible City! Quick as a flash, the name ploughed through my memory, and I recalled the first time I had heard those words, many years ago.

We used to play at the old quarry – an open, colossal pit that perched on a hill in the Montsià Mountains and reluctantly emptied into the sea, down by the bay. We would race through the rocks and dirt canals, dwarfed by the size of the quarry, stopping when we came across basins of damp, greenish mud, where we gathered clay and fashioned figures with wild grimaces. Sometimes one of the group would slip and fall into the mud and his coat would turn a rusty colour.

Then someone would shout:

"We've found another entrance to the Invisible City."

"No! These are the rocks they were going to use to build the Invisible City, but instead they threw them in the sea. That's when they built the port."

"That's a lie! The Invisible City exists. My brother told me that some friends of friends discovered it: it's under the town. A tunnel leads from the Palau del Canal to the square, and another—"

"Rubbish!"

"You idiot!" And a ball of mud would be aimed at the sceptic. Yet in this way things returned to their course, the group once again on friendly terms.

"The schoolmaster showed me the plan of the Invisible City," the pharmacist's son blurted out in a low voice, his glasses greasy, lopsided like the scales we saw at the fair every year.

When I got home, I repeated the news to my grandfather, who glanced up from his football pools long enough to announce:

"If you mention the Invisible City one more time, no more playing with these friends of yours. Wasn't what happened at the canal enough for you?"

I never again spoke of the Invisible City at home, but our group continued to uncover evidence of its existence, or its disappearance. With time I came to realize that what we lose still exists, whether that be cities, lovers or parents.

One day, disobeying family rules, we headed south along the beach, and after quite a while we reached the rocks and grottoes. We combed the area beneath the finger-like fronds of the palm grove, and behind the dancing leaves of a fig tree we discovered the mouth of a cave. We could only make our way a few dozen metres into it, but that was proof enough that we had stumbled across another passage leading out of the Invisible City. This gallery must have linked the beach to the Casa de l'Hort del Rei, the House of the King's Orchard, which was never actually built. Or perhaps it was destroyed, who knows? It all happened during the King's reign, a time wrapped in obscurity.

The passage must have also led to the Palau del Canal, where Jonàs and I made our great discovery: the Invisible City! We had crossed the canal that divided the fishermen's neighbourhood from the rice fields and then ventured further, walking between the white limestone walls and pale-orange tiles that separated the fields. The high walls were Cyclopses, or perhaps we were dwarfs. We followed the edge of the canal until we reached a spot covered by grass and cane where the terrain bulged and cleaved. Branches emerged from the crevices – fig, palm, agave – that had to be moved aside in order to squeeze our way into the belly of the earth. Trees had shattered the arched roof of a storehouse that had been built parallel to the canal and was now hidden by dense undergrowth. Once inside, we discovered metre after metre of impenetrable silence with only faint traces of light filtering through the foliage above.

Our discovery and the mystery enveloping it resonated among our friends. Rumours of the Invisible City spread.

One by one, Jonàs and I began to lead a few privileged friends to our den of extraordinary proportions, the amazing, abandoned nave. The legend grew: during the war planes were assembled and hidden here; not so, said another: the ships that set sail for America were built here; yet another: the endless passages connecting the main sections of the Invisible City started here.

These subterranean galleries lay at the foot of the equally ruinous and forgotten Customs House, the elegant neoclassical building which presided over the area: the beautiful image of a dream that was thwarted before it could be realized. We played among the ruins of a dream.

On rainy days when it was impossible to play football on the street, a select few of us would race to the Invisible City, where our screams and the sound of the ball ricocheting off the walls and columns echoed in the half-darkness creating a wild, cavernous scene. At times, when we had exhausted the afternoon and needed to get home quickly, we would untie a fisherman's boat that was docked nearby, the whole troupe would pile in and we would glide down the canal, speechless with fatigue. When we reached the sea and the shallow waters of the bay, we would hide the boat among the canes, assuming that sooner or later the fisherman would discover it.

One day, however, the owner was on the lookout and caught us in the act. Our families were alarmed and began to investigate, and our secret was disclosed. From then on we were forbidden to go anywhere near the Palau del Canal, and our brotherhood lost its identity, its flame extinguished. The aura of mystery remained: we had only to pronounce the enchanted words and the provocative, menacing shape appeared in our minds. The Palau del Canal. The Invisible City.

Why did we stop exploring? Why didn't the schoolmaster show us the map that the pharmacist's son said he'd seen? Why were the adults silent, why did they silence us? Inevitably time follows its course and the change in generation occurs. The moment arrives when the days that had once been ruled by fear, uneasiness and pleasure vanish, transported to the territory of dreams. Where they remain.

As an adolescent, the memories would only resurface while I was swimming. As I did my laps in the sea I would make plans to return and explore the remains of the Invisible City, but as soon as I left the water, I would forget, or just let it drop, embarrassed at the idea of continuing with my childhood games.

From time to time, my grandfather himself or my mother or aunts, even a teacher – all having warned us not to visit the quarry or the Palau del Canal silos or the distant bay – would murmur, "Of course, the King's Orchard," "Right, the King's Beach," "Down by the King's House." It was almost a litany, as if they were using words they did not understand themselves, words whose meanings they had forgotten years before. What king, what city, if ours was a coastal town filled with life but excluded from all the great events of history, with no trace of its past? We seemed more a town that had always been without a king, without a thing.

* * *

A few years later as we stood in the bright, freezing school corridor – the sound of the howling wind whipping through the trees, blending with the clamour of youth – Armand Coll burst out laughing when I suddenly spoke of the Invisible City.

I had met Armand the day I arrived at boarding school. I was twelve years old, and my grandfather and my mother had just dropped me off at the door of a stern edifice that resembled El Escorial. The school was set on one of the hills that surrounded Tortosa, the regional capital and episcopal see, far from the familiar streets of my town – which I would now visit only on the weekends – further still from the Invisible City, the banished giant of my childhood. I stood alone in the quiet afternoon under a ravenous sky. Fortunately, I did not know then what a young boy could not possibly know: that he will grow up, acquire new friends and play football, learn the periodic table of elements and Latin declensions, travel and fall in love. But the new experiences would not safeguard him from the danger of being forever alone, of waking up on a stormy night in an unknown city, a young body lying a few centimetres away, and realize that he is in fact alone – and he will remember finding himself abandoned before the school door one late-summer afternoon.

On that September day – the sky streaked with reddish clouds that announced a wind from the mountain – as I stood before the impenetrable building, making an effort to seem natural, trying my best not to know what I should not know at that age, Armand Coll strode past, bouncing a basketball. He didn't seem to be aware of my presence and was almost out of sight when he stopped, held the ball a moment, bounced it once and threw it furiously at me, pointing to the basket.

"Come on, I challenge you to a game of twenty-one!" he shouted in a manner that suggested that he would not take no for an answer. Basketball was only just beginning to be popular at home – "twenty-one" I'd never heard of. Both were incomprehensible to me.

Coll became my guide through this palace of Cartesian architecture, which offered the empty solemnity of great pavilions. He was older than me – a student of what was called the "Minor Seminary", an institution located in the same building as the school – and, as such, he had the authority to spare me the consequences of some of the bullying which was so frequent in boarding school.

On one occasion, some classmates and I climbed into the attic under the gable, above the room where thirty sleeping boys would come to life as soon as the lights were switched off. We had sneaked out to conduct an experiment in combustibility: we were going to set fire to the gas from an aerosol insecticide. The flame lit up our faces, making them wonderfully strange. Everything went well until one of the boys carelessly stepped on the wattle-and-daub false ceiling of the dormitory, rather than on a solid joist, and was on the verge of taking the direct route to the floor beneath. A huge commotion ensued. I still recall confessing, one by one, all the details of our rebellion as we were summoned to the teachers' room.

That was before we had reached the extreme of dangling the most brilliant classmate out of the second-floor window. The boy was from Valencia and knew every detail of Hannibal's journey with his elephants across the Alps, almost to the gates of Rome; the precise causes of the collapse of the Napoleonic army after the incredible Battle of Borodino at the outskirts of Moscow; all the circumstances of the violent skirmishes in the Spanish Carlist Wars. Perhaps that was why we called him the *Tigre del Maestrat* – the Tiger of the Maestrat region of Valencia – despite the fact that he was gentle and good-natured. The Headmaster was giving a Chemistry exam in the classroom on the lower floor that day when suddenly he glimpsed the Tiger hanging upside down, waving his arms uncontrollably, yelling all manner of curses, blasphemies and threats. Tiger abruptly grew silent as he confronted, in decidedly unfavourable conditions, the Headmaster's frightened, menacing eye. Just as we managed to pull him back into the room, ashen and cured of his cursing, the door burst open and the shouting, shaking Headmaster, the school's highest authority, appeared, first scarlet with anger, then on the verge of collapse.

Had it not been for Armand's pacifying intervention, I doubt if we would have survived that one. It must have been around that time when, out of the blue, I mentioned the Invisible City of my childhood games.

"Your Invisible City, or the part you haven't invented, is one of the few remaining vestiges of the Royal City of Charles III, which is Sant Carles. La Ràpita, as you call it. Sant Carles de la Ràpita!" Armand Coll exclaimed as he laughed.

"The King, of course. But what does that have to do with it?"

"One of the mysteries of history. It's as if we can only see a few scattered tiles in an immense mosaic. That's all that remains, the rest is mere speculation. Fertile ground for the imagination!"

"I don't know what you're talking about, but maybe it has something to do with the Invisible City."

Armand laughed, as he always did, at my insolence; I played at being more ignorant than I was, and he at knowing more than he did. His explanations filled me with excitement, and we wandered away from the raucous schoolmates. Without my realizing we entered the Seminary area, which was off limits to young students like me. Armand didn't seem to notice either, not even when other seminarians greeted him and gave me a puzzled look. We reached his studio, heated by a stove, where he had a burner to heat milk or water for tea.

Armand began examining the volumes of his encyclopedia, searching for information about the eighteenth century, the Enlightenment, the reign of Charles III, his minister Floridablanca, the architect and engineer Sabatini. He would look for a page, then read it to me out loud, or hand me a book opened at a particular entry while he tried to locate another. After a while, he began to speak as if he were one of those books.

"In short: two hundred years ago, Charles III arrived from Naples, where he had reigned... having inherited the land from his mother, Elisabeth Farnese... became King of Spain when his brother Ferdinand VI died, organized an ambitious plan of public works throughout Spanish territory – another aspect of his enlightened project. Some of his works were carried out, others got lost along the way, including the construction of a new city at the mouth of the Ebro River that was intended to promote the development of the area of Spain irrigated by the river, and encourage commerce between this region – previously closed to trade – and America. For all of these reasons and more, he needed to build a canal that would connect the Ebro to the sea in a controlled fashion."

"And what happened?"

"Just what I was telling you. Sant Carles de la Ràpita constitutes a mystery within the failed projects of the Enlightenment. It was first designed to be a grand, new city, but at some point the project came to a halt, no one knows exactly why, and what was not yet a reality soon became a pile of ruins. These are the ruins where you and your friends played and scattered pigeons. Very little remains: a few urban traces of one part of the town; the enormous porticoed square along the lines of the Royal Seat of Aranjuez – just to give you an idea of the grandiose dimensions of the project – the canal which apparently never really got under way, the buildings by the port, the New Church, the magnificent, unfinished neoclassical temple…"

"So, you're saying the Invisible City exists, we didn't invent much of it?" I said, not certain if I was comforted or disillusioned. I felt almost as if I'd been awakened from an enchantment.

"The surprising thing is that there's really no collective memory of what happened," Armand explained. "If you think about it, we're only talking about your great-grandparents' great-grandparents. It's absurd that no recollection exists among the townspeople, not even a distorted, transformed version of the events."

I mentioned the hushed comments the adults made when we children were told to leave: the King's Orchard, the King's House, the Palau del Canal, the King's Beach.

"That might be a clue, but I'm not sure. The unskilled workers who stayed on after the plans were abandoned were the least informed. The architects, delegates, engineers, the ones in charge of the project, they all left. So, what remains is some sort of mythical echo, or not even that, a collection of terms that have lost their meaning."

Boarding students were not allowed to leave school during the week other than for exceptional reasons, but a couple of times a month Armand managed to get permission to take me to the city where we would visit a philatelist as he searched for stamps for his impressive collection. One day we pushed open the shop's door and, as usual, heard the bell ring. It was a pleasant place of carpeted floors, light walls, wooden cupboards. When the philatelist saw us, he slipped his glasses down on his nose while the lithe, beautiful figure of his daughter disappeared like a frightened deer into the room behind him. The atmosphere was electric, expectant, filled with the girl's perfume. With his shiny tweezers the philatelist picked up the stamps Armand had ordered and placed them in an onionskin envelope, then gave me a cunning look as he said:

"Did you know I have a plan of the Invisible City?"

13

I gave a start.

"Your friend says that's the name you give to the Sant Carles ruins. Would you like to see it?"

Without waiting for a response, he disappeared and returned a moment later with an enormous folder. He untied the ribbons that bound it and opened it flat on the counter. I immediately recognized the outline of the Bay of Alfacs and the Banya peninsula. The gentleman began to point to other places on the paper, offering explanations about them: the outline for the Navigation Canal from the river to the site of the future city; the defence battery by the port; the large, horseshoe-shaped square. At this point the girl reappeared from the rear room, her hair now pulled back, porcelain-white skin, moist eyes, large pink lips – the colour of a fingernail – a rather arrogant stride. The bell rang as she slipped out into the street, leaving me engulfed in her lemon perfume, distressed by my inability to ask her name or make myself visible. It was as if the entire world had quietly marched by without taking the slightest notice of me.

When I recovered my senses, the gentleman had put on his glasses again and was closing the folder that held the map of my dreams, the map of the impossible. He gave me a tetchy glance and I caught a name, one I had never heard before, one the seminarian didn't seem to think important to our research, for he never mentioned it again. Tiepolo. Giambattista Tiepolo.

That was all. I never returned, and the stamp-dealer's shop closed several years ago. I never again caught sight of the girl who perhaps exists somewhere today, perhaps still preserves the beauty that took my breath away. Or maybe not. At that point, Ariadna had not yet appeared in my life.

In the meantime, my conversations with Armand revived my interest in the Invisible City, but in a way quite different from my childish fascination. It was almost the opposite now. As a child I had visited the Invisible City, shouted as I raced through it, possessed it. Now I approached it from a distance, making elliptical circles around it as if I were a satellite orbiting an unknown planet. I read articles and books that recreated the political, cultural, artistic moment in which the idea of founding the city and constructing it out of nothing was conceived. I looked for precedents and similar accounts. I tried to analyse why this place was chosen and not another. I studied the characters that would have intervened, searched for references in the field of historiography.

Tiger, too – having recovered from the window incident – participated in my exalted interest, overjoyed, actually, to discover that he wasn't the only one swept away by historical concerns. I can remember him during our last year together at school, the two of us walking outside in the rough garden, beneath the enveloping sky that beckoned us on to the pressing, unfamiliar future that was university life. Tiger – with a cigarette hanging from his lips, sunken chest, jutting jaws, his short-sighted eyes hidden behind thick, square glasses – enthused as he explained the Esquilache Riots, the Anglo-Spanish experiences in Menorca, the exceptional figure of the Peruvian Pablo de Olavide. But something strange happened: everything that appeared in books or through explanations provided by Armand or Tiger was extremely eloquent, until we drew near the concrete issue of Sant Carles. At that point everything turned to paralysis, mirage, a dearth of documents or information, historical silence. I can only assume that, confronted by the impasse, my interest in the subject continually frustrated, I gradually washed my hands of the issue, distancing myself from it all. Or perhaps it was just that other matters struck my fancy and absorbed my time, my mind.

I am reminded now of something Tiger asked me during one of our last nocturnal strolls, always the perfect scenario for shared confidences. The question was left hanging, like a flash of lightning seen on a calm night and immediately forgotten: "Have you never wanted to discover who your father was?"

But that was much later. From the day I met Armand by the school door, he became the older brother I had never had. With him beside me, I discovered a means of channelling the turmoil of adolescence: the early-morning sun lighting the sea as it rose, a silent valley overrun by pine trees, the summit of a mountain reached after a six-hour hike, the force of a river racing through your legs and stomach as you cross it, the communal song that rises on a star-studded night. I am fish, I am fowl, I am gazelle. I am son of the wind, son of God. Armand was at my side throughout the exalted energy of my adolescence. He offered me protection, made it possible for me to experience a familial warmth denied me by the icy walls of the high-perched school, whose thousand windows would rattle when the north-westerly mistral wind wailed disconsolately in the night.

That was the paradox. At home, in town, I never knew the warmth of a family. It is true that I was accustomed to the tenderness of my aunts, the affection of my neighbours, was always surrounded by women offering me *cócs de brossat*, baked sweet potatoes or pomegranates with sugar, yet it seemed as if they had organized a silent conspiracy to keep me from realizing what had happened. My mother responded to any question of mine with a list of interminable instructions, giving the impression that it was always urgent to finish a particular task, after which another would arise, or the day would draw to an end. The hour never arrived when one could stop and consider if something better might be done, or even if it were possible simply to do nothing, possible to contemplate the clouds or your son's face as he gazes at you. My grandfather's presence on this earth seemed to be exclusively justified by his mission to set the norms of our existence, almost without the need to utter them, norms that could be summarized as follows: things are as they are and must continue as they are. In any event, none of the people who surrounded me were in any hurry to divulge the cause of their silence, their coldness, their sternness – and when they did, I no longer needed it.

Many years before – as many as I was old – at the end of August one surprisingly rainy summer, my mother fainted behind the counter of the family wine shop, where she had been helping her father, after an illness had suddenly taken her mother's life. She was just beginning her secondary education, something that would remain beyond her grasp for ever. This was a time when families in the village were constantly concerned that their unmarried daughters would get pregnant. In this case, the family consisted of father and daughter, and they decided to wall themselves in and bear the stigma alone. Apparently, it was impossible to locate the passing man who had danced with the girl on the beach one August night. Was he French? Perhaps Belgian? I finally got the gist of the story, although shrouded in vagueness. Never uttering one word louder than the other, I grew up beneath the admonishing eye of my grandfather and the shattering silence of my mother. Withered, sad and pensive, she would run her hand affectionately through my hair on Monday mornings as I headed to the bus that would drive me to school, along the thirty kilometres that separated the village from the county capital. I spent the five days every week longing for the smell of the neighbourhood, the noisy streets, the lights at the harbour.

Many years later, I found myself living in Barcelona, trying to reconcile my freedom with the study of humanities – something that was to delay my career in the world of art. During this period my usually desolate inner self alternated between being briefly engaged and unengaged, though at times it was totally subjugated. One day, I received a phone call from my former headmaster, Father Patrici, the one who had glimpsed Tiger's body dangling at the window. I had stayed in touch with him through Armand. He was urging me to return to Tortosa.

"Your mother is very ill, and I think you have a right to certain information. I'm referring to the person who paid for your schooling. I know she hasn't discussed this with you, and I don't know how to explain it to you, but I don't want to keep this from you and then have regrets when it's too late for you to speak to her."

"Well, I suppose it was my mother who paid, or maybe grandfather. It's all the same."

"No. That's what I think you should know."

I remained lost in thought when Father Patrici paused, but could not guess what he was about to say.

"Emili. Emili Rossell, someone else paid for your studies. Someone who was not your mother or your grandfather."

"Who was it?"

"I'm sorry. That's all I know. She's the one who will have to clarify this, but I think it might be important to you."

But my mother did not live long enough to explain if I had had a French or Belgian father who had undertaken to pay for my schooling. I didn't dare torment her with the matter as I accompanied her during the last days of her squalid life of self-denial, the life she had chosen – it seemed to me – of hardship and contrition. When we embraced for the last time, I wished intensely that things might have been otherwise, and swore at the same time to bury the troubling story that no longer belonged to me. I swore that I would move far away.

It's surprising that I have been able to live so long without understanding my mother's behaviour, my grandfather's attitude, but even more surprising is the conscientious effort I made not to recognize the motives behind their behaviour, what led them to be the people they were. Something was telling me that it was better to distance myself from that poisoned chalice, better not to know, not to be concerned, not to let myself get trapped. Too many shadows, too much silence and oppression to venture into, with little guarantee that I could emerge unscathed.

One thing was clear: both my mother and grandfather had been trampled by a power stronger than themselves, something tragic and invincible. I drew the crucial and desperate conclusion that the further I was from this black hole, the greater my possibilities of leading a free, full life, capable of embracing the world rather than fearing it. But is it ever really possible to escape?

To follow now the threads of *Memoirs of the Invisible City* could mean opening wide the doors to my demons, but I do so convinced that these represent my own labyrinth and that the time has arrived to take that risk. My curiosity has also been aroused by a strange coincidence: the document by the Italian architect reached me a few weeks ago, about the time that my old friend Sofia Mendizábal paid an unexpected visit to my art gallery in the Gothic Quarter of Barcelona.

I suspect that the slightly cross-eyed glance the woman gave me as she entered my office brought with it the realization that the moment had arrived. It had been many years since Sofia Mendizábal had focused her eyes on me, those subtly mischievous eyes that gave her a seductive, hypnotic air.

Sofia, with her sardonic half-smile, positioned herself at my office door, her hands on her hips, a mock attitude of defiance that no longer affects me, though I admit that I still find it intriguing. What could have caused Sofia to appear now, after so many years of only exchanging the slightest of courtesies?

Knowing that Sofia doesn't usually want what she pretends to, I initially believed her reply a mere pretext: she had come seeking my advice about opening an art gallery in Barcelona. She was backtracking. Fifteen years before she had been on the verge of carrying out a similar project. She was the one who introduced me into the city's art circles, but then she left town and moved to the Ebro delta – a migration in the opposite direction from mine – where she married and started an extremely prosperous real-estate business.

Despite the fact that I didn't believe a word of what she said, I kept up with Sofia during the following weeks. She never ceased to amaze me: not only did she carry out her proposal for the gallery – following my advice in general – but she made a huge economic investment and showed tremendous artistic ambition. This raised considerable expectations and suspicions in a city accustomed to the comfort of familiar faces. Sofia had told the truth, the question was *why* she had spoken at that precise moment, and why to me. I realized then that the moment had arrived.

Every year I plan to spend the summer just south of the Ebro River, in the house which I bought on the Bay of Alfacs, having sold my mother's place when she died. I toy with the idea, roll it around in my mind as the winter months pass and warm weather approaches, but when the moment arrives for making a decision, I rush to find a better alternative. I finally choose a holiday quite different from what I had planned: instead of dropping anchor, I move further away. The right moment had not presented itself. My summer visits to the region are often limited to a couple of days – similar to the quick ones I pay all through the winter – just long enough to prove to myself that the house continues to exist and that I have no time to renew old friendships, as I'm pressed to return to Barcelona, to get back to the art gallery that requires my attention.

These last few weeks, however, have provided sufficient reasons to suggest that I should disregard my abstruse reluctance to return. The old, always ignored appeal of familiar places and people had resurfaced, and I felt the strong stirrings of curiosity. Perhaps it was just impatience. No matter how well-braided the rope of the years appears to be, its knots well tied, strands tightly woven, there is no denying that the fibres grow frayed, the ends unravel in their attempt to be free. The years that should have strengthened the rigging have suppressed all the mornings of broken promises, the afternoons of curtailed friendships, the nights of a nameless father, the evenings of a city discovered, then reburied.

The time has come to test the ropes. As long as there is wine to be drunk, no doubt it will flow freely at the party given by the wealthy, influential and still beautiful Sofia Mendizábal and her husband Jonàs. My dear friend Armand Coll will also be there, the fashionable politician of the moment who insisted that I could not miss the occasion, *the* social event of the summer. Everyone who wishes to be anyone will be there.

We will all be there, representing what we are today and what we were ten or twenty years ago. I am going primarily because my intuition tells me that among this swarm of people I will discover the origin of the anonymous package that has led me back to the Invisible City, a vision I had not contemplated for years, except perhaps in my dreams.

2

Naples

From Memoirs of the Invisible City

Giambattista has taken the opportunity to inform me that now is the moment to redact the history of my travels, the account of my adventures, the experiences that have left an impression on me. To my objection that he has never done the same, he answers convincingly that though the thought does trouble him, his hour is past, while there is still time for me. "You, Master Tiepolo, have written on canvases and vaults and, as such, you should in truth find consolation." Giambattista momentarily abandons his melancholy and with glistening eyes replies, "Of course, of course, Andrea, as you will do with your buildings. But these oil paintings and frescoes that are scattered throughout Europe, works I will never see again, are not entirely mine. By that I mean: I have not been wholly able to say what I wished, as you will not wholly be able to state what you wish in the palaces and churches you build."

This history commences in Naples some ten years ago, the ten years that my lord, King Charles, has ruled in Spain. He has undertaken many prodigious endeavours during this time, but one of his great achievements is the Italianization of Spanish cities. He has brought Naples to the Iberian Peninsula, brought the Mediterranean to the centre of the high plain at Madrid. His wife, the melancholy Doña Amalia, arrived in the rank, dark, ill-smelling city that was the capital of a pale Spanish empire, far from the elegance and ample scale of the Palazzo Reale of Naples and the bright Portici. Here she withered and pined away for her beloved city. How little does the small town that she first encountered resemble the city that today boasts the Paseo del Prado, the Museum of Science, the new Puerta de Alcalá. In spite of the newly established grandeur of Madrid and the hurriedly finished Royal Palace, Charles III fled from the city and from the riots that led to the downfall of the Marquis of Esquilache. The King greatly preferred Aranjuez, El Escorial and La Granja to Madrid; not simply because he could more easily indulge his fancy for the daily hunts, but most especially because the town was far away.

Charles III of Spain and the Indies made of Madrid a new city, yet the King dislikes Madrid. Nothing he has built can give him back the pleasure of life in Naples. He comes to this realization as he recalls his morning strolls along the coastal slopes of the Palazzo Reale above the Bay of Naples. With the first light of dawn he would glimpse the silhouettes on the horizon as they slowly emerge from the waters and acquire substance. At noontide the Capri protuberance and the Sorrento coast become visible; towards the Levant, the bluish silhouette of the menacing Mount Vesuvius; to the west, beyond Castel dell'Ovo, the cliffs of Posillipo. Ischia completes the curve of the Bay. During the last period of Charles's Neapolitan reign – a time of peace – the bay would be filled with sailing boats, the port bustling with activity, the city on the watch for news that reached them by land or sea. Naples had no rival in the Mediterranean.

Perhaps my portrayal will seem idealized, for Naples was also – like every other place – a city of plague and filth, thieves and tragedies, but the image of the capital of the Two Sicilies that I will always guard is the one I contemplated when I had not yet lived there for a year. The bay lay before me, filled with emblazoned ships bidding farewell to their king on that morning of 1759 as he set sail for Spain. I was beset by doubts and regrets. The entire city was a fête, albeit a sad one, as it paid its tribute to a king who had changed the course of its history and re-established an independent kingdom, raising it up from the prostration caused by centuries of foreign domination. It is true that Charles had become King through the habitual bargaining between Italian and European powers, but for more than two decades he had been King of Naples, not merely the envoy of an emperor foreign to the country.

I could sense in my own person the joy that raced through the streets, the colours that invaded port and bay, the abundant wine, the shameless glances of wenches. My own regret and uncertainty only increased, for with the departure of the King, the circumstances that had induced me to come to Naples could well suffer a reversal.

Ten years ago I was but twenty and had arrived in the Vesuvian city with considerable anticipation to work alongside one of the most venerable architects in all the kingdoms of Italy. Having satisfactorily concluded my studies of architecture in Rome, whence I had ventured from my native Arezzo, the moment drew near when I should commence my true apprenticeship under Luigi Vanvitelli. I was to collaborate in the construction of what was considered at that time the greatest undertaking in Europe: the Caserta Palace. The Bourbon King Charles had commissioned the construction only after devoting much thought to the endeavour. Even the choice of Vanvitelli, my master, was the result of shrewd negotiations with the Pontifical State, from whom Charles sought a papal benediction.

Caserta was much more than a palace: it was an ambitious urban and political project. Beautiful Naples was also crowded, asphyxiating Naples; the King thus planned his palace twenty miles from the town centre, far from the bustling capital, safer by reason of its distance from the coast, a fact that would also encourage the city's expansion. When I joined the project, Caserta was no longer a mere dream. Construction was well under way, advancing quickly with hundreds of well-guarded labourers – free men and forced. The work was carried out by building workmen, supervised by specialists, equipped with extraordinary scaffolding and machinery, aided by horses and camels – elephants even – that facilitated the transport of rock and marble. Caserta was a swarm of bees, and the building proceeded under Vanvitelli's demanding control and the monarch's delighted eye. Could I wish for a more advantageous baptism?

As I approached Caserta for the first time, passing through orchards of orange trees, from a distance I had a glimpse of what the palace would become: a magnificent edifice, a rectangular plan with four inner courts created by two intersecting pavilions. The harmony and grandeur of the palace were visible from many leagues away. The soft colours of the façade, tiles, stone columns, balustrades, friezes, etc., rather than overwhelming you with a sense of the building's monumentality, have a calming effect. Luigi Vanvitelli has managed to create the impression of human proportion in a building where everything is prodigious. The monarch's desire to erect a triumphant statement of his power would have daunted the intelligence of the best of architects. Though inspired in part by the magnificence of Versailles – the palace built by the King's grandfather – Caserta seeks rather the majesty of Bernini's sensibility, coupled with a vague recollection of Palladio.

When the work is finished, the gardens reaching as far as the mountains, the monumental avenue leading all the way into Naples, Caserta will create an unequalled effect. It will be the geometric centre of a world where reason and order reign.

Vanvitelli, however, never ceased to speak of the staircase, the masterpiece that will bring glory to his name and that of the Bourbon King Charles. Once you have passed through the entrance, a gallery connects the straight line of the avenue with the straight line of the future park. The four inner courts will lead from the vestibule located at the centre of this impressive perspective. The main staircase ascends from this focal point. Looking down from the first floor, the spectator will observe the arches of the first and second vestibule, as if a phantasmagoria of stone were brought to life by the geometric play of the columns and the careful, obsessive choice of colours for the marble.

I cannot fail to remember the edifice in all its magnificent detail now that I am in Madrid and frequently find myself at the Royal Palace, the worthy but lesser imitation erected by Sabatini, Vanvitelli's disciple. Ten years have passed, yet the geometry of Caserta still serves to orient me on the labyrinthine paths that lead to the tumultuous region where my soul dwells. At Caserta, amidst the scent of orange blossoms and perfume of lemon trees, Cecilia Vanvitelli was but a child. In Madrid today she is a woman, today she is Cecilia Sabatini. His Majesty announced to me in Naples and Pompeii that he had taken notice of me, Andrea Roselli, the humble architect from Arezzo who dreams now the same dream as his king. A city, a woman, a king can at times seem equally fickle, fragile and inaccessible.

In Naples I lived in a continuous state of exhilaration as I participated in Vanvitelli's undertaking. I felt myself engaged in a project that would last for all time. I spent my days and nights obsessed with the building of the Palace of Caserta. One thing alone did I prefer: Portici, the seaside *reggia*. From time to time I accompanied Vanvitelli there to wait upon His Majesty. If we seek to encounter a human scale, that would be Portici. Here a new passion had arisen amongst noble families: the wish to live beyond the confines of the city, between the sea and Vesuvius, quite forgetting that the mountain was alive. Danger stirs passion; it is almost as if we need to devour the beauty of the world before it disappears. Or we can create it: herein lies the spirit of the Neapolitans.

Close to Pompeii and Herculaneum, I find myself reflecting that the recently commenced archaeological work will permit the ideal world to be restored to us, shown as it actually was, the world that we have studied, imagined and yearned for. The excavations, enthusiastically funded by the King, have confirmed the dramatic account by Pliny the Younger: the torrent of ash that buried the city.

I paused for a long while to regard the sky after noting whole houses that remain intact, preserved beneath the ashes as they stood on a morning one thousand seven hundred years ago. It is one thing to retain your faith, quite another to retain it in Pompeii. Will anyone contemplate my house in this same fashion, one thousand seven hundred years from now? Where will I be when strangers take possession of doors and walls, beams and furniture, as they observe the site of my agony and murmur, "Here lived a man"? I believe firmly in what we construct with our minds and raise with our hands, in the determination of a few to guide the effort of the many to prevail over the past and the catastrophes of nature.

My parents died in Arezzo when I was very young. Their countenances are lost to me, but I carry with me always that of my uncle, who raised me, funded my studies and travels. In some affairs our intervention is ineffectual; in others we have the capacity to transform life and the face of this earth. This is what interests me.

On one of my summer evenings in Pompeii, I separated myself from the group that was visiting the excavations and wandered through the houses that were beginning to emerge among the hillocks and vines. How great was my dismay; I had lost my way when a cat caught my attention as it clambered out from behind a parapet. I drew nearer the knoll and was dazzled when I confronted on the opposite side of the wall one of those miracles that can occur in Pompeii.

The wall displayed an almost intact fresco, or rather a portion of a painting no larger than two spans of my hand. From beneath the vegetation and rocky ground, the gracile figure of a girl had been uncovered. She wore a pale-coloured robe and appeared to be rehearsing a dance or salutation. She was all delicateness, her face reflecting a gentleness of expression. The girl was dispensing flowers, which gave the impression that they would never fall to earth, but would remain suspended in the air, luxuriant. Purple, pink, yellow flowers. Her tunic, evanescent, pale-green like the shallow sea floor. Such grace, such perfection, such harmony of gesture and innocence of regard, I had only observed in Botticelli of Florence. Yet for centuries the flowers of Pompeii had flourished, cascading gently. I did not know at that time that one day a great sovereign would ask me to describe this vision to her.

At night, upon my return to Portici, everything changed abruptly. We would leave the *reggia* after the mandatory daily hunt, because His Majesty would devote himself to family, always following the strictest of customs. Not even the heat of summer could distract him from his inflexible schedule: he retired early, rose at dawn, a habit he has continued in Madrid. This seemingly absurd rectitude was, naturally enough, not followed in the neighbouring seigneurial villas. In one of them I attended a reading of Virgil, the Roman poet buried in Naples, whose verses were declaimed by a girl of large eyes and dark hair, her hips and breasts pronounced beneath a veil that resembled but little that of the adolescent's tunic in Pompeii. In the Neapolitan night, beneath the star-speckled sky, the distant silhouette of Mount Vesuvius, I walked with her barefoot along the beach.

The praises I heard of His Majesty's public works during the midday meal changed to poisoned darts some hours later, after dinner, abetted by the wine and poetry. The philosophers believed that the King banishes them and only favours flatterers; the engineers opined that Naples offers too many palaces whilst there is a great want of roads; the merchants believed they pay too many taxes which benefit but a few. Even one religious person present that evening imprudently issued a long-drawn statement about the city whose streets were filled with the destitute, thieves, drunks, whores, rubbish. I was young and all of that lay far from Portici, far from the beach of the idyllic moon…

When Master Vanvitelli invited me to Naples, he spoke to me of Elisabeth Farnese, mother of King Charles. She had presented her son with the new kingdom, and as he quit Spain bound for a country he did not know, she had described it to him as "the most beautiful crown of Italy". I too had quit my home in search of Naples.

Caserta lies far from the urban life of the capital, and on summer evenings in Portici, or at winter festivities in the

Teatro di San Carlo, it is good to remember that the city itself and the life of gallantry existed long before we did, and that, while we are moved by the passion to build what does not yet exist, it is likewise necessary to cultivate and enjoy the present moment. Let us take a look: here we contemplate ladies in exultant dresses, their insinuating glances of submission offered with no effort on your part. You are fully aware that their eyes are directed on you whilst the aria lasts; you know they linger in the vestibule in order to be present when you leave the theatre. Is it not a discourtesy to God and Nature, to established forms of social communion and personal ingenuity, to ignore such marvels of life?

Naples is the ideal place to partake of life and surrender yourself to it. Why else were Virgil, Petrarch and Boccaccio brought hither? Why else would the Roman emperors build such enchanting villas here? A stroll through Chiaia, along the shore that stretches from Castel dell'Ovo as far as the cliffs of Posillipo, provides the most propitious entry into the prodigious world of delight that beckons Neapolitans under any pretext, or for none at all.

A more rational pleasure exists: for example, contemplating the treasures the King removed – with considerable protests from the population – from Piacenza, Parma and Florence. These gems were part of the inheritance he received from the Farnese and are displayed in his palaces now. I have had the privilege to spend hours contemplating Titian's *Danae*, a painting that Michelangelo himself viewed at the Venetian's studio in a visit recounted by my compatriot Vasari.

If to this we add the work undertaken for the Palace of Capodimonte, located above the city, and the Albergo dei Poveri – the almshouse the King had built at the insistence of Father Rocco in order to care for the thousands of hungry people throughout the kingdom – and a multitude of other public works, many left unfinished, it is understandable that Naples began to long for Charles as soon as he had left the port for Barcelona. The splendour of the city had never been as great. Its fame throughout Europe had not been so illustrious since the era of Alfonso the Magnanimous, three centuries before, when the Catalan King had established the centre of his Mediterranean empire here, his court had welcomed the first humanists, and he had built the beautiful Triumphal Arch between the massive towers of Castel Nuovo, the city's most visible symbol.

The city and I were one and the same. I too felt forsaken as I glimpsed His Majesty's vessels sail away. He had abdicated in favour of his son Ferdinand, who was but a child, though the real power rested in the hands of Bernardo Tanucci, who guaranteed the continuity of Charles's policies of reform and construction, activities which were beginning to bestow on His Majesty the epithet of "The Good King". The finances of the kingdom must not have been as solid as they appeared, for Tanucci immediately showed signs of curbing the resources destined for Caserta, provoking disputes between himself and the surly Vanvitelli, who refused to impoverish a project born for perfection.

Tanucci had not changed; it was simply that the King's obstinacy was no longer driving forwards the works. In politics, something similar happened: Tanucci and the

EMILI ROSALES

other ministers did not alter their policies, it was the King's prestige that had maintained peace and the balance of power with foreign nations. Charles III had protected trade and opposed the Inquisition. The new king was a pale shadow of his predecessor, capricious and lacking in understanding, childish and incapable of assuming what had been handed him. The want of food after a bad harvest raised further doubts about the finances of the state and threatened to degenerate into a popular revolt on a day in which not even the huge Albergo dei Poveri, built by Ferdinando Fuga, could hold all the hungry people. The Neapolitan chapter was drawing to an end.

The proposal I received from Francesco Sabatini – who had moved to Madrid with King Charles and his minister, the Marquis of Esquilache – was timely. All the travels I had undertaken, experiences undergone, events that had almost made me forget who I was, the many days of work spent at the service of a royal plan I could not fully comprehend – all of it had been as a preparation for my high mission: Charles III's most ambitious project and the most fabulous commission that an architect of my time could receive.

3
Lights in the Bay

A beacon blinks during the insatiable summer night. If you look carefully you will see two, then three, four lights. Perhaps you discover a boat that is returning late, taking the shortest route possible. Exhausted waves tumble gently onto the beaches, lapping against the rocks, as if the August day has emptied them of their fury. If you leave behind the bright lights by the shore, the vivacious noise of strollers and the festive terrace, you will enter a silent, still kingdom.

The Bay of Alfacs is smooth as glass as it gently rocks a dozen boats that have braved the night. You count the lights again, discover a few more, all around you. These same sleepy waters that each morning witness the departure of the noisy fleet of fishing boats welcomed more than two hundred years ago the King's engineers, sent here to embark on an enterprise that was scarcely commenced, and never to be finished. The magnitude and precise intentions of the undertaking are unknown, but traces of the Invisible City have reappeared in my life with a force that I believed forgotten for ever – gone, faded. History is like the blinking of a beacon, the instant in which past and future are worth nothing. Or perhaps they are everything.

EMILI ROSALES

I have come to the house on the coast this summer, having decided that the right moment has finally arrived for me to spend some time here. During the day I devote several hours to the translation of *Memoirs of the Invisible City*; at night I enjoy contemplating the silent sea charged with stories, such as the one that leads me to the Mendizábals' house for the most celebrated event of the summer.

My friends, the hosts, have become the eminent proprietors of one of the largest real-estate companies in the area. I had seen them only sporadically over the last decade, but they have reappeared in my life, ever since Sofia showed up at my office in Barcelona.

I've driven cautiously up the winding road to the house, through the brush, accompanied by the exhausted, shrill sounds of cicadas. Flanked by bluish mountains, I catch my first glimpse of the house as it begins to emerge above the yellowish green of the pine grove, the silvery green of olive trees, the slender green of cypress. I knew that the Mendizábal family would neither maintain nor restore the old farmhouse set in this oasis in the middle of the dry, scorched Montsià region, but I must confess that the house they have built is not what I expected. My admiration for the location intensifies with the climb, fanning my envy as I approach the entrance announced by the gently swaying palm trees. My thoughts are suddenly interrupted by Sofia Mendizábal's warm words.

Sofia praises my car, tells me how tanned I am, Sofia likes my shirt, finds me younger than ever, Sofia embraces me like a schoolgirl while she laughs and enthusiastically addresses first me, then her husband Jonàs, who joins us a moment later. As the three of us walk towards the house, I realize by the sound of voices that I had miscalculated the number of guests who would respond to the Mendizábals' invitation. Far from the twenty-odd that I had expected, I notice a large throng of people around the swimming pool, whose reflected light casts a snowy pallor on the guests, creating the impression that they have wings, are almost floating. Sofia points to them without bothering to disguise the fact that they are her spoils, her conquest.

"The European Commissioner for the Environment has decided to spend his holiday on the delta to demonstrate how sensitive he is to ecological issues," Sofia tells me with a wink. "So you can imagine, as soon as word got out that he was coming to the party, everyone was suddenly available!"

"Excellent!" I reply, playing along with her. "Is he here?"

"Not yet, darling, but don't worry, he'll make an appearance," Sofia says with pride and a nervous half-smile.

"Well, we should certainly toast to the success of your new venture," I tell her to keep her from being anxious. "Definitely the best surprise of the year, that you've returned to the projects of your youth. I didn't think the business would ever leave you time to—"

"I know, but I've finally extricated myself. Real estate is Jonàs's thing, I'm interested in art. You know what I mean, buying, selling. Yes, I worked for the family business at some point, but for a while the only thing I've been doing is helping a friend who's starting up as a painter. The gallery is the real thing. So, I'll toast to that."

We are beginning to discuss her new undertaking when Jonàs approaches with a glass in each hand and cordially drags me away from his wife. We walk a few metres to another terrace, overlooking the distant bay above the olive trees. He taps me on the shoulder and points towards the south, to a nearby hill.

"Mola Erma, the huge wasteland. Remember? All brush and thicket, dry rocky terrain. We bought it, and will start developing it after the summer. A hundred and twenty lots. One of the most complex operations we've had. For years I've been fighting a thousand obstacles. We'll transform the wasteland into an orchard and call it 'Mola Verda', the green land. We've dug wells, commissioned studies as to which trees will take root better. We'll have to plant them everywhere. The truth is I have more than a hundred people interested even before we start, and since I know how you love this area, I've reserved you one lot with a view of the sea."

"Mola Erma... But a hundred and twenty houses?"

"It's all up to snuff. A real ball-breaker trying to get all the permits. I should be given a prize. That's why I'm thinking of providing the press with the information. I finally want to make a good impression."

Fortunately someone calls to us before I have time to reply, and we look up from the pitch-dark hill that the next year – or the following – would be turned into Sunset Boulevard. As we spin around, we notice a group of people, laughing, dressed in loose, semi-transparent clothes, who had been friends of Jonàs's and mine, and now are making extravagant displays of how long we've gone without seeing or speaking to each other. We hardly have time to speak when we hear a commotion at the other end of the walkway that links the patio by the swimming pool to another area of the garden, by the row of cypress trees on the north side of the house. The first notes of a string quartet are beginning to sound. Those who do not yet have a drink grab one. The soft ground lights make everyone seem taller; the music breathes oxygen into conversations.

You see a familiar face talking to someone whose back is to you and you play at guessing who it is. You draw near, she turns around, you sense the weight in your chest that you used to feel before the wild, impossible cry of feminine beauty. This happens in two seconds, the time it takes you to greet effusively the man with the beautiful woman, the painter Malaquies Tarrés, then lower your sails and stop short before the triumphant smile of... What *was* her name?

"A real pleasure to see you, Emili Rossell. Sofia says that without you she would never have been able to set up the art gallery," Malaquies exaggerates. "And I needed a change, do something different, unexpected, none of that inaugurating a new show in one of the usual places!"

"You're right. Bold decision! But it'll work out fine. Sofia's great, as you can see," I say, pointing to the large crowd.

"Ten years ago, no one would have believed that you could stage a launch party like this, two hundred kilometres from Barcelona. But Sofia had an inkling that it would work. Brilliant idea, huh?"

"That's what we call having a good nose," I say, as I remind him that I had travelled in the opposite direction. Both of us laugh.

"And don't think for a moment that she won't find her Tiepolo."

Malaquies Tarrés lets this last phrase drop as if it were the most logical of things, as if everyone were *au courant* with the news. Before I can question him, Sofia Mendizábal herself joins us, stands between the two of us, her arms on our shoulders, and guides us in the other direction, leaving behind the angelic young woman who has accompanied Tarrés.

The quartet, to which few have paid any attention, has taken a break, and little groups, like the three of us, head down the stairs to the ground floor, which opens onto the olive grove, actually a basement if you look at it from the north side of the house. Accompanied by Malaquies and Sofia, I enter the living room, where a large window separates us from the trees outside. On the wall hang a sampling of paintings, three, part of the exhibition to be held at the Barcelona gallery, one of the big autumn events no doubt.

Malaquies Tarrés has travelled half the world before settling in the Ebro delta, where the light is blinding by day, unpaintable, but takes on a fibrous quality of infinite subtlety in the early and late hours. Malaquies assures me that the explosion of light at midday, fuelled by the absence of mountains, means that there is no continuity of images from one day to the next. The raging sun burns everything and what emerges when the fury of the star grows tame is like a film fade-in, utterly new, unencumbered by memory. Tarrés the painter is also consumed by a mystical relationship with colour, by certain turbulences of artistic composition, by the excesses of his love life.

Africa changed him. He spent two or three winters in Tangiers – maybe part of them in Paris – never had a show the whole time, so on his return he organized an impeccable campaign with the Barcelona and Madrid press about his years of contemplation in Africa, his visions, a sort of fakirism or abstinence, the kind of thing that makes a huge impression every few years on the enlightened, guilt-stricken representatives of the city's affluent society. It all fit perfectly with the artist's athletic build and rather lean appearance. He reappeared with these paintings of Turner-like epiphanies that had a certain expressionist quality. After a string of successes, Tarrés became fed up with the never-ending engagements in Barcelona and started looking for a place to escape, and discovered the old house on the delta plains.

How did Malaquies know Sofia? No telling. Living here, it wouldn't have been difficult to meet at some point, but it was inconceivable that Mendizábal would be able to launch her gallery with a show by someone so well known. The entire art world had their eyes on him.

"You haven't been to my studio for a long time," Tarrés tells me, glossing over the fact that I have never had that pleasure, but he does recall that we publish a trilingual quarterly magazine under the gallery's name, circulated almost exclusively among critics, gallerists and people of the art world.

41

"Well, you're a long way from Barcelona…" I say, playing at swapping roles, I of course being from the delta, he the man from Barcelona. Malaquies laughs loudly, as if I had just told a great joke.

"This was a calculated gamble. Maybe it's a risk to have a show with these people," he says lowering his voice, "but I'd like to present a comprehensive image: painting, place and people. Quite original, don't you think, to announce the show here? Now that the delta's a European symbol of a nature reserve that must be protected, it's as if I were turning the whole delta into a work of art."

"Brilliant idea, Malaquies. You have half of Barcelona buzzing with curiosity, with no idea of what you're up to."

"That's exactly what I was hoping for! And when the show opens in Barcelona in the autumn, everybody will be all fired up. I'll have all the interviews take place down here at the farmhouse, make the journalists scramble through irrigation ditches and canals, and I'll try to emphasize my perception."

"Sounds good: that should get you at least two paragraphs filled with admiration for the countryside you've chosen to depict, the labyrinthine character of the approach to your sanctuary." Tarrés, you're a genius, I think to myself.

Soft lights focus on the three large murals. The sparsely furnished room lies in half-darkness; the other walls are bare. The yellowish light of Malaquies's paintings dominates everything. I begin to get a hint of the social scope of the Mendizábals' event: the affluent, both from the region and Barcelona, who have hastened to reserve a place for themselves in the last remaining stronghold of nature along the one-thousand-kilometre Mediterranean coast. Some of them must be real-estate customers – buying land or houses – others soon-to-be customers, who will purchase works of art. Some are politicians with their eye on the Spanish Congress or the Catalan Parliament, and the odd person who has realized that holidaying on the Ebro delta carries extra political weight. Sofia's party is a good place for people to notice that they are here.

Among them we find Armand Coll, more intent on surviving than navigating, a Member of Parliament in Madrid who has appeared in the press rather more than he would like to in the last couple of years, if that is possible for a politician. He gives the impression that he's a bit uncomfortable among so many fat wallets who can afford to buy a painting by the international artist Tarrés. He is saved by the women, who shower him with courtesies, all of them a bit more elegant than their husbands (is it the jewellery?), who seem to have dressed down in order to convince themselves that they are on holiday. The politician, on the other hand, looks a bit stiff from a sartorial point of view.

Armand, who guided me through the blazing corridors of school, exchanged his religious faith years ago for a faith in history, a field that had always interested him. He didn't abandon the Church because the pressure of desire exceeded the limits imposed by priesthood. Nor was it a crisis of faith, but rather an intellectual transformation linked precisely to the idea of redemption. He came to the realization that the liberating mission the Church had entrusted him with could only be carried out from a layman's position and, ultimately, from a political stance.

Armand has spotted me. He's on the other side of the room, flanked by two women who don't seem inclined to give him up easily. Engaged in the energetic defence of Greenland seals, Patagonian whales, Pyrenean bears, they have just recently discovered that the whole of the Ebro delta is a live, endangered species, in need of defence, especially now that their investment-minded husbands are intent on building their mansions here. The two women, accustomed to dealing with important politicians in Barcelona or on the Costa Brava, where they spend their summers, are familiar with the policy of "You scratch my back, I'll scratch yours". They feel rejuvenated, emboldened to find themselves face-to-face with Armand Coll, the elegant but forceful opponent of government projects that threaten egrets, ducks and the migration of flamingoes.

"So you think, sir, that the European Commission will put a halt to this? The plan seems a bit third world..."

"Please call me Armand, Senyora Riudellots."

"Sorry, and you call me Cati."

"The European institutions have a lot at stake; it's a matter of prestige, no doubt about it. Brussels can't give their support to a plan that would put a nature reserve in danger... But let's see what the European Commissioner has to say. He's around here somewhere."

"The fact that he has also," the plump, dyed blonde says, accentuating the *also*, "decided to spend the summer on the delta must mean something, don't you think?"

I dare to join them at this point, something that may please Armand if he wants a break from his daily speeches – or maybe not. It's clear: with one quick move worthy of

the best American basketball player, he shakes my hand;
with the other on my waist, he twirls me around as if we
were dancing. Suddenly I have the impression we are a
hundred metres from the spot where he had been speaking
to the women.

"So, how are you? About time you showed your face
around here. Me? I'm absolutely fed up with all the talk
about the interbasin water transfer from the Ebro!"

"Well, Armand Coll, you're famous now!"

Many years ago, when he lost his priestly vocation but
not his faith, the wish to help others had led Armand to
identify with socialist positions, almost a political derivation
of his redemptive notion of religion. His speeches were
passionate, much more so than others' – along the lines of
the intellectual university movement of the time – because
Armand himself was deeply contrite and felt that he had to
redeem himself.

He was from a family of small landowners from Tortosa,
most of whom spent the war hiding in a farmhouse after
Armand's grandfather's brother was murdered. He was
walking back from the café when a jovial bunch of anarchists
driving along the road shot him, then killed a dog and a rat
on the same street. Once the carnage of the war was past, the
outcome clear, Armand's family became fervent followers
of Franco and held positions in the municipal government
for decades; one was a renowned man from Tortosa who
became a politician and represented the interests of the
region in Madrid. Another family member who was a
Franco follower secretly used to organize festivities where
the Catalan dance, the Sardana, was performed and even

gave Armand a subscription to *Cavall Fort*, the juvenile, diocesan magazine associated with Catalan nationalism.

Later on, for years Armand – anxious at the thought of causing a family scandal – was a socialist in Barcelona, but when he returned to his hometown he assumed the "Tortosa role", meaning the position represented by the Colls. At some point, however, several members of the Socialist Party, including Armand, were elected to serve in the national Congress in Madrid, but by then sufficient time had elapsed for even his ninety-five-year-old grandmother to announce with unheard-of spontaneity: "A politician is a politician, for crying out loud!"

In the end, Armand has come to represent the thundering voice that rages against the central government's hydrological plan, the interbasin water transfer from the Ebro. He is not simply the spokesman for a progressive political position or the shadow of the Minister of the Environment. He is the voice of the entire Ebro region in Madrid, the last hope for the people of Tortosa. The entire town stands behind the man, as it had forty years previously for his grandfather.

Armand – who had saved me on that lonely afternoon by the school door – and I wander away from the spot where Sofia and the painter have requested people's attention and are about to speak.

When they finish, Armand and I agree that we'll meet a moment later on one of the terraces, and I search the different floors of the house for a bathroom. At this point it dawns on me what the night might have to offer. Just an intuition.

As I am strolling down one of the corridors in half-darkness, only a pale glow from the garden outside, I open a door thinking it's a bathroom, then close it impulsively – almost a defence mechanism. The sort of "didn't see, don't know" reaction. The episode in the school attic when we set fire to the insecticide sneaked into my mind. Jonàs was only at the school for a year and a half, but he managed to participate in our escapades: our school-kid eyes lit up by the flame, faces suddenly ablaze.

It was so fast I couldn't tell how many there were: four, maybe five, a dim look on their faces as they gazed at Jonàs, who was leaning down to sniff a carefully drawn line on the mirror. My reaction was so automatic that I sensed they hadn't even noticed my fleeting appearance.

A moment later, as I'm going up to the terrace, I ask myself why I had acted as I did, rather than greet them in a natural way. I'm embarrassed to think that if they did see me, they'd take me for some naive schoolchild, easily scandalized. But my reaction is the result of so many suspicions and so much evidence.

It all started with smack. Jonàs hooked on heroin. Jonàs looting the generous but not exuberant coffers of his fisherman family. Jonàs threatening his mother with a knife. Jonàs in detox. Jonàs back. During the years that I studied and travelled, I would occasionally feel a shadow of guilt for my detachment; I rarely asked about him, always from a distance. I recognized the plague and wanted no part of it. Few managed to survive those years. A generation was foolishly decimated, the first generation in Spain that grew up having everything they needed, the first to decide of their own accord to die before their time. A biblical curse. I know Jonàs disappeared for a few years, supposedly to Jamaica, and returned cured of his addiction, to everyone's amazement.

When he returned from the Americas, all bright and shiny, smiling from ear to ear, talking non-stop about the marvellous paradise he had left behind, Jonàs used the tiny inheritance from his father – who never recovered from his son's departure – and tried to set himself up in real estate, renting apartments and studios he had managed to snatch. He floundered at first, but didn't seem too upset about it, though the business was in ruins. Then Sofia appeared on the scene.

Sofia Mendizábal was the sixth of eight siblings; she decided early on to step away from the century-old family enterprise in La Rioja, the vineyards and wine. When I met her in Barcelona she was finishing her degree in architecture. She had been stubborn in her desire to distinguish herself from her family, and at university she did distinguish herself from everyone. She stood out. With her long legs and arms, slow stride, self-assurance, she seemed to be from another planet. We visited galleries together and spent time at the art studio that belonged to a friend of hers. I could not have fallen in love with Sofia. She produced in me the same intellectual and sensual sensation as certain works of art. She made my head spin. I would never have planned to go to bed with her, but it did happen a few times over a certain period, not often, random occasions, like a series of unforeseeable storms.

The problem was that these continued even after Sofia had started a relationship with Jonàs, something I wasn't aware of then. I introduced them. She wanted to visit the Ebro delta and inevitably we ran into my newly reborn friend. The day he found out that Sofia was having fun with both of us, he turned up in Barcelona furious as hell. It's possible that I wasn't very inspired that day. I insisted on my ignorance and innocence, and washed my hands of the whole matter, offering practically no objections to Jonàs's demands that I say goodbye to the woman we were sharing and never again cross his path. Sofia was so offended that I gave Jonàs so many guarantees that I never saw her again.

I was disturbed by the contempt Sofia showed at my lack of interest and cynicism. Was I supposed to have defended my rights beyond what was rational? Should I have changed a passing attraction and, yes, a true friendship, into a cause for war that would have forced me into an absurd commitment? Should I have told Sofia exactly who Jonàs was? With what conviction could I threaten, what arguments could I wield? Not a word was said about Ariadna.

It took me a while to recover, but with the passing of time, things returned to normal, the knots untied, the experience faded into the background. In the meantime, the distinguished Sofia and the surprising Jonàs joined forces – her money, his talent – to build one of the most prosperous real-estate enterprises in the region. Something we are celebrating today, our wounds having healed long ago. Or we had been celebrating until a moment ago, when I opened a door by mistake and caught a glimpse of the nightmare that Jonàs might represent.

* * *

The ex-seminarian politician is waiting for me, a Scotch on the rocks in his hand, leaning against the railing of the terrace that overlooks the bay, almost touching the olive trees which seem to exhale into the night air, sending up their scent, the smell of earth scorched by summer, in the realm of crickets.

Some guests have already left, and the European Commissioner hasn't made his appearance, but the party seems to have been given a new burst of energy. Everyone is gathered around the sofas on the garden patio. The people who have just come upstairs after examining the paintings are engaged in lively discussion; the ones who have just come down with Jonàs are standing about. The glimmering blue lights of the swimming pool separate Armand Coll and me from the group. The August night is serene and, as Armand speaks, I observe the lights moving in the bay.

At first I think they are beacons used as sea marks to signal the jutting Banya peninsula, but I realize immediately that they are moving, and fast. In a few minutes a light on the open sea has travelled the seven miles that separate Salines from the entrance to the bay, where it vanishes. In the meantime, a new light has appeared; I didn't notice where the boat had set out from, the bay perhaps, and it has crossed the harbour and reached the point where the other disappeared at the Punta de la Banya lighthouse. It vanishes too.

"Do you know what Jonàs does?" Armand asks me in a confidential tone.

"What do you mean?"

"I mean, before the party I took the liberty of asking—"

"Come on, Armand, let's not have any stories here. I've known Jonàs all my life, know all of his pranks. What he did when he was twenty has nothing to do with now."

"I'm not talking about when he was twenty. I assume your friend didn't have a penny, and the money for the Mendizábal real-estate agency—"

"As the name shows, it's Sofia who—"

I break off the conversation, because I catch sight of a third light that has just left the port and is moving rapidly across the bay towards the open sea, or perhaps to the Banya lighthouse. When it has covered half the distance, the two boats that had switched off their lights when they met at the lighthouse turn them on again and head out to sea, one in front of the other, followed by the last boat to leave the port. The third catches up with the second and they stop alongside each other. At some point I lose sight of the first one, which has disappeared into the open sea.

The survivors of the party are seated on sofas by the swimming pool or in armchairs facing the same general direction. There is a moment of calm; the music has stopped playing, no more murmurs of people conversing in the background. The patio is like a balcony over the vibrant, luminous, star-studded sky – a probing sky almost. Then, as if the mere sound of ice tinkling in my glass could provoke a cataclysm, I venture to say:

"So, in the end he didn't come. The Commissioner didn't show up."

"Just what do you mean by that?" Sofia hisses at me, as if the spring on a jack-in-the-box had been released. "What exactly do you mean?"

"Nothing. Simply that he hasn't come."

"What else did you want? What were you expecting? Now our *senyor* has realized that the Commissioner didn't show up and he makes a comment, just for the sake of commenting. All the people who did come were not enough for you? Want me to read you the list?" Sofia's voice doesn't sound like her, hits a false note, she's drunk.

"It wasn't my intention—"

"Oh, I know, an innocent comment, no offence intended. Well, I *do* know how to irritate people, I'm great at annoying. But you, on the other hand, shut away in your little art gallery in Barcelona, you think you don't need to trouble people, you have enough with what you have and what you know, but then you find any strategy that wants to go beyond the ordinary suspicious, because me, my gallery, in only a few months…" She breaks off, realizing that she's saying something inappropriate, that I was an ally of hers. But Armand speaks out in her defence.

"Sofia, with the gallery and selling land, her social activities, is doing more than most to draw attention to the Ebro delta, providing a wider cultural recognition, which – by the way – you clamour about in the articles you publish every I don't know how often, where you always seem so full of yourself. If the Ebro delta existed as a cultural icon, no one would dare lay a finger on it – you wrote something like that as I recall. Excellent, but in order to create this acknowledgement, we have to convince people, attract them, invent what we still don't have."

The present situation is absurd. It's not clear what I'm being accused of, but I have to follow the argument, because these drunken, wandering conversations sometimes provide precious information, and I have to search for the Invisible City through unlikely channels.

"That's fine, Armand. I wouldn't argue with that; you do the same from the political trenches," I say, giving in stoically.

"I know. I hate the shows I have to put on, but I help guide things in what I think is the right direction, give things a push."

"Good for you!" I say, as Sofia makes a grimace that first seems to indicate a lack of comprehension, then antagonism, but is really only a mixture of exhaustion and alcohol.

"But you're caught up in your own world, protected by art and refinement, and you feel yourself qualified to judge anyone who attempts to do anything, as if your behaviour were extraneous to the whole comedy, I mean, as if you weren't part of it all."

"That's true," adds Jonàs, who has come rushing in from God knows where, speaking fast, not articulating. "I just offered him a fantastic investment opportunity, and instead of being grateful, he reproaches me. Emili, you dropped anchor somewhere during the crossing, but the world continues to revolve, revolving around you, right under you!"

Everything revolves, and my friends are less mistaken than it might appear. Jonàs is bright, and his sharpness tends to move faster than his interlocutors', so he is always able to anticipate other people's intentions and take advantage of them. Yet he is not moved by any particular idea of where he wants to go, but by his need to generate debts – in every sense of the word – greater than he can handle, a situation that leads to greed, mental agility, a quick eye. Armand, on the other hand, sees the world as a collection of imperfect realities which need to be acted upon. Work must be invested to improve these situations, yet he seems to have lost sight of which models are flawed; and he's overwhelmed by a sense of fear, an anxiety caused by the constant threat of not being sufficiently sensitive, efficient or grateful. So he becomes dependent on outside factors that could lead him in a direction he might not have wished. Sofia is certainly more complex, maybe even a mystery. Her aspiration is to control all the moves in the game, no matter what it is, but she never lets down her guard; she doesn't proceed in this manner merely to benefit from it, but for the reaction it causes in her once she has emerged victorious, been flattered, recognized, praised. Sofia never wavers as she carries out her schemes, which are often no more than a game, a habit of hers that is of no particular consequence, though revealing, symptomatic.

She taught me some of her skills many years ago. But before I knew her, long before, I had discovered in myself a mechanism that was perhaps neutralized by Ariadna, but reappeared with Sofia. This was the period of icy classrooms and draughty corridors, the period when I first heard the name of Tiepolo. This was my first aesthetic awareness, or rather the oldest memories I have of what might be called an aesthetic awareness. Does a child even have one? A young boy? Doesn't having an aesthetic appreciation of something or someone also mean, paradoxically, to draw back, separate yourself, distance yourself? I remember vividly how I had looked down on a classmate or valued him purely by the lines of his face; I became friends with someone because I liked the way he dressed or combed his hair; I was repelled or attracted for this reason. I suppose it was the same reason that led me to cross the street to greet someone or pretend I hadn't seen him. In reality it was often simply that the place where I was offered me a sense of harmony, or the opposite. Sometimes I reacted to a person whose clothes I didn't like, or to that person's smell. Today I find this grotesque.

Some will think that an element of this – conscious or not – exists in any decision we take; I admit that, but what I'm talking about is that intense, overwhelming impulse that would tempt me to kick a member of the opposite football team, or the contrary, offer him the ball. I've often suppressed these impulses, of course. I'm guessing that I learnt to restrain them or conceal them. Could it be that I wish to continue viewing the landscape of the Ebro delta as it was before, for the simple reason that I like it, beyond any moral, social or acquisitive motives for which some want to preserve this area and others to raze it?

A bit later, the party languishes and roles have been switched. As Sofia and I dance, suddenly I become aware that she has begun to sob, her supple body caught up in tiny convulsions. I step back so I can see her face, but she refuses to let me. I don't insist, but I notice her tears dampening my neck. Now what? I glance around and make sure that I have no need to worry. I don't see anyone who might notice what is happening: they have all either left or are lying on the floor or lolling drunk in armchairs. Sofia stammers something, almost as if she didn't dare make it intelligible:

"I'm scared rotten," she seemed to say the first time, but then I clearly understand. "I can't put up with this any longer; I don't know what's going to happen."

We're dancing near the railing on the terrace where Armand and I watched the play of lights on the bay, and I try to divert my attention by letting my sight dwell on the valley that lies between the hill where we stand and the town below. Something tells me not to relax: I glimpse the bluish lights of two police cars that are climbing the dark road to the house. And the Invisible City?

4

Venice

From Memoirs of the Invisible City

The proposal was too good to refuse – which is not to say that I was not grieved to leave Naples. The work on the Palace of Caserta had progressed slowly, but Charles III was tired of living in the retreat in Buen Retiro and ordered that his new Royal Palace in Madrid be quickly finished. If everything proceeded as it should, he would soon have to choose the lavish decoration that would adorn the palace. The King had resolved to rely on artists capable of reflecting the grandeur and glory that he sought. The ceilings of the new palace would display the art of the greatest muralist of our time. His Majesty wanted Giambattista Tiepolo.

Venice: the delicate green of the lagoon and its many-coloured façades – peach, straw, pomegranate – white Istrian stone, the bell tower.

The mission entrusted to me called for prompt action; yet, in spite of the urgency, I was granted authorization to sail as far as Livorno and stay a few days in Arezzo, where my uncle Alessandro continued in his renowned gold and silver workshop. To him I owe the privilege of having studied in Rome. My uncle had been father and mother to me, and I wished to embrace him before it was too late, as

57

my passage through Venice would be followed by a long interlude in Madrid.

My uncle – a plump, elegant man who wore his eyeglasses low on his nose, a kindly temper behind his resolute manner – looked dubious: "There was a time when men were from only one place, you understood their dealings, they carried in their hearts the affection of their families, a debt to their fellow citizens, a bond with the streets that had seen them grow. But now, as it has been reckoned that the world goes round, so it would appear that men likewise find themselves inclined to go round…"

It was not my uncle's intention to sadden me, still less to reproach me. His lament turned to warning: "Pay me no heed. You must seek your own world, create a world adequate to your needs. Clearly, the situation offered you by this Charles of Bourbon will suit your taste, but be alert: you know now how to flee Florence, pinching all that you can! Be wary that the games of the powerful never catch you by surprise, for their interests are not ours – that is to say, not yours. We must always move with a vigilant eye, be on the watch, see if we can cozen something, never allowing ourselves to be flattered, never believing that we are one of them, because if you do and they turn on you, you will find yourself drifting like a ship without a mast. You see this, don't you? Remember my words, Andrea: profit by what you can, but never lose sight of the plain truth that our interests are different from theirs."

He must have believed that I understood, for he added no more words of advice and asked that I speak to him of Naples: the music at the Teatro di San Carlo, the Roman marvels from the excavations at Pompeii, the Farnese treasures appropriated by the King in Parma and in our own region of Tuscany. Yet, what most stoked his curiosity was quite a different matter. When I confessed to him that in spite of all my courting in Naples I had never surrendered my heart to anyone, he led me into a room behind his workshop and opened the door of an old oak wardrobe, turned the knob on the safe and removed a tiny velvet bag.

"Alessandro Roselli of Arezzo makes you a present; you alone will know for whom it is worthy. When the moment arrives, place this ring on the finger of your beloved, and may God and your family bless you."

As I left my ancient city, I experienced a strange mixture of pain and joy, a sensation unknown to me until that moment.

The watery paths lead me to Palladio's marvellous churches, first to the delicate gracefulness of San Giorgio Maggiore – which bestows a subtle verticality on the broad lagoon, its façade smiling in the twilight – and then to the temple of Il Redentore on the Giudecca, where year after year the Doge arrives from Dorsoduro over the bridge of barges to give thanks for delivering the city from the plague that had decimated it. The two Palladian buildings stand in striking contrast to the gleaming baroque Santa Maria della Salute, with its boldly triumphant architecture.

I never tire of speaking of Venice, of the welcoming sight of the Palazzo Ducale – which seems to float, elegantly perched between the lagoon and the piazza – or the Byzantine brilliance of San Marco. But I had travelled to the city to carry away the man who had painted the ceilings of churches and ballrooms, sacristies and private chambers. I came hither to rob Venice of the finest painter of this century.

In Dorsoduro, facing Il Redentore from the other side of the canal, stands the church of Gesuati, where we find the most fascinating ceiling fresco painted by the artist I have come to meet. The high perspective of the Institution of the Rosary causes onlookers to lose their balance as they gaze upwards. The Mother of God observes from the clouds as St Dominic offers the Rosary to an exultant multitude who are clad in vividly coloured garments, lying on a staircase which makes the ceiling appear to open onto a celestial arch.

Tiepolo's work in the Würzburg residence, far from Venice, has spread his fame over the whole of the continent. Monarchs and great lords aspired to enlist the services of a painter who knew how to control large spaces, infusing them with majesty and strength. In Italy, Tiepolo was initially considered to be an imitator of Veronese because of the theatrical nature of his scenes, the mixture of worldliness with the sacred, the sheer vastness of his compositions. Soon, however, it became clear that Tiepolo was following his own path, or if anything he carried Veronese's tastes to other extremes. The frescoes in the Palazzo Arcivescovile in Udine, one of his first triumphs – or the Venetian church of Gesuati itself – demonstrate that he was a marvellous painter of religious themes; yet later in the Palazzo Labia he allows himself every freedom in depicting the passion of Antony and Cleopatra, grandiose and ironic, mythological and irreverent.

By means of a letter of recommendation from the Count of Montealegre, Charles III's ambassador to the Republic of Venice, I was invited to the Palazzo Labia which lies at the confluence of the Grand Canal and the Cannaregio. The palace is evidence of the commercial power that this family of Catalan origin had commanded; they were among the first to purchase their nobility from the Venetian State, whose coffers were then depleted. At their height, the Labias were renowned for their lavish existence; there were even tales that the gold plates used for a famous banquet were thrown into the canal. The Labias of today no longer possess the glowing opulence of their ancestors, but they endeavour – as does all of the old city – to give the impression of being as wealthy as before. Maria Labia, widow of Giovan Francesco Labia, has inherited the finest collection of jewels in Europe, and is said to bestow them generously on certain visitors. She wishes to show herself as beautiful and magnificent as the Cleopatra painted by Tiepolo.

The first time you contemplate an oil painting or fresco by Tiepolo, it produces a strange reaction in you, almost one of repulsion. There is something about the strokes, about the figures' expressions that initially seems shocking, but the longer you observe the painting, the more obsessed you become by it, until you understand that Tiepolo has painted faces that look contradictory. He has pursued the chimera of presenting us with something in these remarkable heroes that is unstable, changing.

The mission I was charged with was not easy. Signor Giambattista Tiepolo, who had been chamber painter for

Doge Giovanni Cornaro when he was but twenty years of age, now was over sixty years old, and he believed that his days of travelling abroad were long past. Nothing could tempt him to quit the golden retreat of his Venetian home and commence another adventure that could bring him only discomfort in exchange for hardly more glory.

Striding up and down his studio where he had asked us to convene, Tiepolo affirmed that the age of the greatest artists was past. Naturally, he wished us to convince him of the contrary. Why should the era of grandiosity have passed? The era for the representation of beauty will never pass, I argued: the manifestations of grandeur that mankind had created through the power of its imagination could never fade. Admiration, I continued, would always exist for his *Apollo and the Continents*, the immense vault frescoes above the staircase at the Würzburg residence, which I had heard about from the ambassador, the Count of Montealegre.

Apollo, accompanied by the Hours, raises his head to heaven, the resplendent morning sun behind him. The four continents represented at the edges of the fresco are illuminated by the light from the sun, the vital force that moves the days and years: America, surrounded by exuberant nature, rides a huge crocodile; black Africa is seated on her dromedary; sumptuously dressed Asia, the cradle of science, rides atop an elephant; and Europe, home to the arts, is enthroned beside an ox.

As I have now observed many of Tiepolo's paintings in palaces and churches in Venice, I can see them in my mind's eye. Bodies that defy gravity and levitate, strong arms that restrain and rescue, faces that light up in horror or dismay;

airborne hoofs of a giant horse with a silvery rump; golden jewels; amphorae and wind-swept flags; blue capes and ruby silks; trumpets and torches; ample, swollen bosoms; splintering columns and half-viewed temples; clouds that swirl, filter the light and announce a tempest. The age of Tiepolo. The age of the Titans.

Flattered by our praises of his vaults, the elderly painter spoke with passion about the difficulties of painting at Würzburg and how he had resolved each problem. When he realized that he was supporting our argument – that the age of the Titans had not passed and he should end his career with another great work of art at the palace of Charles III – he pointed out his age, which made things difficult, and the countless dangers of such a long voyage.

Signor Tiepolo had arranged for us to meet one week later, thereby leaving me time to visit another of his marvellous creations: the frescoes of Villa Valmarana in Vicenza. As I was leaving Venice, the ambassador told me not to be too worried about contracting Tiepolo, all his circumlocutions were only meant to let time pass so as to negotiate a higher salary. After all, he had a large family. For many months the Count of Montealegre had done all that was possible to press Tiepolo. He had recently learnt that the master would be completing the frescoes of Villa Pisani in Stra in half the expected time. The decision had already been taken: Tiepolo would accompany me to Madrid. We were in the final stages.

All the more reason for me to make my stay in Vicenza as pleasurable as possible. I was attracted both by the possibility of examining the paintings in the Villa and contemplating

Palladio's buildings. Many would think I had taken leave of my senses if I explained how the outline of the distant buildings drew tears from my eyes when I first glimpsed them from my carriage. I had studied the plans of these constructions, had admired them in engravings, but never actually seen them. Perhaps only Palladio has been able to create in a house the ideal we have dreamt about: the art of the ancients transposed to our time. We may erect palaces and cathedrals, temples of power and faith, the embodiment of majesty and glory, but we do not get a step closer to the lesson of well-being and harmony, of humanity and beauty displayed by these villas. I ordered the coachman to stop several times before reaching the beautiful city of Vicenza, in order to study the buildings erected by the master of the *Four Books of Architecture.*

Once again, through the mediation of the ambassador, I was able to visit Villa Valmarana, where Master Tiepolo has painted a collection of images, illustrations of scenes from Homer and Virgil, Ariosto and Tasso. Here, the paintings are confined to a much narrower space, but Tiepolo has created another dimension by means of false columns and perspectives that expand into seemingly real landscapes, into the open sky, with figures who peep out from architectural elements, giving the sensation of depth. Thus, Agamemnon hides his face to avoid seeing his daughter Iphigenia sacrificed so that the winds will favour the Greek army and lead them to Troy; but he does not glimpse the cloud advancing towards the centre of the scene, bearing a deer that will be sacrificed in the girl's place thanks to Diana, who has taken pity on her.

The colours of the faces, bodies, flags, clothes and capes are luminous, light and soft, giving the paintings an air of transparency, of warmth, quite different from the dense scenes of some of the Master's oil canvases. Although the rooms are not very spacious, the muted shades bring the viewer gently into the atmosphere. A work of genius.

Our final meeting with Tiepolo was adjourned once more. This allowed me to become acquainted with other Venetian masterpieces I had read much about and often heard of. Some of them caused in me such a strong impression that I can still remember them in great detail – Bellini and Giorgione, Titian and Veronese.

I also had time to visit some of the extravagant salons of this Adriatic city, where the music of Antonio Vivaldi was the fashion and the ladies dressed as if they were Cleopatra. Conversation is, alas, not my greatest skill, but as it is considered impolite simply to observe without contributing to the general banter of the occasion, I was obliged to invent excuses and abandon the parties at an early hour. I would then ask my gondolier to take me on long detours before returning to the house of my affable host, the Count of Montealegre. From the water, Venice is a window from which light streams, a house from which music escapes – it is sudden laughter spilling from a doorway, the rippling sound of the gondola cutting through the waves.

No ladies were ever out in Venice at night: they were all parading themselves, richly adorned and gleeful, at the salons. On leaving one of these sumptuous parties, I might easily sink into a state of melancholy that I could not allow to last, for I had to be alert. As I had had occasion to observe, the dark alleys and empty piazzas were places frequented by thieves.

On the day of the arranged meeting at Master Tiepolo's house, it was a very quick affair, as the ambassador had predicted. We were quite impressed when the painter produced a sketch entitled *Glory of Spain*; based on this and the suggestions given to him, he would fresco the ceiling for Charles III's Throne Room.

His conditions followed immediately thereafter. He would travel accompanied by his sons Giandomenico and Lorenzo, who must also be contracted, as he would require their help. His wife Cecilia Guardi would remain in Venice with their four daughters and the other son, who was a priest. The painter then came to his main point: the remuneration offered him was far too little. The ambassador agreed without hesitation, at which point Tiepolo doubled the figure. The Count of Montealegre rose from his chair, approached the window, tried to negotiate, glanced at me and grew flustered. In the meantime, the painter had begun to cover the sketch of the Throne Room with a cloth. The ambassador yielded without giving the painter everything he had demanded. Tiepolo seemed distracted as he followed the explanations impassively. The ambassador grew silent. I perspired. Finally, the count offered Tiepolo his hand, a faint smile crossed the painter's face, and we began discussing the details of the voyage.

The journey with the Tiepolo family lasted more than two months. Spring was beginning to break in the Veneto countryside when we departed on the thirty-first day of

March, and a precocious summer had swept over Castile when we arrived in Madrid on the fourth day of June. It was an epic journey with Giambattista, his entourage and the tools he had refused to leave behind. Tiepolo's age – his sixty-six years – made this a wildly imprudent expedition. He suffered attacks of gout, was haunted by the spectres of failure, demanded constant guarantees concerning the treatment and the attentions he would receive. He was too intelligent not to recognize that in the year 1762 his artistic career would not rise beyond what it already had; he knew that fashion was driving art in new directions, and the branch that he had cultivated, virtuous and lofty, could not blossom further. It was time for pruning.

The ambassador left me to attend to all the details and accompany Tiepolo first to Barcelona and then to the Court of King Charles. I was eager to arrive in Genoa, where I had made arrangements to sail for Catalunya, but when we reached the coast of Liguria a strong, frightening wind from the Levant appeared and Signor Tiepolo began to recoil. It was impossible to make the passage by sea.

It proved extremely difficult to find a coach for such a long journey by land, but during the days that I was occupied in procuring us transportation, with the Tiepolos installed in an old manor house by the port, I was able to observe the transformation in Giambattista. Strong winds created clusters of flaming clouds; mild ones gave rise to purple streaks. I would find him absorbed in the contemplation of the orange-coloured twilight sky or pacing anxiously up and down the room as if he were called upon to perform a mysterious dance.

Tiepolo returned to the sketches he had begun. He drew new ones. He asked me to tell him about Francesco Sabatini, the architect with whom I had collaborated in the building of the Caserta Palace until he had left Naples with King Charles to work on new projects in Madrid.

We finally arrived by land in the Catalan city, after what seemed like an interminable passage – not so much due to its length and discomfort, but because I saw how the elderly Giambattista Tiepolo suffered. Ventimiglia, Nice, Marseilles, Montpellier, Perpignan, Girona... Fortunately, he had the support of Lorenzo and Giandomenico, otherwise we would still be travelling.

What was the first impression Barcelona made on me? Coming from Naples and Venice, Barcelona struck me as a small, noisy city in comparison, confined within its walls, still recovering from the open wounds of the War of Succession. It was a centre of extraordinary maritime and mercantile activity. Unrestrained commerce seemed to be the only weapon the Catalans possessed, but it didn't seem to have caused any significant transformation in the architecture or the people. A torrent of projects and ideas flowed from the mouths of the leading figures of the city's Commercial Council, who received us with all honours.

Thanks to their explanations and comments, I came to realize that the Bourbon victory in 1714 was still seen by many Catalans as their downfall – their city razed, their rights abolished – but also that Charles's accession to the throne (he had chosen to disembark in Barcelona on his return from Naples and had shown himself receptive to the demands of the Catalan merchants) could be construed as a positive event. In spite of the fact that Charles III had reigned for three years and the promises he had made were fading away, I did not have the impression that the notable citizens of Barcelona were willing to consider themselves defeated. As soon as we mentioned Naples, even the eyes of the most illustrious men shone – the Catalan city of Naples that Alfonso the Magnanimous had transformed into the capital of his Mediterranean world, the Triumphal Arch of Castel Nuovo that announced the arrival of a golden age of architecture and art.

The Catalans of today are not satisfied with just the Mediterranean: they constantly insist that they have the right to trade with America, an activity which the Crown thwarts but does not obstruct – according to what I have found – as the Catalans are allowed to use Cadiz as a bridge to America. This was, or is, their battle, whilst mine is to accompany Tiepolo to Madrid.

I will not dwell on the discomforts and hardships we suffered during the last stage of our travels, even though we were accompanied by a royal agent. He was supposed to make the contingencies of the passage easier, but revealed himself to be the most useless of guides, full of romances, constantly bowing, but lacking in any practical sense. The agent was as good at inventing complicated justifications for the setbacks we faced during the journey as he was incapable of foreseeing them or solving them. By the time we had reached Saragossa, I seriously doubted if Giambattista Tiepolo and his family would ever make it to the Castilian Court.

During my week in Spain, the country had presented me with so many charlatans, knaves and incompetent, ignorant people that I was almost willing to submit to the pleas of the elderly artist and turn around and return to civilized Venice. How was it possible, I asked myself, that in a country that had dominated Europe and subjugated America one could not travel more than thirty leagues without being robbed, where swindling was the standard conduct in roadside inns?

As we travelled further into the Peninsula, the feral aspect of the people produced even greater displeasure: they covered themselves head to foot with terrible clothes, all in tatters, and many were toothless, to the point that it required an effort to discover if you were confronting a man or a woman. Can an entire people lose their grace and subtlety in this manner? The truth was we could not possibly find ourselves further from the smiling, haughty, winged or enraptured creatures painted by poor Tiepolo, who had ceased to complain a few days before and contemplated everything with a frightened look of amazement.

Having watched all of this, the plebeian atmosphere of Madrid, poor and insalubrious, was no surprise to us. But we would have to wait before we could discover the manner in which the Spanish Court would receive a foreign painter who had been invited to stamp his seal on the Royal Palace. At the very gates of Madrid, by the old Puerta de Alcalá, we were informed that the Court was at Aranjuez for the season, as was the custom each spring. We had presumed, however, that Minister Esquilache or my esteemed friend Francesco Sabatini would have arranged to have some trusted person receive the painter, in the event that they themselves could not. It was not to be. It would seem that the sultry heat that had descended on Madrid that fourth day of June of 1762 had encouraged them likewise to remove themselves for a few days to Aranjuez.

As I discovered the many inauspicious circumstances facing us, I pondered how to explain them to the great Tiepolo – to him and his sons, who were hiding in the coach, not daring to set foot in the filthy city. I imagined that the painter would order me to accompany him back to Barcelona and from there to his own country.

I was at a loss, perplexed to an extreme. Either we had been left to ourselves or the Royal dignitaries believed that our journey from Barcelona to Madrid would take longer. Knowing how disappointed Tiepolo must be that no one was waiting for him, it occurred to me that I might be able to cheer him up by means of a sentimental ruse, and I ordered the coach to take us to the Venetian embassy. A grave mistake, for here we found but a few people, who announced that the ambassador was also in Aranjuez.

Giambattista and his sons were finally given a room in the embassy of the Most Serene Republic of Venice. As I busied myself searching for a house for him to stay in while we awaited the appearance of someone from wretched Aranjuez, I realized how difficult it would be for Tiepolo to make his mark in this final stage of his career.

When Francesco Sabatini finally appeared and learnt of the Venetian's poor health following such an abominable trip, he sent a letter to the King and Minister Esquilache recommending that Tiepolo should not travel to the Royal

Seat of Aranjuez to present himself to the monarch. I was a stranger, lost in what seemed like a plague-infested city, but much of my distress came from the humiliation suffered by the greatest painter of vaults and ceilings that my century had known.

I could not anticipate then the days of glory and torment that this city would procure me. I had not yet recaptured the affections of the girl from Naples who had become a woman in Madrid; nor had I watched a king proclaim his dream on the brightest of days.

5

He Did Love Her

I had been absorbed for some time by the translation of Andrea Roselli's memoirs when I heard someone knocking on the door. I should have seen Armand approaching – I was writing in the shady, cool area of the porch which looks out onto the road coming up from the bay – but the vicissitudes undergone by the architect from Arezzo, his mention – not yet fully explained – of an extraordinary new project, the appearance on centre stage of the Venetian painter Giambattista Tiepolo (Tiepolo again!) had transported me to a distant world. The engineer's text is suggestive, provides subtle distinctions, becomes still more insightful and penetrating as I advance slowly, episode by episode, through the translation, to the point that I have even been able to forget about my phone conversation with Chloe that morning.

Chloe takes the photographs for the quarterly magazine the gallery publishes, but it's only a pleasant diversion for her, something she does on the side that distracts her from her usual work of snapping photos right and left for a lifestyle magazine. Chloe is not at all pleased with my decision to spend the summer – really just the month of August – in the house on the Bay of Alfacs. She's aware of

Sofia, and even though she knows that it's all water under the bridge, she's not totally convinced: she suspects the old lioness is up to some trick. Chloe isn't even on holiday now, so she can't expect me to stay quietly in Barcelona, though she would be happy enough if I had left for any other place on the planet.

Chloe is the kind of person I used to hang out with some time ago, one of those people you don't really know where they're from – the sort of people who show up in Barcelona or London and get by with very little money thanks to a precarious network of contacts that always provides them with a place to sleep and often a rather unconventional job: student interns, would-be designers, idle photographers, aspiring writers, actors on an indefinite pilgrimage, or sometimes just a bunch of grouchy individuals – an itinerant tribe I was once part of, but never felt completely at ease with. Family holds no ties for them, friends are everything; they never have any plans for the future, only a perpetual interest in pleasure and discovery: a devotion to sincerity or simplicity has taken the place of any established form of relationship. My rather chameleon-like character adapted to these changing colours until I discovered that to be Mediterranean or from a small town or have a Catholic background was not something to be despised.

But Chloe, a Caribbean who had spent time in the British capital, did fit in. She was a true feline, from her alert, eager little head to her agile body and lively imagination. I suspect that going out with her I've been somehow disloyal: I've devoured the freedom she offered me, her youthful sensuality, but when the tables turned and she tried to claim me with a possessive jealousy, I couldn't respond. I can't be tied down. She's not one of my kind.

In the meanwhile, I must let Armand Coll know that I've heard him and I hurry to welcome him. It sounds as if he's trying to knock the door down. He speaks franticly, as if he's just returned from sorting out the misfortunes of the world, keeps running a nervous hand over the rebellious tuft of hair that rises from the centre of his increasingly bald head. Armand reproaches me because I seem so unconcerned and hadn't bothered to leave the house all this time. What else could I do?

Armand is anxious, wants at all costs to prevent the newspapers from talking about the party and the names of the guests from being made public. He is determined in his effort. If yesterday the European Commissioner for Environment had shown up, Armand would have been suspicious, and asked himself why the event had been so widely circulated, so much energy invested in publicly displaying how close he was to the painter Malaquies Tarrés. After all, the autumn exhibition will be an effective international campaign to denounce the dangers facing the Ebro delta (which has been proclaimed a European natural-heritage site) and the atrocity the government is preparing to commit.

It must have been around midnight when I was standing on the terrace at the Mendizábals' beside Armand, watching the lights on the bay. A fast motorboat coming from open sea had approached the Banya peninsula – a sandy, deserted strip of land, far from any port – to deliver several bags of cocaine and ecstasy pills. At the arranged time another boat had set off from a secret point on the Bay of Alfacs and headed to the tip of the peninsula, where the exchange had quickly taken place, according to the usual procedure. But someone lost his nerve, or maybe there was an argument about the amount of money agreed upon. In any case, the delay afforded some time to the Guardia Civil, and their boat, which had been hiding in the Sant Carles de la Ràpita port, raced towards them.

The men who had arrived from open sea saw the police and tried to grab their money and make off, but the others – seeing themselves duped – attempted to stop them, giving the police even more of an advantage. Both boats desperately gunned their motors and tried to get as far from the coast as possible – an impossible task for the boat that had set out from the bay: neither the size of the boat nor the engine could compete with the police. They were quickly caught, while the suppliers escaped.

The four occupants of the boat put up no fight. They couldn't – besides, they had already thrown the drugs overboard. But there were two things that they had not foreseen. First, several bags didn't completely sink in the shallow water by the beach, and were spotted by the police. Secondly, two more people had also been arrested on the peninsula, where the drug-dealers had their base, the point from which the boat had set out. Here the police found a simple dock among the canes in the salt marsh, a farmer's hut and a vehicle waiting for the distribution of the drugs.

The Guardia Civil had been following their movements for some time and had carefully planned their course of action. They questioned the arrested men, and a third person was taken into custody, presumably the head of the operation: Jonàs Sauler, universally known by his wife's surname as Jonàs Mendizábal, as was his real-estate company. It must have been around two in the morning when this happened.

Fortunately, Jonàs offered no resistance. The euphoria from the cocaine had faded and, like many of his guests, he had stretched out in an armchair. Sofia took her husband's arrest with surprising stoicism, considering that only minutes before she had wept on my shoulder while dancing with me. The rest of the guests didn't make much of a fuss until a little later, when they realized what had been going on. We all excused ourselves as best we could and filed out.

Armand's anxiety was growing as the radio stations kept broadcasting the news of the arrests. There was a huge commotion in Tortosa: many young people from the town were involved. But, as yet, no news had leaked out about the guests at the party, about the well-known people who had attended the event.

"You've got nothing to worry about," I tell him. "You'd already left by the time the Guardia Civil got there. Right?"

"Well, I tried to warn you that Jonàs was up to something, and you wouldn't listen to me. I left when I left, but that doesn't mean that some smart alec isn't going to tell a reporter that I'd been there."

"Come on, Armand, you know as well as I do that there were reporters at the party. We'll have to see if the ones who were there want to spill the beans or not. Besides," I say, slightly annoyed, "the fact that you were there doesn't make you a drug-dealer."

"Of course," Armand says, clearly not pleased with my comment. "But you know as well as I do how much damage it would cause if my name were to be linked to the Mendizábals."

"Hold on a minute… They've arrested him, not her…"

"I know, and I found out this morning that there are no charges against Sofia. So now it's a matter of waiting a few hours or a few days, until the news moves away from the party and focuses on the real-estate scandal that's bound to come up… Yet another scandal."

I'm not keen on spending my time with Armand, who's frightened, mean-spirited, and only worried that his public image might get damaged. I end up inviting him out to lunch so we can talk about it calmly. After a couple of hours, we tackle the problem again.

"I've got used to moving carefully, being alert. Even more so now, with the huge mess about the interbasin water transfer," he says, more relaxed now as we sit at the table.

"Well, according to the latest polls, the fact that you're one of the driving forces behind the opposition to the project has turned you into one of the most highly esteemed Members of Parliament."

"But that also means I'm forced to speak out all the time; I can't live the way I want to."

"I don't understand you. You're lucky enough to be able to defend what is yours…"

Armand becomes serious, and gives the impression that he's searching for something in the recesses of his memory. He stops eating and says:

"You know me. I've always tried to be rational in politics. I thought it was possible—"

"But that's what you're doing, isn't it? Environmental sustainability, territorial balance—"

"Rubbish! All the hydrological studies I've carried out since I've been in politics, the facts and the information I'd previously gathered, point to one thing only: if we look at the big picture, see this as a broad peninsular project, then channelling water from the Ebro River to other basins is logical and even advisable…"

My spoon stops mid-air.

"What are you saying?" I manage to stammer out. "Are you out of your mind? That's the government's argument, and you're the main political figure who disputes it!"

"You have to remember that I am a member of the opposition party, and since I am the only Member of Parliament from around here, I'm the one who has to be visible."

"Which means?…"

"Which means that if I were part of the governing party, I'd apply the hydraulic plan the progressive party supported a decade ago."

"If the thousands and thousands of decent people you drag to your demonstrations could only hear you now! They'd be up in arms."

"We don't organize the demonstrations: we only show up if the activists invite us."

"You participate and support what they say. You are their voice in Congress. Don't give me that bit about hydrological studies, Armand – everyone sees you as the most zealous defender of the Ebro."

"I know, and the truth is I do oppose the conservative government's plan."

"But it sounds like it's the same thing your party would implement."

"Well, yes, but we'd do it to support a political cause, to contribute to the overall development of the region, whereas they are motivated by pressure from the large construction companies that will derive huge profits from the work. Which in the end means the banks."

"So you're saying that the people who just congratulated you will be sent to the slaughterhouse, by one party or the other."

"The Ebro delta's receding, the crops and wells are saline... it's impossible to navigate the river because there's not enough water... and none of that can be attributed to the transfer of water to Murcia or Almeria, because that hasn't been done yet. It's all been caused by the reservoirs from forty years back, from the time of Franco's regime."

"And the situation would only worsen with your party's reservoirs."

"Right now we're the opposition, and we're against the plan. If we were elected – which is unlikely – we'd continue to oppose the plan for a decent length of time..."

"But Armand, you're from here. When all of this is over and you're sixty years old – like the fisherman who just embraced you because he believes you defend him – and you come back here and discover the disaster caused by your party or by the others, then—"

"Don't feed me the same speeches I have to make! Let's cut the bull. I have two good arguments. For one, if I ever publicly support this project from the opposition party – or from a governmental position – it'd be because it would represent the greater good, something that would benefit ten million people and hurt a hundred thousand, even if it is a hundred thousand of 'my' people. And secondly: the disaster you mention is nothing more than a return to the original situation, the delta of two hundred years ago, where rice – such an important crop now – wasn't grown at all and the area was full of salt mines."

"In other words, what we need to do is improve Charles III's plan for the delta – the enlightened despot will be your model."

I wasn't trying to accuse Armand: it was more a matter of complicity. He was the one, after all, who encouraged me to study the failed plans of the enlightened king who indirectly promoted the colonization of the deserted delta. For a moment Armand Coll seems to reconsider.

"I really appreciate being able to say what I think for once. I can rarely do so – at times I feel like I'm going to go crazy."

"If what you say was ever published," I tease him again, "the hardcore Catalans would be delighted. They can't understand how all of you can spend so much time supporting a cause that in the end – when you have the opportunity to govern – you'll abandon."

"For the government it's even worse: their people in the region are completely cornered. Defending the river was their natural argument, a nationalistic argument, and they had to sacrifice it for political reasons, the same kind of pressure that construction companies and banks put on the conservative party."

Armand Coll smiles – he's enjoying himself. I have to admit that the only thing that at one point attracted me to journalism was the possibility of knowing stories from the inside, from all different angles. The only difference, contrary to fishermen or painters or drug-dealers, is that as soon as you discover a politician's strategy to deceive you, you start getting bored.

When I was at university, I did a bit of journalism to earn money. I can't complain, things went well. What I most valued from that period in my life was the possibility of acquiring certain friendships that I wouldn't have otherwise. But when my mother died, I discovered to my surprise that the inheritance was more than I thought – the truth is I was expecting nothing – so I decided to leave the newspaper, where I had slowly come to be in charge of the cultural section and art supplement, and invest the money in an art gallery where I could lead the life I wanted. I sold the family house in the village and bought the one on the Bay of Alfacs, knowing that it was both a refuge and a trap. I knew I could always come back, but that it would be better if I didn't. It served as a magnet and a repellent, a situation that suited me reasonably well until very recently. When I saw Sofia walk through the door at the art gallery, I read it as a sign that the hour was drawing near for me to return to the labyrinth. I never expected, however, that my first days back in the town would coincide with a friend locked behind bars.

"So, Armand, if you had reliable sources of information and knew about Jonàs's activities, and that his bad reputation could affect your political image, why did you come to the party?"

"For the same reason you did."

"Which is?"

"Because Sofia invited me. But unlike you, I'd been going to their summer parties for some time. The same as other politicians, builders, the same as the painter Tarrés. You have to be there."

When we part, Armand again shows off his insider information by reporting that all the men arrested the night before have been moved to Tarragona. When I mention once more my concern that Sofia might be caught up in the scandal and my intention to visit her, Armand tells me I won't find her at home. Seeing my puzzlement, he reveals that she's at Tarrés's farmhouse amid the rice fields. I knew what he was driving at, but acted as if I didn't, and he didn't dwell on it. We got up from the table quite late. This evening I'm not planning to visit anyone other than a man named Andrea Roselli.

The day after my lunch with Armand Coll, I decide to go to Tarragona to check on my arrested friend Jonàs. Why should I? For a number of reasons. For the Invisible City, for all the afternoons we played there before I acquired a notion of the beauty of objects and before Armand Coll had told me that the place had been a silo, used for storage, but actually built two centuries before as a warehouse for the great port that was going to be built at the mouth of the canal that would connect the Ebro to the sea.

Jonàs was always the sharpest, the quickest of the group. When we organized a football match, he was the first to choose who would be on his team. He knew all the strange names of nautical gear and would frequently spit out whole lists: thole, trammel, rudder bar. His pranks were famous – everybody was a target for his jokes, riddles and challenges. Had we been animals and had there been a fight for survival, he would have been the one to outlast us all.

So, what happened? At some point in his studies, Jonàs lost his drive; his shrewdness was no longer useful. His vitality had kept him unfettered, until he reached a point where he couldn't grow any more. It was as if the boy's star had prematurely begun to wane.

It wasn't a material limit, but a moral one. Jonàs lost interest in what we still had to learn, lost all motivation to study. He felt – or he was told – that it wouldn't be of use to him or it would be beyond his reach. At that point, the innate advantage he had always counted on vanished, became an obstacle; he was left helpless in an unfamiliar situation. He wasn't prepared to stop being the fastest, the cleverest, the most brilliant, and his reaction was to compensate by being cocky, aggressive, putting on airs. Except for the mirage of our golden youth, when his character and attitude made him the natural leader of a gang of kids, it was a slow road to marginalization.

The companion of my childhood games, now a petty Mafioso. He was sucked in by the irresistible promise of the easy money he would gain as a drug-dealer, something that would restore his sense of superiority – economic of course, but also social and, especially, sexual – while the rest of us poor insects were scrabbling around in studies which would only benefit us at some point in the future or in employments that paid next to nothing.

* * *

My friend's startling physical decline surprises me today: his sunken eyes, bent shoulders, trembling hands. Just before I enter the sordid cell his lawyer – a good one – informs me that he's not optimistic. I find Jonàs lying in an almost fetal position on a kind of bench; he gives me a glance that says he is both annoyed and pleased that I've come to visit him.

"You have to be patient. It's only a matter of a few days," I tell him with little conviction.

"Who knows, maybe it was my time? The worst thing isn't being locked up in here, it's not being able to pump anything into my body. I don't suppose you have—"

"Of course not."

"Then get out of here."

"I'll leave if you want."

"No, wait," he says, making an effort to look at me.

"With the real-estate business going so well, why did you have to get mixed up in all this?"

"It all looks so easy from the outside. I was in so deep, I couldn't do anything except keep playing. The whole thing just got out of control. If I couldn't put my hands on a large sum of money, the entire business was going under."

"What about the Mendizábals' money?" I ask, at the risk of complicating things more.

"Sofía pulled the plug some time ago. All these people who've been rich all their lives, they won't take any chances, and if they let you have a few pennies, it's for investing it, and they want to see results immediately."

"Well, I doubt if it was just pennies."

My comment gets Jonàs all worked up.

"What the hell do you know about business? You don't have a clue. Those of us who are out there on the front line, the ones who know how to turn a profit, sometimes we just have to take short cuts, break a few rules that were made for the crowds. So maybe you're right, I blew away a small fortune that belonged to Sofia's family. So what? Right now, I could do with a line. Any chance you'd help me out?"

"Not with this."

"You're just like her, exactly like Sofia, you stupid bastard. All she needed was this artistic whim. You know what? You should have kept her."

"Jonàs, don't be such an idiot!" I was finding it harder and harder to put up with his pathetic rant. I'd much rather he attacked me – licking his wounds doesn't suit him.

"Sofia's not up to this. She can't keep up with me. I've let her have her way with the gallery and all that about the art work. It could turn out to be good for me, we could share clients…"

Fortunately, now that Jonàs was wallowing in the mud, I was told that my visiting time was over. But when he heard the guard, he counter-attacked:

"I'm telling you, you should have kept her!"

"Maybe you're right, Jonàs," I say, knowing I won't be seeing him for a long time and wishing to end on a conciliatory note, "but she chose you!"

"The hell she did: you got scared because I threatened you."

I smile. It's true and it's not. Sofia was special, dazzling, but I wasn't going to get myself killed for her.

"Good luck, Jonàs. I hope this will be over soon."

"No need for you to hurry, it's too late. Sofia's probably with Malaquies right now. She's been cheating on me for some time."

"That's enough, Jonàs. Bye!"

I closed the door softy. Years ago, when we raced together through the Invisible City, we were in a similar situation. None of the group could have known what lay ahead of us. Sometimes I think that Jonàs is what I might have been, and I have the absurd feeling that the worst part of myself was passed to him, in concentrated form. Perhaps for this strange reason I went back into the room and stared at him in silence. He was still talking, as if I'd never left, his eyes curiously fixed on me and the door.

"But I'll tell you one thing. This painter with the shitty exhibition, he won't last long. The only thing she wants, the only thing she's ever wanted is the Tiepolo. I did love her."

Having said that, he crumpled down, like a building that collapses after years of being riven with cracks.

As I drive along the motorway, heading south this time, I think about Jonàs's last words. To my left the sea is blackening as a mass of dark clouds swells, growing so dense one has the impression it is palpable. As the windscreen fills with drops, I continue driving as if in a trance, with only an outward appearance of calm.

"I did love her" could mean a million things. That Jonàs used to love Sofia but doesn't love her any more. That Jonàs loved Sofia but she didn't love him. Or something quite different: Jonàs – unlike me – did love Sofia. One thing is clear: Jonàs once loved Sofia. Curiously, it is this fact that brings me a sense of peace. It sort of redeems him after all the dirty tricks he's pulled on everyone, as if having loved her excuses him. I'm probably just swept away by the whole thing: seeing Jonàs in prison, knowing Sofia's screwing Malaquies, and I forget about all of Jonàs's capers over the years.

Why would he accuse me of not having loved her? Or does he only mean that it was a fitting destiny for Sofia to be handed to him? Somehow, I know that this accusation is related to the other thing he said, and that it'll be a difficult issue to unravel: Sofia is only interested in Tiepolo. Tiepolo? What does that have to do with all this? Jonàs is jealous of Tiepolo, he scorns Sofia's love of painting, and believes that this is what has kept her from loving him. It seems an oversimplification, but I can understand. What I refuse to accept is that a bastard like Jonàs has the right to pass judgement.

The drops on the windscreen have changed to a deafening downpour, the sea has disappeared, and the smell of earth seeps inside the car as I drive, my eyes glued to the lines on the road. Some cars have pulled over to wait for the deluge to pass, but I continue, still haunted by what Jonàs meant by his words. I suddenly realize that he didn't say that Sofia was only interested in Tiepolo, rather she was only interested in *the* Tiepolo. A specific Tiepolo. As if it were a particular painting. I repeat the words to myself: it's the only thing that she's *ever* wanted. In this case *ever* means, at the very least, as long as he's known her, as long as they've lived in Sant Carles. That's what he was reproaching her about:

the painting was more valuable or important or fascinating than Jonàs was. What Tiepolo? And what does Malaquies Tarrés know about it, since he bothered to mention it at the party?

I first met Sofia when I was beginning to interview people for the newspaper. In the '80s the interest in fine wines was no longer confined to a small circle of connoisseurs, but was gaining ground among professionals and people who could afford to pay for it. So the newspaper commissioned a series of articles on the subject. Sofia was an interesting character, part of an old, well-known line of wine makers, but she had her own point of view about the wine world and, besides, she lived in Barcelona. She was dazzling.

We became friends, and she reinforced my interest in painting by introducing me to her painter friends, thereby providing me with the possibility of viewing private collections that otherwise I wouldn't have had access to. My relationship with art was intellectual, aesthetic; Sofia's was one of familiarity. She had seen paintings of value hung and unhung in her own home; at times she was charged with the acquisition – or sale – of paintings that formed part of the family patrimony. I'm trying now to remember what pretext she gave for accompanying me to the Ebro delta. What an absurd idea: there was never a Tiepolo.

It's stopped raining by the time I reach Sant Carles, and a multitude of restless people have flocked onto the streets to spend the rest of this strange August evening. It proves difficult to drive through the centre of town, but I finally reach the bay. Before I can get out of the car to open the gate, a slight figure waves an arm at me by way of greeting.

It's Valeriana, Jonàs's mother. Her face is furrowed with deep waves of wrinkles, which are more concentrated around her tiny dark eyes – eyes that seem to be hiding from the world. She's dressed in black, head to toe, including a scarf around her head that's tied at her chin. All the old women used to dress like that, but you rarely see it any more. I explain to her that there is very little chance that he'll be let out, and she'll have to get used to the idea that she won't be seeing him for a long time.

"I never see him anyway," she tells me. "And I worry a lot less if he's in prison. If he's out and about, he'll just get into trouble again!"

Valeriana has no idea just how right she is. She's anchored in the past, still remembering the period when Jonàs caused her so much trouble and anxiety. But that was a long time ago.

"He killed his father, all those worries," she adds.

I can see them both, husband and wife, walking along the wharf, Jonàs playing nearby. The father jumps on the boat, helps the son on, then Valeriana. Once on board, Jonàs senior's every gesture is gentle and loving; he's always in high spirits when he and his son are on the boat, as they will be in the future when they head out together to fish every morning. This is Jonàs's family, his people, and he has destroyed all hope and goodness.

I look at Valeriana and I think that nothing I can say or do will be of any consolation. Both the torment within her and the public humiliation she's had to endure have driven her to the edge of insanity. She loves her son as much as she did when we were young and she'd catch us in the canal on the way back from the Invisible City. But she's turned into a ghost of her former self now that she knows that Jonàs is in danger again.

"What happened to the witch?" she asks me abruptly.

"What witch?"

"The one you brought him."

"I didn't bring her to him. He went looking for her," I tell her, smiling at the old woman's expression.

"Of course. He wanted everything you had, wanted to be like you." She's suddenly become so lucid that I start getting anxious.

"I don't know what you're talking about."

"Ah, if you knew how much he admired you, how he imitated you... From when he was little, he wanted to comb his hair like you, wear the same shoes, he'd repeat the same phrases you used..."

"Where did you get that impression?"

"It's not an impression. It's what happened. You never realized. I had to send him to that school because you were there. That's when he started falling apart."

"But I didn't—"

"He couldn't keep up with you, and that made him furious. He tried going to sea with his father, but that didn't work. He'd talked about you as if you were from a different world. You *did* live in a different world. We lost sight of you for all those years. You could have helped me set him straight; his father only knew how to use his belt on him. And Ariadna, how could you—"

"I didn't know how—"

"When he found that girl, I thought he'd straighten out.

It's true, he loved her and things got better. But they never even came to see me. A real witch."

I see it all now. He had found a way to be me at last: he must have been thrilled to steal Sofia from me, or to think he had. I can't believe it, I can't believe I've lived all these years with someone shadowing me, scrutinizing my every deed, gesture, my life, blowing it all out of proportion, interpreting it in his own way, assigning a value to things that had none for me, distorting the words that I would casually throw out, mirroring, emulating, envying me.

"After a while people started to talk. They'd try to cover it up when they saw me, but I could tell. I saw it coming. I knew he was up to his old tricks."

Valeriana didn't want me to accompany her home. I watched her climbing the road from the bay and disappearing into the night. I was left alone with all the ghosts that her words had evoked. How many people are there in the world like Valeriana? Armand is worried about what the newspapers say, but they never mention people like her, all that frustrated dignity and goodness. The emotion and compassion aroused by Valeriana could make me have even greater contempt for Jonàs, but her words were also a warning. I was right by the hornet's nest and I didn't even realize. And what was that about Ariadna?

For one reason or another, I know I can't just wait until my holiday ends and pretend this week didn't happen, go back to Barcelona and bury myself again in my work at the gallery and the magazine. If there is a way to unwind this enormous skein, it has a name: Tiepolo. *The* Tiepolo. In other words: Andrea Roselli.

6

Madrid

From Memoirs of the Invisible City

I managed to procure suitable quarters for the Tiepolos in a house in Plaza de San Martín, where they have resided since they left the Venetian Embassy. Once I had found the lodgings – with the help of Francesco Sabatini – I was able to relax and visit the capital of the kingdom with less angry eyes. The architect contributed greatly by inviting me to see the final work on the Royal Palace and admire the decoration. He was filled with passion as he provided details about the many projects that would change the entire face of the city and the court, some of which had been carried out during the last few years, while others would be finished shortly: the Royal Customs House, the General Hospital of Atocha, the Church of San Francisco el Grande, the new Puerta de Alcalá. Even the sewage system and road paving were being extended throughout the city.

Sabatini has applied to these buildings – it matters not that they are for public service, hospitals and churches – the Roman architectural model of the last two centuries, and as he has the royal coffers at his disposal, the results are splendid, so that the Spanish capital has begun to acquire an air of elegance and distinction previously denied her by the precarious buildings that prevailed. Nor has Sabatini neglected urban improvement, thanks to which Madrid has seen avenues, boulevards, fountains, squares and parks spring up; with time they will erase the memory of the weary, decrepit town that in 1762 received a frightened Tiepolo through the back door.

Sabatini is shrewd. He has found the opportunity to distinguish himself and leave his stamp on the Royal Palace: the construction of the magnificent main staircase, following the lines of Caserta, designed by our master, Luigi Vanvitelli. The one in Madrid is without a doubt imposing and elegant, but it lacks magnificence and light, which keeps it from rivalling the perfection of the Neapolitan villa. While visiting the palace – where architects, painters and sculptors were all busy at work, surrounded by a multitude of workers and members of Charles III's Court – I began to understand why no one had come to receive Tiepolo on our arrival in Madrid.

As Sabatini had gained the confidence of the monarch, so too had Anton Raphael Mengs, a painter from Bohemia who had met the King in Naples. Mengs was trying to secure royal commissions for himself. He seemed almost a hermit – living alone, his family in Rome – and he worked as if possessed. He frescoed at dawn and prepared cartoons at dusk. I had at first felt the same kindliness for him that I had for Tiepolo; both were devoted to their art – their religion you could call it. But I soon came to discover that he was consumed by an ambition for power: he wished to gain control of the Academy and impose the strictest of artistic principles, as if they were the new Tables of the Law which had been revealed to him alone.

Mengs was sullen, expressed his ideas with great severity, was blunt in his dealings. In spite of that, he was esteemed and admired, in part because he had garnered considerable respect with his brief treatise *Reflections on Beauty and Taste in Painting* – which few had actually read, as it was published in German – and in part because human nature tends to feel itself comfortable following the dictates of others, avoiding thereby the risks of freely thinking for itself.

Nevertheless, Mengs's treatise does indeed help to understand and appreciate painting and the training of painters. The Bohemian has in his favour the fact that he has seen sublime manifestations of art in Parma, Florence and, especially, Rome. One could object, however, that he seems to consider his theory more important than the painting itself, issuing statements entirely too categorical: "Raphael chooses expression, finding it in the composition and design; Correggio searches for what is pleasant in shape, and predominantly chiaroscuro; finally Titian embraces the semblance of truth to be found in colours. The most sublime of these three must of course be the one who possesses the most essential part, which is, without a doubt, expression. Raphael is, therefore, unquestionably the best."

The arrival of Giambattista Tiepolo might well endanger the Bohemian's hegemony. Mengs – who will never belong to the category of painters such as Tiepolo – had striven to demonstrate that the Venetian's paintings were antiquated, lacking in merit when seen in the light of new currents of thought. We can observe in Mengs's paintings a parallel to his aesthetic ideas: his portraits are correct, neat, recall in some notable cases an attention to detail, but his art never soars beyond what he represents. We could say, perhaps, that he draws well, but is a painter wanting imagination and genius.

As he could not always succeed on canvas, he tried to triumph in the field of theory and in personal intrigue, and attempted to take control of the Real Academia de Bellas Artes de San Fernando, the Royal Academy of Art. When he realized that his supremacy was not complete and his health declining, he obtained permission from the King to spend time in Rome with his family. Later on, he developed a new strategy by forming an alliance with His Majesty's confessor, Father Eleta, who had greater influence over the monarch than anyone foreign to this court could possibly imagine.

All of Madrid was surprised – is surprised – to have a king as devout as Charles, something that was accentuated by the death of his wife, Queen Maria Amalia of Saxony, shortly after arriving in Castile. Everyone is aware that Charles is a very chaste man: they even say that since he was widowed, the King displays this virtue by escaping from all temptations of the flesh, to the point that he sleeps on a bed hard as stone; and if, in spite of this, he occasionally feels agitated at night, he rises and walks about barefoot to dissipate his evil thoughts. His Majesty refuses the idea that a new wife be sought, and is enraged if it is suggested to him that he follow the easier route of taking a lover, a practice so frequent among his acquaintances.

As in Naples, hunting is almost as sacred to the King as prayer. It affords him some distraction, without a doubt, but there is a further reason. It has been suggested to him that frequent exercise could help avoid the streak of insanity that has ravaged his family. The strictness of the royal calendar is proverbial, but equally strict are the dates regarding places of residence. The exact day is established on which the King will be moved from one royal seat to another: winter in El Pardo, spring at Aranjuez, summer at San Ildefonso, autumn at El Escorial, with but brief stays in the Royal Palace in Madrid, the residence where he spends the least time. If I had only known this when I arrived in Madrid with Tiepolo!

In the meantime, the indefatigable Francesco Sabatini was supervising a great number of architectural and urban works, and I followed him about. From time to time I mentioned to him that I would have preferred to concentrate on one project, for example the Royal Palace or the Hospital, but he would only become elusive, refusing to give me a clear response. At times I managed to draw from him some comment, such as "This is not your mission". "Do I have a mission?" I asked myself. During this time rumours began to spread around us – rumours that left me both worried and flattered – according to which I was becoming the master's right hand.

It was true that I worked in the shadow of Sabatini during my first years in Madrid; they were the culmination of my training in a city teeming with new projects and reform, filled with architects, painters, writers, with a king and minister disposed to renovate the country. I often visited the elderly Tiepolo, who bravely made progress with his work on the palace vaults. I would find him on the scaffolding or at his home in the Plaza de San Martín. Señor Giambattista pretended he was not aware of his disdainful treatment by Mengs and his group, as well as by the Royal Academy of Art; or perhaps in truth he was not aware of it, engrossed as he was in the work of Titans, the real emblem of the palace.

If anything could represent the animated, creative and bold atmosphere in Madrid at that time, it was the images frescoed by Giambattista, which I examined from one end to the other, lying close to the ceiling, on the same scaffolding from which Tiepolo painted. First he finished the *Apotheosis of Aeneas* in the Guard Room: the hero ascending a spiral of clouds and light towards Immortality, aided by his mother Venus, who is seated beside Cupid offering Aeneas a helmet.

The masterpiece, however, is in the Throne Room: *The Apotheosis of the Spanish Monarchy*, in which the monarchic institution is exalted by heavenly beings, assisted by the Virtues and surrounded by the various States. The fresco overcomes the difficulty of the gigantic dimensions of the room by creating different focuses of attention, at the heads of the room and along the cornices, whereas the sky draws together all these areas of the painting, creating tension among them – a sky whose light explodes among great castles of clouds where a rainbow peeps out – a sky that illuminates and attracts seemingly weightless, yet decidedly corporeal figures, inundated by a glow which shows them attired in a dazzling range of colours.

* * *

With time Sabatini grew to be one of the most influential men in the new capital, and he kindly proposed that I settle in a detached, empty wing of his mansion, which was to become my home. He had got married by proxy to the daughter of Luigi Vanvitelli, and I accompanied him as he awaited her arrival from Naples. Francesco was upwards of forty years old; Cecilia had just turned eighteen. The news of her beauty had preceded her, and all of Madrid was expectant.

The arrival of the Neapolitan could not have been more unsettling to my friend and mentor. Cecilia announced with a show of arrogance that she refused to accept the marriage to an old man. Apart from his age, I should add that Francesco's appearance was not that of the fair Adonis. Cecilia's brothers – who had also settled in Madrid and directed the works that Sabatini supervised – moved heaven and earth to convince her of the benefits to be derived from the union and the scandal that would occur if she did not consent to it. Nothing, however, could make her change her mind.

Francesco Sabatini, the great man of the new city of Madrid, was pensive and dejected within doors, but when about his work he tried to look as if nothing troubled him – the same energetic man, a trifle petulant perhaps. The days passed, and his Cecilia still would not listen to anyone or relent, not even after all the gifts the architect sent her. She refused to see him. At that point Sabatini pleaded with me, implored me to speak to her, talk to her about my friend and master's many virtues – some of which might not be apparent on first sight. I should tell her that he would be generous and accommodating: she would have all the freedom she needed. Sabatini said that she would listen to me, because I had nothing to gain or lose in the matter; moreover, he had confidence in my ability to convince her because my age was closer to hers.

Obviously I could not refuse, though I had very little faith in my powers of persuasion. What I never suspected, however, was that this errand would change my life for ever.

I met Cecilia Vanvitelli in the park. She was wearing a light dress and holding a parasol, showing bare arms and a bare neck, the low-cut neckline revealing the swell of her breasts. She had large, keen eyes, a certain alertness in her glance – she was an intelligent, educated woman. A foreigner. No lady in Madrid would be quite as daring. A young lady, a girl.

She smiled, and her companions smiled and bowed slightly as they greeted us. The group moved along slowly, and we spoke of yesterday's concert, the good weather, until little by little our escort fell behind, and Cecilia and I walked together alone, though observed from a prudent distance.

I had the impression that my entire life until now was a whirlpool that had swept me up and delivered me to this moment and place. Cecilia twirled her parasol and gave a sly smile.

"I remember you well from Naples. My father said you were his favourite disciple. But I am sure you never noticed me!"

"I was in awe of your father, and I was only just out of the egg, so to speak."

"Ah, Caserta! La Riviera di Chiaia! What sin have I committed to be exiled to this infernal city? Have you also been sent by Sabatini to convince me?"

"No, I just wanted to greet you. I can make this city more pleasant for you."

There we were. How could I talk about winter to someone in the springtime of life? I swear that I did make an effort: I named all of Francesco's virtues, all the benefits she would derive from the marriage. I appealed to her interest, her heart, her vanity and sensibility. The only responses I received were smiles and a few angry comments. How pleased I was to observe that she resisted all my exhortations! How pleased I was to see that she did not love him and would not be persuaded. Should I be considered a bad friend for not being more convincing, for not putting more warmth into my arguments? Should I feel guilty for not conquering for someone else the person I desired for myself?

Each new encounter with Cecilia made it more difficult for me to ignore the dictates of my feelings, to turn a blind eye to the enticing charm issuing from her eyes, her voice, her gestures, her young body, her insolent beauty. Still, I resisted, even though I could perceive a spark in her eyes, a certain involuntary inflection in her tone of voice indicating that the attraction was mutual. It was mad, reckless for us to persist in our encounters. She grew more and more intrepid in separating from the other ladies' company, more and more daring along the labyrinthine paths we wove through the gardens in our attempts to escape.

The present situation could not continue. I had to stop this, or I could be exposed to shame and impropriety, something I could not allow to happen. I resolved to be honest, and informed Sabatini that I had failed in my mission to favour his interests. That same afternoon I would see Cecilia to bid her farewell. I had done what I could.

When she received the news from me, she flew into a rage and railed against the institution of marriage, her father and Sabatini – against everyone except the Pope and the King. Then she started sobbing, and begged me to help her, telling me how cruel I was to abandon her to that man, calling me cynical for denying the evidence of her love for me.

"I'll do whatever is needed not to lose you," she said after a brief pause, both of us lost in our thoughts, unwilling to leave our sheltered spot in a remote part of the garden. "If necessary, in order to be close to you, I will consent to marry Sabatini. You can tell him that he has won."

Francesco Sabatini was ecstatic, and so grateful for my diligent collaboration that he requested that I continue to occupy the rooms in his house, despite the fact that with Cecilia's arrival the number of servants would have to be greatly augmented. Still dazed and in a state of numbness, I wasn't able to decline his offer. As soon as the move had been completed and the celebrations ended, the skirmishes began. My head was occupied with Sabatini's urban projects, my heart pounded at the thought of Cecilia's proximity. I tried to avoid her by not frequenting the places she loved, choosing hours when I knew she wouldn't be there. Cecilia, however, had but one idea in mind, the opposite of mine, and she contrived to appear in the places where I was forced to be present.

We once met in the garden. The evening light filtered through the branches amid the scent of lemon trees and music from a nearby concert, our faces half-hidden by the rows of oleanders.

"You said you would not abandon me, Andrea."

"That is what you said, dearest Cecilia, not me. This is terribly imprudent—"

"I am alone, far from home. And you refuse to help me."

"Francesco is my friend, my—"

"I told you I would marry him to be close to you, and now you—"

"That's not true. You had no choice! The marriage had already been arranged."

"Don't be so cruel to me. Can you not be more gallant, as other gentlemen are?"

"What do you mean? What gentlemen?"

"Andrea, my dear, surely you do not think yourself the only one who can keep me company?"

I squeezed her well-turned arm, pulled her towards me – her hair was swept high and I kissed her bare neck. Our lips touched and we embraced, as the drawn-out notes of a violoncello sounded nearby. A shadow moved in the bushes a few steps from us: we both pretended not to have seen it, powerless as we were to control our passion.

The scene was repeated in another garden, then in a secluded parlour, later in my room. You may think I had gone mad. I had indeed. And I would have many days on which to recall Cecilia's enticing, triumphant song, her naked shoulders, the inescapable attraction of her breasts, her insolent joie de vivre. On the ship that would take me to my destiny – my doomed mission – I would have considerable time to reflect upon the intoxicating weeks that had finished so quickly.

One day Francesco announced that the Palace had requested an audience with us. I should prepare myself for an important commission, he said: my hour had finally arrived. I remember thinking at the time that I had been living in Madrid already for four years. I must confess that I was shaking as I sat by Sabatini in the carriage that led us to the Royal Seat. I was assaulted by the fear that Francesco had discovered us – yet I found it strange that he would act as he did if this was true. Still, I was consumed by shame knowing that I had betrayed the confidence of my friend and mentor. My mental state was such that I did not even notice we had arrived at the Palace: everyone was waiting for me to step down from the carriage. With a fast stride we entered the building, crossed the Arms Courtyard and reached the main staircase – a replica of the one in Caserta that had been built by Vanvitelli, Cecilia's father! The name of Cecilia rang like an accusation in my ears. Cecilia!

On this occasion, I had no time to glance at the ceilings by Mengs and Tiepolo. Esquilache himself, the man who had requested that I accompany Giambattista from Venice to Madrid, led us to the King. The warm, placid midday light, unfiltered by curtains, flooded the room where the

King was signing documents, surrounded by secretaries and ministers, the majority of whom were asked to retire when our presence was announced. Minister Esquilache, royal architect Sabatini and I bowed, as a smile crossed His Majesty's face. Charles III's large nose gave him a look of fragility, one that almost suggested piety, though his noble height lent him a majestic air. He put aside the business that had occupied him and came up to us.

"I wished to speak to you, Señor Roselli. I remember you from Naples, especially from Pompeii."

"Your Majesty, it is an honour for me to—"

"You carried out successfully the task of accompanying Señor Tiepolo to Madrid. The frescoes are almost finished... magnificent paintings."

"The Palace is worthy of them, Majesty."

"Señor Sabatini's efforts have proved to be splendid, and we have built a grand palace, as did our old friend Vanvitelli at Caserta; the work there was proceeding well before Vanvitelli's arrival, but his involvement provided a touch of genius. Your efforts in trying to make Madrid a more beautiful place are commendable, yet much remains to be done throughout the kingdom. Do you not agree?"

"It is so, Your Majesty. The magnificent public works you have commissioned have the additional advantage of enhancing the architecture of the entire country."

"Señor Roselli, I have asked Minister Esquilache and Señor Sabatini to train you as an architect and engineer, so that one day you might be able to direct the most ambitious undertaking of this kingdom."

"I am pleased, Your Majesty, to be able to serve you."

"But that moment has not arrived yet. I wish to send you to Russia to study how Tsar Peter built his city. You are then to return here, prepared to erect a new city that will glorify the country and contribute to the economic progress of Spain. Use your best endeavours, Señor Roselli; go to St Petersburg and learn all their secrets, see if the marvels we hear about are true. On your return, we will decide where the new city shall be erected, so that it might best reflect the benefits we seek, and have the most suitable shape. As of this moment, the city of St Charles exists only in the minds of those who are present here today."

All the year's seasons flashed before my eyes as I saw the transformed countenance of the King: he had now abandoned his timidity and fragility and assumed an air of determination and joy only imaginable in someone who has a dream and knows how it can be achieved. His Majesty let fall these last words as he walked towards the light streaming through one of the great windows, and repeated in an unrestrained voice close to ecstasy: "St Charles! St Charles!" It is not often that a king can proclaim in the bright light of spring the birth of a dream. Esquilache and Sabatini likewise smiled. The former was troubled by the difficulties of government as he attempted to apply the monarch's reforms, yet he smiled, for it was his duty to please the King. As for the latter, it was easy to imagine why he was smiling. No doubt it was Sabatini himself who persuaded the King to send me as far away as possible. Could any place be further than St Petersburg? A masterful move on his part, certainly. I was dismayed and overwhelmed by a series of emotions: euphoric at being entrusted with the most important mission I would probably receive in my entire life; delighted with the confidence the King had placed in me; disturbed because this confirmed that Sabatini had discovered us; deeply distressed that, as a result, I must part from Cecilia.

The preparations took only a couple of weeks. The travel plans, the credentials, the letters of recommendation – everything seemed to have been arranged before the audience with the King. There was a certain urgency about the mission, and I went about my affairs in a state of intoxication, engaged in frenetic activities, overwhelmed by the powerful emotions of my leave-taking and the atmosphere of unrest in the city. On the streets of Madrid, and in certain aristocratic quarters, the air of revolt was palpable. As the King advanced along the path of his radiant dream, the kingdom prepared for a Vigil of Arms that would lead it once again into darkness.

My light was not St Petersburg, but Cecilia. She appeared in my private rooms before I had the opportunity to announce the news to her. Perfumed, arrogant, she spoke with an accusing voice:

"Write to me and describe the dresses and salons of Catherine of Russia."

In that moment I realized my Neapolitan lover had undergone an inner transformation. From then on, nothing that might happen would affect her deeply; events would simply represent a challenge for her. She would never again be a person living in the shadow of anyone or anything; her alert eye would be capable of turning any obstacle in her favour. The discovery of this attitude in her both attracted and frightened me. From this moment on, I knew that Cecilia Vanvitelli – or rather Cecilia Sabatini – would be capable of anything.

That afternoon we made love for the first time, with bites and cries, with the fury of those who know that the same fortune that brought them together was now separating them, with the frenzy and pleasure of those who perceive that life is but a moment of exultant joy or a disheartening shadow, a brief moment that has been given to you.

7

Along Old Paths

St Charles, Sant Carles, the city of Charles III! I am finally getting close to the heart of the mystery. Andrea Roselli must be the man chosen by the King to carry out his project on the Iberian coast: the construction of the city that would in time go by its Catalan name of Sant Carles. The memoirs of the Tuscan architect seem to indicate that the moment for deciding the exact location of the future city is still distant, and his sentimental entanglement could represent a serious obstacle – after all Cecilia was the wife of Sabatini, the royal architect! Whether at the King's command or forced by a cheated husband's revenge, Roselli has set sail for St Petersburg, which is to be the model for Charles III's new city. Sant Carles an image of St Petersburg? And if these events were recorded, it must be because Andrea was encouraged to do so by Giambattista Tiepolo, who apparently had a great influence on the architect.

I sigh as I think that I have Tiepolo close at hand, as well as Sant Carles, although for the time being there is nothing to indicate that the city of Sant Carles planned by the King was actually located by the Ebro River. And, somewhere, a painting by Tiepolo has disappeared. Jonàs said Sofia had always believed in its existence; apparently even Malaquies had heard of it, as well as the stamp-dealer in Tortosa, who mentioned Tiepolo the day he told me he had a plan of the Invisible City. All together, this strikes me as a bunch of unconnected stories, guesswork, loose ends. Yet, a distant throb somehow seems to be growing nearer, as if a sleeping truth had been awoken, one that had been awaiting me for a long time in the quiet darkness – as if the moment had now come for this story to be revealed. I still don't know how the Roselli manuscript came to me, or if someone simply decided that it was time for me to know this.

I awake early. Valeriana's words stirred up old demons that troubled me during the night. From the bay the regular sound of gentle waves lapping the beach reaches me. It's the sing-song quality of the waves that strikes me. When you are at peace, the sound comforts you; when you are anxious, the waves seem to break relentlessly against you, as if they were an echo of the conscience – yours or someone else's – a reproach. I try to block out the bitter voices by walking along the beach, which is still deserted. The reddish finger of land extending into the sea appears on the horizon, on the other side of the bay that perhaps Charles III imagined similar to the Gulf of Naples and the salt marshes of Pozzuoli. The cool water on my feet stimulates me – my mind races, but I'm thinking clearly now.

Last night, after I talked to Valeriana, I phoned Chloe, and she scolded me for letting myself be dragged again into Jonàs's problems, everyone else's problems – *di tutti quanti*, as she put it. Maybe I'm only imagining it, and she's just a little sour because she's still in Barcelona while I'm down here jumping from party to party. Or from prison to prison. There's no logical reason for her to be anxious, yet she feels that there is. Is she off track? Possibly. She's always suspicious of what she doesn't know: and here on the delta I'm a different person, or rather, I'm a person she doesn't know.

I sit down on the porch of my simple, whitewashed house in the middle of the little bay, and it's as if I were stripped of everything I have accumulated far from here. No art gallery or trips, nothing that ties me to my work, no Barcelona. I was horrified the first time I discovered how little time I needed to rid myself of all the layers that enveloped me. It was as if I stood on the edge of an abyss, as if in a few brief moments everything that I had learnt through years of effort, what I meant to others, everything that had contributed to the creation of the image of myself could be taken from me. You've imagined that this appearance is like a solid wall erected stone by stone over many years as you are constantly engaged in changing yourself, disguising yourself, as you come into contact with people and work. You assume that the social network in which you are ensconced, which maintains you thanks to a succession of small conquests and compromises, is as solid as the time invested in building it. When you see yourself divested of masks and shields, your very core stands naked. You discover you are fragile, vulnerable, abandoned, as if the angel that accompanied you until that windy afternoon by the enormous school door has fled; but if you can bear to face your own life, you'll see that once the fear has gone you can slowly lift your head and grow more solid, blissfully free.

* * *

This morning I returned to an old concern of mine. My phone call was answered by the warm, convincing voice of Father Patrici Domènec, the priest who had been headmaster of the school that resembled El Escorial, a person still very close to the progressive politician, ex-seminarian Armand Coll. Father Patrici had known how to channel our adolescent exuberance towards religious faith – a free, full faith that resembled very little the rigid, corseted system favoured in certain ecclesiastic quarters. We were lucky. Those of us who learnt to see God in the sunlit beams of the building, the icy streams, the holiday songs, the freedom in our dress code, the sense of brotherhood, the knowledge that affection was more important than any rules and regulations – those of us who experienced this were able to escape the obsessive anticlericalism that characterized the intellectuals from previous generations, an attitude still occasionally found in our own time. I thought of this as I spoke to Father Patrici on the phone and we arranged to meet. I should be grateful to him that I didn't have to waste a third of my life disparaging God and his mother, as most of my friends do – that noble, cathartic crusade of our time.

Father Patrici retired some time ago from his pedagogical career and now directs the new Diaconal Archives of Tortosa, a treasure trove of historical documents, only recently open to the public after the enormous task of cataloguing was completed. This is what led me to believe that it must have been Father Patrici who had sent me the Roselli manuscript.

I stroll through the streets of old Tortosa – the southern capital of Catalunya, a city forever turned inwards with the crumbling façades of its Renaissance palaces, the exuberant baroque cathedral – and finally come face to face with white-haired, alert Father Patrici, a kind-hearted man who doesn't want his kindness to be trumpeted around. He shuns my long stare. We haven't seen each other for many years; this would be the chance to talk at length, but the archivist avoids any familiarity and goes straight to the point. Perhaps he still remembers our meeting when my mother was dying and I showed up from Barcelona, bewildered when he tried to point me towards the discovery of certain truths that I refused to pursue; perhaps it weighs on him that I didn't respond very well to his rather unsettling frankness. There is, however, not the slightest air of reproach about him.

"The most unthinkable things can surface from these bundles of documents and old papers. We've only studied about five per cent of what's here," he tells me as we walk through what appear to be very unsteady stacks.

This is encouraging. Father Patrici stops in an aisle that is better illuminated than the others and pulls out a folder as his glasses slip down on his nose; he shows it to me, then puts it back in its place.

The ex-headmaster laughs softly from time to time; it's clear that he knows perfectly well why I've come, though he elegantly tries to hide the fact. Once we've left the stacks and are back in a well-lit room, I decide it's time to stop playing cat and mouse. I admit to him that I've been snared, and that the Roselli memoirs have led me to him. I tell him it was a clever way of summoning me, that I'm very excited about what I'm discovering, and that if my expectations are fulfilled the historical importance of this one document more than warrants the huge amount of work devoted to classifying the archives.

Instead of looking evasive – as he used to look when he reluctantly scolded me at school – or filled with enthusiasm, like when he encouraged us to take our two-day mountain hikes; instead of the saintly smile he would have as he blessed us, he stood stock still, an expression of surprise and incomprehension on his face. He asked me to explain.

There was no point making him repeat that he had no idea what papers I was talking about: his face said it all.

"I'm really sorry I can't help you. The document was not from our archives, definitely not. But, from what you say, it sounds like it could be quite important."

"When I saw how happy you were when I arrived, I thought it meant that this was your doing and that you were smiling at how well your strategy had turned out."

"Why would I have sent you the document anonymously? I would have phoned you, told you to come and see me. I was smiling because I was happy to see you – I haven't seen you for a long time."

"I know I don't come often," I say in an apologetic tone and with a touch of sadness, because I have a feeling Father Patrici doesn't have many visitors.

"You've got your own life…" he says and stops, thoughtful, as if considering whether it's prudent to continue. "But I'm not at all surprised that you're interested in this Roselli, quite the contrary…" And he pauses again, as if looking for help in what he wants to say. "When I enter this silent, empty nave, I often think that the people I've just seen walking down the streets, talking, people who live their lives with passion, aren't attracted to these piles of paper we have in the archives. By that I mean that they have no interest in their own past."

"They say that's a sign of health!" I point out laughingly, hoping this will help Father Patrici to make his argument.

"I clung to the hope that you were different," he says, surprising me with his comment. "And you are, in a certain way – but in a very strange way. The information I shared with you when your mother... you never looked into it, did you?"

"No. And I don't plan to."

"That's your choice, of course. You don't want to see your own, recent past, yet you're running after these eighteenth-century documents, as if you think that the truth you are looking for can't be found fifty years ago, but rather two hundred and fifty years ago."

Father Patrici's words amaze me. He seems to have devoted more thought to my problems than me, and to know them better than I do myself. It had never even occurred to me to view things from this perspective – maybe he's right. When I try to improvise a clumsy, garbled response in my defence, he cuts me short:

"I trust you know that the road to peace, or whatever it is you're seeking, can't be found in any calendar, in any particular deed that took place in a particular year."

Truth. Salvation. Redemption. Father Patrici is inviting me to take part in a dialectical game which seems harmless enough – after all, he's only offering me his sympathy and his blessing. So I leave the archives feeling comforted by the encounter, by having embraced a friend and former master, but no less obsessed with uncovering the mystery of Roselli and Tiepolo.

I walk away from the narrow streets, the decadent houses, the robust façades in the Episcopal quarter of the city and find my way to the broad avenue along the dwindling river. I find the light unbearable, the heat annoying. As I drive back to Sant Carles I listen to the three messages left on my mobile phone while I was visiting Father Patrici. The first is from a weeping Sofia, the second from an inquisitive but animated Chloe, the third a silly query from the gallery – something that will work itself out without my help.

Once I'm back at the house on the bay and have taken a quick swim during the lazy hours of midday heat while the beach enjoys a moment of respite from the tourists, I finally understand the reason for Chloe's tone of voice. She's found the perfect excuse to interrupt my stay in the village.

"The magazine's commissioned an article on 'Tuscan Towns Seen through Films'. They're paying me for a full week in Tuscany. You will come with me, won't you?"

"So, when is this? What exactly is it?"

"Next week! All I have to do is identify squares, streets, buildings in Florence, Siena and Arezzo that have played an important role in films – then photograph them and write up a short feature article."

"Arezzo?" I say with a start.

"Of course. From *Life Is Beautiful*."

"What?"

"Roberto Benigni's film, the one that won the Oscar!"

"Oh, I see... So it's not for Piero della Francesca's frescoes," I say with thinly disguised rage, seeing that it'll be impossible for me not to accompany Chloe, and upset by this turn of events that draws me again to the Aretine Andrea Roselli.

"Don't be such an ass. I know about the frescoes... but why do you sound so surprised?"

"Nothing, nothing, it just never occurred to me that..." Suddenly a certain diffidence comes over me: I don't want to reveal anything about Andrea Roselli. I don't want to talk about it with Chloe – not for any particular reason, just that suddenly, when I heard the name Arezzo, a chill went up my spine.

I hang up, certain that Chloe will do her best to transform our trip to Tuscany into an international forum on our relationship – what we are and have been or should be, all of it minutely analysed. I should prepare for the trial, but I'm going to do exactly the opposite. I'll spend every possible moment before the trip poring over the memoirs of the globe-trotting Aretine engineer.

Sofia – lonely in her mansion in the mountains, or perhaps with Tarrés in his farmhouse over the delta waters – doesn't sound like she's willing to let me off the hook either. I'd like to feel indifferent to the scandal she's involved in, be able to ignore her, but Jonàs's words keep coming to my mind: "The only thing she's ever wanted is the Tiepolo. I *did* love her." And here we have Tiepolo. But who the devil is this Roselli? How did these papers reach me?

"We said we'd meet up," Sofia tells me from the other end of the line, clearly in a bad mood.

"You're high-maintenance…" I say with a laugh, hoping I can ease the tension.

"This is no joking matter, Emili. I'm dead serious. I have very little time and we have a lot to talk about."

"Well then, let's talk." But as soon as the words are out, I realize that it sounds as if I'm saying the contrary. I said them without thinking, impatient to know what was so important to talk about.

"I know you went to see Jonàs in prison."

"No reason to hide the fact, is there?"

"Don't be so childish. You have no idea what a mess your friend's in – and me too, thanks to him."

"I'm not saying he's a saint."

"Well, on top of this huge scandal, I can see you must have listened to him – he must have fed you a bunch of stories." It's strange to hear Sofia speaking like this: she's worried, nervous.

"Why are you jumping to conclusions?"

"I'm not. It's Jonàs who told me he made you believe that Malaquies and I… the painter and I, I mean—"

"Stop now, Sofia. There's no reason to give me any explanations about anything. It has nothing to do with me."

"No, no. But you, you're capable of believing it! Can't you see he's like a poisonous snake?"

"Sofia, I have no idea what's going on between the two of you, but I can tell you that when I got to your house the night of the party, I definitely didn't have the feeling that you were at war with each other."

"Emili, I'm tired of covering up for him, protecting him, helping him financially... and now it's all been blown to pieces."

"Look, I don't know what your problems are, but Jonàs was absolutely devastated."

"I'm sure he was, but he's going to bring us all down with him," Sofia says, lowering her voice, as if she'd just made some sort of Biblical proclamation.

"He spoke to me of a Tiepolo."

"What?!"

"Jonàs told me you've always been after a painting by Tiepolo. He said something like that – that you only wanted Tiepolo. I had no idea what he was talking about."

"Emili, I told you, we need to talk, but not on the phone. The problem is I'm leaving for La Rioja today. I have to take care of something for my parents, but I'll be back in three or four days."

"And then I won't be here. I'm going to Tuscany with Chloe."

"I'd rather not wait that long, but if there's no other way... Promise me we'll see each other when you get back. I have to be in Barcelona next week."

"Then we'll talk about this in Barcelona."

Sofia hangs up and I stand for a moment holding the receiver in my hand. Sofia never gives the impression that she's alone or helpless – not even now, when she truly is. Her pride won't let her show how fragile she can be. If she'd only insisted a little, I'd have raced over to see her, tried to help her out, or just listened to her. Sometimes just listening is enough. Talking and explaining, going over details helps to bring out issues, put them in order, take control over them. Isn't that what Roselli tried to do by writing his memoirs? But Sofia is proud, and I'm probably indecisive; besides, those strange memoirs written two hundred odd years ago are calling to me as if they held the key to an enigma I haven't even discovered.

I was disappointed not to learn anything from the archives and Father Patrici. Clearly Sofia is either trying to gain more time or she's lost track of the Tiepolo; Chloe at least seems placated by my promise to go with her to Tuscany. So this means I will have a few days to continue translating the memoirs and to revisit the Invisible City and do a bit of investigation among the ruins, what remains of them – the Customs House at the canal, the wrecked silos, the unfinished neoclassical church and the porticoed square that still today proclaims the grandeur of the original project. It looks like I'll finally carry out my plan to spend some time in Sant Carles.

I am attracted to this new idea of investigating the old ruins, but at the same time I can also sense, in the calm offered me by the house on the bay, a conflicting pressure – one that is difficult to suppress, related to my past, like a distant, relentless wail: Ariadna.

It's time for me to get back to my work – the benign punishment I've been sentenced to. Having excluded any connection between the archivist and the Roselli memoirs, I begin to sense, behind all this, the sarcastic laugh, the glowing eyes and the lit cigarette of Tiger. Daniel Cabrera lives in Madrid, where I often go for work. We frequently meet for lunch and have long conversations, which inevitably end with us being thrown out of the little restaurant on a narrow street near the National Library, where he works. How could it take me so long to realize that it had to be him? Who else would have had access to or could locate a document like this, knowing that I'd be interested and intrigued? Who would have the ingenuity, the diabolical inspiration to give it the title *Memoirs of the Invisible City*? He must have laughed his head off thinking how excited I'd be reading the title, which I am sure he must have written, trying to imitate Roselli's calligraphy. And now he must be waiting in silence, curious to see how long it will take me to realize and phone him to congratulate him on his triumphant discovery. Tiger!

I give him a quick call to make sure he's in Madrid and arrange to have lunch the following day at our usual place. It takes me five hours to drive there the next morning.

"I prefer to take my holidays off-season: in the summer the city's empty, really pleasant," Cabrera tells me with a grin that makes me think he knows why I've come. But on the other hand, it's his usual grin. "No need to worry about the town of Morella – it's not going anywhere."

"I've decided to spend my holidays in Sant Carles this year. I wanted to read, not travel around." Tiger doesn't even blink. "But it started off with a party at the Mendizábals', which has made my life even more complicated than it already was. I told you Jonàs ended up in prison and Coll's all involved in his political intrigue."

"I haven't heard from him in ages," Cabrera says. "He probably thinks I'm a lost cause because I supported the hydrological project, or maybe now that he's a big shot, he thinks a historian, a civil servant at the National Library, is not even worth the time. Besides, I read that the European Commissioner for the Environment – the one who will decide if Europe will finance the project – is holidaying on the delta. What a mistake. It questions his neutrality – though it also seems good from our point of view, if you see it as a consolation visit—"

"Let's not get started on the interbasin water transfer! As I was saying, I want to spend a few days in Sant Carles and—"

"So it still hurts," says Daniel, the confessor and psycho-analyst who feels he can poke around in my soul.

"No, well, yes... I mean, now that I see how her brother has turned out... His mother came to see me – she looked really old, exhausted. I can't stop thinking how Ariadna—"

"That's a thorn in your side you'll never rid yourself of. Why don't you pretend it's not there?" Tiger says firmly, with the pragmatism of an honest person.

"That's what I've done for years. I thought the pain and guilt had disappeared, but when I went back, saw Jonàs and Sofia... But I'll do as you say... I already have: I'm going to Tuscany with Chloe."

"I must say I've never envied you, but even less so now... I have enough on my plate with a wife and two young daughters. And look at you: now it's Ariadna, now Sofia, now... what's her name? Chloe?"

"Cut it out, Tiger. One thing has nothing to do with the other."

"Maybe not, but why put your head in the lion's mouth again? When you told me this winter that you were helping

Sofia to set up an art gallery, I thought, 'Oh no, not again.'"

"Well, actually that's why I wanted to talk to you and tell you what made me think that this was the moment to make a fresh start, enter the labyrinth..." I try out various formulas and looks of complicity to see if Daniel will show his hand without me having to show mine. But Cabrera listens in silence, increasingly amused by my verbal tricks, which I interpret as a confession.

"So, it was you who—" I start to say, laughing.

"It was me who what?" he cuts me short with unfeigned sincerity, to show he's not playing games.

"Andrea Roselli. The memoirs. The Invisible City."

"Ah, your Invisible City. But unless you tell me what you're talking about..."

As I begin my explanation, Daniel Cabrera's face takes on an expression of feverish curiosity and excitement.

"Just a moment, Emili Rossell! It's time for cognac and Havanas. Do you realize that if this is true, it would be the most important historical document discovered in many years?"

Daniel wants more details, then begs me to continue, to repeat one of Roselli's anecdotes or opinions. He stutters, smokes like a chimney, but he's on cloud nine. He reproaches me for reading the manuscript so slowly, for not having finished studying it, for not having brought it with me. Once I've told him everything I know, he comes up with his own interpretations and hypotheses, speculating on the story that remains to be read, the revelations it might contain, the light it might shed on the whole historical period.

"I assume you have it in a safe place?" he asks in alarm.

"Of course," I say to keep him happy. "But, Daniel, you were not listening to me: it's clearly a copy, not the original."

"Of course it's a copy, but don't lose it!"

"I don't know if you understand. I have no idea who sent it to me; I thought it was you. Who else – if we exclude Father Patrici and the super-Member of Parliament – would make the joke about the Invisible City in the title?"

"I don't know, but I wouldn't trust Armand."

"All right, but even if I don't trust him, it makes no difference. Who could have uncovered the document? Who could have sent it to me, and for what reason?"

Silence falls on our table; once again we are the only ones left in the restaurant. The smoke that envelops us is punctuated by streaks of light from the lamp. Tiger seems to be reflecting on what I said, but he can't work it out. He's so excited about the idea of the discovery that he's totally at a loss. He doesn't care about the title or who might have wanted to play a hoax on me.

We toast again, this time with cognac, and take the last puffs on our cigars. We should leave, but the expression on Daniel Cabrera's face changes as he carefully stubs out his Havana.

"There's one thing I've always wanted to talk to you about, but I've never known how to broach the subject. You were reluctant to discuss it. Maybe now that you say you're ready to face—"

"If it's been preying on your mind for so long, Daniel, just say it – no need to beat around the bush."

"But I don't know if you want to talk about this. I remember very well when I brought it up the last time you didn't want to know… We were still at school in Tortosa… Your father…"

"Nothing's changed. Mother was bitter, I am not."

"I'm sorry if—"

"No, don't worry. I know you think it's something I refuse to admit, but it's actually the opposite: I don't want to know, I don't want to be harmed by the person who made my mother's life miserable. If she was able to carry the burden and resign herself to it, I can go one step further: I can forget about it, erase it from my life, purge my life of what can weigh me down, hurt me."

"Sorry about all this," Daniel says apologetically.

"Don't feel bad about it. When Mother was dying, Father Patrici and I had a long chat. He encouraged me to ask her. He gave me the impression that he had certain information, but that I should talk to her about it. I didn't though, out of pity for her, because I didn't want to torment her, but also for my own mental sanity and personal dignity. Someone who chose not to be there does not exist. It's over."

I said these last words as we walked out of the restaurant, trying to end the conversation on a lighter tone and alleviate Daniel's embarrassment. The apocalyptic, fierce light of a Madrid summer afternoon awaited us outside.

"What time are you leaving tomorrow?" Cabrera – the perfect image of a good-natured soul, ungainly, panting – calls to me after we've separated and are headed in different directions. "I'll send over to your hotel the magazine you left me with the article on Catalan regional history of the '60s."

* * *

The galleries I usually visit are closed. I take refuge in my hotel until sunset; in the evening I stroll over to the little Plaza de San Martín. Nothing remains of the house where the Tiepolos lived, and the San Martín monastery in the same square, where the painter was buried, was plundered during the War of Independence, so there's no telling where his remains are. The great Venetian painter continues to live, however, in the ceilings of the Royal Palace; Sabatini's presence, too, is felt throughout the city.

I was disappointed by my conversation with Tiger. I was hoping to find out who had sent me the memoirs, but then his words excited me even more, making me eager to return to Roselli, and with a greater sense of urgency now.

Even though I rise early in order to be back in Sant Carles by lunchtime, the envelope with the article I lent Daniel a few months ago is already at the hotel reception desk. On the cover is a full-page photograph of General Franco visiting the port of Alfacs in Sant Carles de la Ràpita on 21 June 1966 – the whole village decked out, people in their Sunday best, local and provincial authorities honouring Franco. There's a note from Daniel wishing me a good trip back and telling me: "The photo cut from page twelve was missing when you lent me the magazine." I look at the caption of the missing picture: "The illustrious member of parliament, Señor Juan Coll, being warmly welcomed by grateful citizens." Well, well, someone cut out the photo of the Tortosa Member of Parliament, who was probably the orchestrator of His Excellency's trip!

When I reach my house on the bay, I know the perfect way to escape from everything: Roselli, bound for St Petersburg.

8

St Petersburg
From Memoirs of the Invisible City

One day in the year 1703, the Tsar decided that he had had enough of Moscow. He and Russia needed a new capital, a city that would reflect the grandeur of the country and dazzle foreigners, that would facilitate trade between his empire and Europe and become a centre of power and universal fascination. The entire Russian State was placed at the service of this idea, as Peter the Great summoned engineers and legislators to choose the ideal location and dictate the appropriate laws. The name has already been chosen: the City of Peter, St Petersburg. The site, at the mouth of the River Neva, made it possible to build a port at the western border of the Empire, one that would taunt Sweden, who had controlled and contested the territory.

If the location of the future city was chosen with great care, so likewise were the layout of the city and every architectural detail. Everything followed the strictest and most carefully considered rules: St Petersburg was meant to be the most beautiful city that humanity had ever conceived. Many years before the city was founded, an expedition of some two hundred and eighty men – one of whom was the disguised Tsar under the assumed name of Pyotr Mikhailov

– had travelled through various European countries to study their political and military organization.

When the time came to start building the new city, an army of men worked under the orders of Dutch and Italian architects at the service of the visionary sovereign. The city was erected among the islands at the mouth of the River Neva, using existing branches of the river or building canals. Swamps were drained and built over. Thousands upon thousands of deported men worked in the mud in freezing weather, poorly dressed, poorly fed, until they died of exhaustion, all for one purpose: to transform streams and whirlpools into geometrically organized canals; uneven terrain and sandbanks into broad, straight avenues; islands into bastions; beaches into fortresses. A silent multitude laboured like Pharaoh's slaves, like an ant colony. At times the river swelled, carrying off a hundred men to the Baltic, or disease swept through the muddy marshes, decimating the hordes of workers.

The city began to rise from the waters, taking shape above the muddy mires, where frozen serfs with pale eyes and flayed hands will lie for all eternity. The imposing Peter and Paul Fortress was slowly erected. The first golden steeple appeared, announcing from many leagues away – from across the plains, from the Baltic Sea – that the City of Peter was the greatest of all, its radiance proclaiming its beauty. And if ten thousand or thirty thousand labourers died, well, they would have likewise died of hunger in their hamlets in Siberia or working the land on the Russian steppes, while here they have died contributing to an immortal work of art.

Noble families from Moscow were ordered to establish themselves in St Petersburg and build their palaces there in accordance with artistic requirements determined by the Tsar's architects. It was only a matter of years until the city became the real capital of Russia and the wonder of European courts. Has humanity ever witnessed a similar undertaking, carried out with such incredible resolution? Every person who entered this new city, by land or by sea, was obliged to transport stone, mountains of stone, to strengthen the foundations of the metropolis built on the Neva delta. The breadth of the avenues and streets, the height of the buildings, the façades of churches and palaces had all been decided on by the Tsar, but Peter the Great also wanted his city filled with vitality and elegance, and to that purpose he ordered that young noblemen go out, walk along the streets, give parties, dress with elegance. As if it were possible to contrive a Paris or a Vienna or a Venice.

Soon the new port boasted a considerable maritime traffic and became an essential centre of trade with Europe; with time St Petersburg replaced Moscow as economic capital of the country. The Tsar passed laws that fostered the arts and sciences with the aim of drawing distinguished men to the city from every corner of the continent.

I have arrived at the Baltic wonder, dazzled by Peter's star, or rather because his star has dazzled the King of Spain and the Indies. In comparison to the journey I made with Tiepolo from Venice to Castile, this one has been free of complications: only one stop of more than a day – in Amsterdam, quite enlightening for it was one of the models the Tsar had in mind as he paved the way for his dream. From Amsterdam I sent my first letters: one to the court to inform that my mission was proceeding well, the other to Cecilia, who was not simply a memory but an almost palpable presence.

It must be spring now in the Mediterranean, but on the Baltic the fog-shrouded month of April is still icy, giving the impression that a thousand eyes are watching you from the waters, from the soaring clouds. A clearing suddenly appears in the clouds, and a silvery-blue beam illuminates a strip of sea – a strip that grows, allowing you to see the sky which is no longer cobalt-blue and leaden, but earth-coloured, streaked with gold. It only lasts a moment. Soon we are again enveloped by a milky-white blanket of fog, and a bold expression returns to the crew's weary faces. The Mediterranean Sea can be treacherous: a cheerful day can suddenly turn about, unleashing a storm in a matter of hours, but on the Baltic you have the feeling that the same weather could last for centuries.

Finally one morning, through the residue of clouds and marine shadows, above the grey lethargy of the sea, we heard the sound of a golden drop, like a grain of sand at the bottom of a bucket of water. It came from the steeple of St Peter and St Paul announcing itself from the distant Gulf of Finland. It was St Petersburg that had appeared, as if out of a dream.

Viscount Herrería, King Charles's ambassador in the Russian capital, is waiting for me at the dock, apparently quite satisfied, almost radiant I would say, and gives orders for my baggage to be taken to the embassy. As soon as the Viscount has greeted me, he informs me of reports from Spain.

"Señor Roselli, I imagine that you have not received intelligence of the events in Madrid that occurred soon after your departure. The news arrived only now, almost at the same time as you, and your journey was quite swift, was it not? Do not be overly concerned, nothing has changed for us for the moment – I mean, here in Russia. But, poor Esquilache! But first, allow me to express my profound pleasure in receiving you. I am aware of the high mission that has brought you here. The embassy is at your disposal."

"Thank you for your kind words, Viscount, but pray tell me what has happened to Esquilache," I interrupt him impatiently.

"I am quite certain you understand the affairs of our countries; reforms can often not be applied as quickly as one would wish. The people of Madrid, incited by those who were opposed to the enlightened works of His Majesty, requested the head of Esquilache. These same people have accused the King of allowing Madrid to be full of foreigners."

"Excuse me?"

"Forgive me, sir, I did not mean to imply that... You have nothing to worry about. St Petersburg is a city of Europeans: Italians, French, Dutch, English. It was already like this at the time of Tsar Peter, but even more so today, as Empress Catherine is determined to improve on her predecessor's design and transform St Petersburg into the most important city in Europe."

"How do the Russians respond to this?" I ask, concerned about the brief but alarming news from Madrid.

"Ah, Señor Roselli, the Russians adore the Tsarina, even more so after the troubled decades following the death of

Peter the Great. He believed that the system of imperial succession was unfair and inconvenient and passed a well-intentioned but ultimately catastrophic law whereby the Tsar would name his own successor. This gave rise to incessant intrigues, conspiracies, murders and assassinations of high-ranking statesmen."

The ambassador broke off his account to signal that we should enter his carriage – where, after comfortably installing ourselves, he continued:

"As I was saying, this method of choosing a sovereign caused considerable upheaval in the Russian Court. In 1762, just four years ago, Peter III inherited the throne, but he lacked an acute mind, whereas his wife was brilliant and shrewd, free of prejudice, and won the favour of the nobility and the army, who roused the people. You can imagine how easy it was to do that: in the end they forced the Patriarch of Moscow to proclaim her Empress of all of Russia, which essentially she already was."

"Catherine the Great!" I exclaim, as attentive to Herrería's explanations as I was to the mansions and palaces that line the avenue filled with people, vehicles and soldiers on horseback. The ambassador guesses what I'm thinking:

"Nevsky Prospekt, Señor Andrea Roselli. This is where the whole of St Petersburg is on display! The Parisian Alexandre Leblond laid out the city along three avenues that converge at the Admiralty, which was Peter the Great's first residence. The main avenue is Nevsky Prospekt, which leads to the Alexander Nevsky Monastery, going from one end of the great, meandering River Neva to the other and across the Fontanka Canal. Forgive me for carrying on like this when you have only just arrived. It's presumptuous of me to talk about such things when you are a master in architecture and city-planning."

"I assure you this is a great honour for me, but you have left me intrigued by your comments on Tsarina Catherine's deceased husband."

"Never was there a husband more cuckolded than he!" the viscount says laughing, and glances out the carriage window at the glorious Nevsky Prospekt. "Catherine used her bed to create alliances, gain favour, destroy enemies. Grigory and Alexis Orlov would be mere military men had she not convinced them to incite the army against her husband and place him under her command. Then Catherine, having received the blessing of the Patriarch, rode her horse to the palace of Oranienbaum, where the dull-witted Emperor Peter had sought refuge, and demanded that he abdicate or simply obey her."

"And the deposed Tsar left for exile, or did he shut himself up in a monastery?"

"Too dangerous. First Catherine had him imprisoned – but that was not enough, and one day he was found dead. But don't worry, the great Catherine was only following a tradition begun by the greatest of all, Peter I, whom I suspect you must admire. He rid himself of his son Alexis in the same manner."

"Yet, with all this, you say the people adore her?"

"My dear Señor Roselli, the people know nothing of this. I will tell you just one thing: it was absolutely necessary that Catherine's husband should 'disappear'. He was an incompetent, mean-hearted rogue, while she is a glowing light, someone who will restore splendour to this city and to the entire empire. Do you not realize this? For once justice has been done, though it has been painful."

"Cecilia! Cecilia!" I exclaim in a silent voice as enormous blocks of ice drift down the Neva. I too feel as if I were a mere piece of ice, carried along by events over which I have no control: Arezzo, Rome, Naples, Venice, Madrid, St Petersburg. I would like to believe that I am more wise, more accomplished, more shrewd with each new stage in my life, that I am learning the rules that govern social exchanges, that I am benefiting from contact with learned, powerful people; but now that I am no longer young, I have noticed that with each new year time passes and does not come back. With each city that I abandon, I leave behind the possibility of transforming it into my city; each month away from Cecilia is a month of bereavement and loneliness.

Some nights I wake up and the worst of suspicions assaults me: I do not belong to anyone, I am from nowhere; the glow of parties, the flashing eyes are quickly extinguished, and no one remembers me or is waiting for me. Perhaps the day will arrive when not even I remember myself or wait for myself; perhaps the day will come when I question the land on which I tread, my voice, my very existence.

Fortunately, night and sleep eventually swallow me, and the following day only a tiny ember remains of the fire that had consumed me, the anxiety that had made me tremble as if I was faced by an ogre. What if it was this fear of solitude and of being insignificant that had driven Peter's or Catherine the Great's titanic undertakings? They say that the Tsar sailed through the desolate swamps at the mouth of the Neva when St Petersburg existed only in his mind, shouting "I am Noah, and this is my ark; here I will build my city!" Catherine's demons of loneliness and regret must have driven her not only to build the most beautiful palaces, but also to surround herself with the most valuable men, whether they be guards who must defend her against conspiracies or thinkers like Voltaire and Diderot. They serve as a confirmation that she is brilliant – that she is alive.

Charles of Spain has lived in a dozen palaces on the Gulf of Naples and the plains of Castile; yet, he must not find this sufficient to keep his nightmares at bay and finds that he must build an entire city in order to testify to his passage on earth.

"Cecilia! Cecilia!" I exclaim in a silent voice as the thaw fills the Neva with a slow procession of white slabs. With Cecilia beside me, in my mind, I do not feel an orphan or surrounded by danger. Why is it that I travel and follow the orders of one or the other, why do I meet with politicians and architects, with sculptors and engineers to understand the plans that have guided them or will guide in the future? Why do I listen to them, flatter them, why am I interested in new ideas and dazzled by every palace in this incredible and captivating city, if I know that every day I am further from my own city and from the person who makes me feel complete? Perhaps it is because in a sense this city still does not exist, it is invisible; perhaps because I know that I have to seek out that city amongst nightmares, as if the dreams were my allies, not the enemy, as if the danger of losing my way were the very compass that will guide me I know not where. To create the world in order to own it, or simply to be in it.

Bartolomeo Rastrelli is one of the people who has done the most to ensure that the world created by Peter the Great is reflected in the most marvellous city in Europe. I explored "his" Winter Palace, outside and inside, as far as I was allowed. I drew sketches of it and studied it in order to understand how he had managed to combine unparalleled grandeur with harmony and balance.

Rastrelli was removed from the frontline when Catherine's tastes had changed. She also wanted to distance herself from Tsarina Elizabeth, who had commissioned Rastrelli to embellish the entire city. He pointed out to me the building's combination of long Corinthian columns resting on those of the Ionic order, the finishing touch provided by pedestalled statues. He designed it thus to create a sense of verticality to the colossal breadth of the palace, which seems to rise from the waters of the Neva and dominate the river – a green-and-white vessel, balanced, majestic.

Bartolomeo could be seen as a symbol of the spirit of this city: he was fifteen years old when his father left for St Petersburg to work as a sculptor with Leblond, but he later left to train as an architect in France and Germany. Rastrelli applied the European architectural models of his century to the Winter Palace, but he wanted to combine the Western trends with the traditional Eastern, onion-shaped domes that he used for his Smolny monastery.

I was thinking about the ageing Rastrelli, my esteemed guide in St Petersburg, as I wandered through the gardens of Tsarskoe Selo on the outskirts of the city, seeking the right angle to observe this huge palace that Elizabeth had also conceived and commissioned. Here the turquoise and white, and the profusion of gold, do not proclaim their triumph above the waters – as does the Winter Palace – but rather clash with the green of meadows and foliage from elm, oak and linden trees.

This splendid summer residence was not the proper place to understand the design of Peter's city and begin to plan Charles's. I needed to study the urban network of St Petersburg, the role the city played in the empire, the methods used by the Tsar to build it. Yet, Tsarskoe Selo was the place to which all courtly activity – as well as much of the artistic – had been moved. The architect of the deceased Tsarina Elizabeth was not favourably received, but my protector, the ambassador of the King of Spain, was, for Catherine wished to see Russian trade expand to all the corners of Europe. She was also aware of the spirit of reform and reconstruction that Charles had put into practice first in Naples and later in Spain.

After Viscount Herrería's description of Catherine's brutal methods – corroborated by other accounts I had heard in the city during the following weeks – I was decidedly uneasy at the prospect of attending the reception to which the Empress had invited the Viscount and me. I had mixed feelings as I followed him into the palace, feelings I had experienced many times in my life: caution and fear, with a touch of curiosity.

Seeing Catherine at the far side of the room filled with gentlemen in uniform who addressed her with great pomp and ceremony, you could understand why she had a reputation for being both intimidating and dazzling. Her arrogant demeanour and brusque gestures, the energetic traits of her body made her the natural focal point of the reception. It was almost as if she occupied the very spot on which the sun rose in the morning, at the precise moment when one can view the whole countryside. Inexplicably, she struck me as less majestic as I drew nearer, her figure less round, her face slightly plump, the look on her face more persuasive than inquisitive, more understanding than determined. This same impression stayed with me as I observed her closely when it was our turn to pay our respects and deliver the greetings sent by the King of Spain and the Indies.

Our visit to Tsarskoe Selo had gone well, but when the reception seemed to be drawing to a close and we were about to withdraw, I noticed a slight commotion, someone whispering into the Viscount's ear. A moment later the ambassador approached me and announced that the Empress wished to speak to us again. As I crossed the large room, I tried without success to imagine why Catherine would want to talk to us.

"I have been told, sir, that you have visited Pompeii."

"That is correct, Your Majesty."

"Speak to me of Pompeii. Did you see the paintings?"

I found it difficult to believe that the face before me, filled with such enthusiasm and anticipation at my humble remarks, could belong to the fiery despot who had spurred her horse to Oranienbaum and had had her husband poisoned. I told her about the young girl in the diaphanous dress who was strewing flowers which seemed to be floating, falling with eternal slowness.

"I shall have a painting of this girl commissioned for one of my rooms," the sovereign exclaimed as I furnished her with all the details I could, hoping she would not be disappointed, noting all the while a look of barely concealed amazement on the faces of the gentlemen around her.

Her Imperial Highness did me the honour of prolonging our conversation for some time, as she enquired about the architecture of Pompeii and requested information about Naples.

"Europe is full of marvellous places that I cannot visit. I am sure you understand. As I cannot leave Russia, I do my best to bring here, to St Petersburg, the finest European artists and thinkers, so they can reveal the secrets of Europe to me."

"What secrets are you referring to, Your Majesty?" I asked, perhaps too abruptly.

"Ah, Señor Roselli, you know very well which secrets I'm referring to. The illustrious Diderot and Voltaire know! The secrets Peter the Great tried to uncover in Amsterdam and Vienna."

"Are you referring to the rules that govern construction and painting, the secrets of beauty?"

"Señor Roselli, there can be no doubt that Pompeii and Roman architecture can reveal the secrets you mention. Pompeii was destroyed when Mount Vesuvius erupted, a natural catastrophe – some would say that it was destiny.

St Petersburg, a meeting place for the finest European art, could in the same way be obliterated by flooding or wiped off the map by an earthquake. The acts of nature are of relative importance – what matters is will-power, the reign of human intelligence. Don't you think this is the real secret?"

"Without a doubt, Your Majesty," I stammer, not wishing to interrupt her.

"We want to import reason and put an end to the inertia that has kept Russia from being master of herself. We are working to build a new set of laws by which reason will triumph over the natural conditions that have decimated the empire. If you remain with us a few more months, you will see this."

Clearly, only a persistent exertion of will could explain how Catherine had managed to reach the Russian throne in such unfavourable circumstances. Tsarina Elizabeth had brushed her aside no sooner than she had given birth to a son, thus securing an heir for the throne; her husband Peter gave her a wide berth and scorned her in private and in public. She had survived all kinds of conspiracies and had learnt to use to her advantage the same arms as her enemies: astuteness, intrigue, favouritism, physical attraction, murder.

After my encounter with the Tsarina I accompanied Viscount Herrería back to St Petersburg in his carriage. I was euphoric, filled with excitement at the attention devoted to me, but so as not to prick the ambassador's pride, I tried to control my enthusiasm and directed our conversation towards the more innocuous, superficial aspects of the ceremony. The viscount engaged quite courteously in talk, until he suddenly changed the subject.

"The Court of the Empress is a nest of vipers. There have been times when the Tsarina had three lovers at once, apart from those she has abandoned through the years, lovers that every now and then show up to claim a debt. In addition to lovers and favourites, there are also the contenders, the intriguers, or those who have been scorned. They have their own circles of influence, and keep close watch over each other; they vie with each other, demand money or palaces or favours. It is true that the Tsarina is particularly fond of artists and writers – especially if they are foreigners and can sing her praises in western capitals – still, it is not advisable to approach her until you are certain that none of the factions will see you as an enemy or as another competitor."

I was at a loss for words. It struck me as totally inappropriate that the ambassador could magnify my ambitions so much and warn me of impending dangers; I also found it outrageous to think that Herrería's words might be motivated by jealousy. However that may be, my pleasure that evening had been marred by the shadow of threat and uncertainty. As we drove through the almost deserted streets of the city, the façades of the buildings gently brushed by the milky light of the languishing, not yet extinguished day, I fretted at the thought that within my exultant heart I could only hear the sounds of the horses' rhythmic trot and the off-key but soothing creak of wheels.

A few days later, accompanied by Bartolomeo Rastrelli, I took one of my exploratory walks through the city and mentioned to him what had happened and what the Spanish ambassador had told me. Old Rastrelli smiled and tactfully changed the topic, but he must have felt that I needed some reassurance, because he picked up the thread again.

"As the wife of the heir to the throne, Catherine – who had been a Prussian princess – bore the title of Great Duchess. She had ambivalent feelings towards her predecessor, Tsarina Elizabeth, who had arranged the marriage to her nephew Peter with the assumption that he would succeed her. Catherine realized that Elizabeth expected but one thing of her: to produce a son for her dull-witted husband, a son for Russia. Little did it matter that Catherine did not share his bed. For this reason, Elizabeth protected her for a while, and when the beautiful, cultivated Catherine finally gave birth to a boy – which everyone knew was not Peter's – the court received him with great celebrations. At that point the Tsarina completely forgot about Catherine – and about her husband too, of course – and from that moment on Catherine was forced to live on her own, ignored, deprived of even the most elementary attentions. But, rather than submitting to this, she began to weave her web, forming alliances, cultivating her spirit."

"Have you had any dealings with her? It must have been difficult for you, considering how fond Tsarina Elizabeth was of you and your work."

"Not very easy, certainly, but I was able to observe how the years had moulded Catherine from within; I came to realize that behind the apparently fragile and fickle courtly person who passed easily from one man to another, there was a woman who had learnt an important lesson."

"A lesson?"

"She explained it to me herself. As Princess Sophia – that was her Catholic name before she embraced the Orthodox faith and took the name of Catherine – she travelled to St Petersburg, where the Tsarina was waiting in order to introduce her to the court. Once everything was settled, she would be betrothed to Peter, heir to the Russian throne, and the news proclaimed. Showing extravagant generosity, the Empress had placed at her guests' disposal (the young Sophia was travelling with her mother) a retinue of a hundred people, including officials, aids, cooks, menservants and pages. The Tsarina had sent the two women a luxurious carriage lined in red velvet, with damask cushions.

"They had left behind the city of Riga, and were beginning the last stage of the journey before reaching St Petersburg, when from her elegant carriage Princess Sophia caught a glimpse of another coach, as if floating in the clouds, going in the opposite direction. It was a dark, desolate carriage, with an ill-boding look about it, escorted by soldiers. The princess wished to know who the unfortunate people travelling in the carriage were. They did not want to tell her, but in the end she discovered the truth: it was the little Tsar Ivan VI and his mother, the Regent Anne, both of whom had been banished by Elizabeth. They had just been deported to Riga, where they would be imprisoned.

"Sophia came to an unsettling realization: she had never stood that close to glory and to ruin. Her road led to glory, little Ivan's to infamy and torture, both through the gracious decision of one woman. When Sophia became Catherine, she knew she should not forget that dizziness, that image of black fortune, and every time she felt dejected, she reminded herself that one small gesture could result in her downfall. Every part of her body, every bit of her being has striven to avoid that dark vessel, while leading a full life without regrets."

Summer was fading away as the splendour of the Tsarskoe Selo balls came to an end – often they were no more than a drunken bunch of men and women dancing in drawing rooms or amusing themselves in the parks – and our evening strolls along avenues and canals, through palaces and gardens grew shorter.

It was during the glacial autumn of wine-coloured forests, when yellow leaves carpet the parks, that Princess Tarakanova made her appearance. Or rather her ghost. A strange and, perhaps for that reason, intriguing invitation came to me through the embassy. I was requested to meet her on a certain bridge on the Moika river, whence we would board a vessel that would take us further out, so that we could talk. The message was blunt and cryptic. It said that the information I would be given would be of great interest to the embassy of which I was a guest; with this in mind, and knowing Viscount Herrería to be out of town and unavailable for consultation, I decided I should at least make my appearance at the designated place. Once there I would decide how to proceed.

At the time agreed upon, a barge loaded with old furniture approached and a person wearing so many clothes that it was impossible to distinguish if it was a gentleman or a lady signalled me to get onboard. Even now I can't understand why I acted with such naivety: I jumped on the vessel as if I had received an order that had to be obeyed. The oarsmen immediately set to work, driving us upstream towards the main course of the Neva. Was that bundle of trousers, jackets, coats and hoods the person who would provide the information mentioned in the note, or was this scarcely human figure taking me to my real destination? It would have been pointless to ask. I was signalled to wait, but my anxiety grew: everything had taken on a dreamlike atmosphere. Maybe it was just a nightmare.

We finally reached the Neva, crossed it and docked on the bank opposite the city, in a large sheltered area beneath the branches of trees. The person in strange clothes beckoned to me, and I followed obediently. We walked a few steps along a path, only far enough for the barge to be out of sight. As my anxiety turned to alarm and I started thinking that I should throw off my passiveness, something extraordinary happened.

The person in front of me began to take off some of the clothes, and a slender lady, graceful in spite of her masculine dress, appeared. She did not remove her hood.

"Señor, you must help me," said a young but determined voice.

"I don't know who you are or what I can do to help you."

"You could arrange for the ambassador of the King of Spain to receive me."

"I am only a guest. I hold no official capacity at the embassy—"

She interrupted me, finally throwing off her hood and allowing me to see a face that would be impossible to forget: eyes green as marble, pale face, pink lips, delicate skin, each feature well proportioned and slightly rounded, hair dishevelled and black as the night, a look on her face that seemed as much a smile as a plea. She took my hand and pulled me towards her, offering me her lips, embracing me. I jumped away from her with the same irrational impetuosity that had led me to follow her.

It was almost twilight and the branches on the trees were fading into the purple sky, but the lady – rather than be annoyed or embarrassed – began to speak, as if she were a statue in a park – motionless, undaunted, beautiful.

She was the sister of Tsarina Elizabeth, daughter of Peter the Great, rejected by everyone, first by her sister and now by Catherine, the great usurper. Every Russian must know this, every European power must know. She had been obliged to lead a clandestine life, constantly hiding, fleeing, moving from one country to another, changing identities in order to escape Catherine's tentacles. One day, she said, they would come face to face and she would recover what was hers, what belonged to her family, the throne of all the Russias.

I stared at the icy figure of the lady with amazement, all the while thinking that this encounter could produce very unwelcome consequences for my stay in St Petersburg. As she put on her outer garments and signalled me to follow her back to the barge, I told myself that I would not breathe a word of the incident to Viscount Herrería. We returned to the city in silence, a freezing chill rising from the waters of the Neva, filling the night with ill omens. Princess Tarakanova's menacing escort left me at the same point on the Moika where I had met her but a few hours before.

I did not return to the embassy alone, but accompanied by my Cecilia. She was further and further away from me, more and more silent, yet she seemed to be present, palpable, as if miraculously Princess Tarakanova's lips had restored Cecilia's to me. I felt as if I – a desolate soul wandering through the streets of St Petersburg – could be seen, understood and consoled from some distant, unheard-of place. It was as if the realization – forceful this time – that I had no country and that no one was waiting for me transformed the desire for them into reality. The imagination creating the world.

I decided not to tell the ambassador about the meeting with the princess and her plea for help until I could ascertain what he knew of the affair. He was due to return to the city in three days. But I did not have time to carry out my plan; two days after my meeting on the Moika, as I was returning from a visit to Vasilyevsky Island, where I had gone on Master Rastrelli's recommendation, I had another, much less pleasant encounter. Three brawny men, who must have been either guards or soldiers, although not by their appearance, stopped me and insisted that I accompany them. I offered little resistance, for I immediately realized there was no possibility of escape. They shoved me into a boat and we headed for the Fortress of Saints Peter and Paul – the odious glow of Trezzini's spire appearing in the dim, overcast twilight.

It didn't take me long to realize that my guards were either mute or did not speak the languages I used to make myself understood. And it didn't take me long to realize that I was soon to be thrown into the most famous prison in the city of the tsars. Why? I was not told. For how long? No one replied to my question. I knew full well that only Viscount Herrería could have me released, but how was he to know that I was incarcerated? The skies of all the cities I had known, at their most sinister, weighed on me as I tried to adjust to the damp, dark, ill-smelling cell where my journey had led me.

9
Don't Forget Ariadna

Roselli is holed up in the court of Catherine the Great, and I am holed up here, trying to decipher his manuscript, which should reveal the origins of the Sant Carles project, a city that was invisible at that time and would become so again. The ruins of the original city are more and more disfigured today, the few remaining traces in the countryside are fast disappearing. From what I've read, it looks like the port of Alfacs, the canal and the square were the design of the Tuscan engineer.

I feel closer to Andrea with each episode in his memoirs. With him I have shared my sleepless nights, when it seemed that the world was turned upside down, as well as my constant guilt, which assumes different masks. Or is it just my uncertainty, the impression that danger is close at hand?

For the moment, I am forced to interrupt my stay in Sant Carles to accompany Chloe on her photographic tour.

Chloe doesn't know why I've come to Arezzo with her. Yes, she has her article on film locations and I have my passion for Tuscan painters of the Quattrocento – this she knows and has taken advantage of. She suspects nothing of Andrea Roselli in the court of St Petersburg – or rather in the dungeons – or of the papers that I couldn't resist bringing with me. Roselli's arms are reaching across the centuries to me.

We're at the chapel where Piero della Francesca's great frescoes can still be seen. His *Leggenda della Vera Croce* can be visited again after years of restoration. Another epiphany. The Emperor Constantine is sleeping in his tent when an angel appears to him, announcing that he will be victorious if he takes up the cross. The light shining from the angel also illuminates the guards keeping vigil over the Emperor, whose body is protected by the camp, although he is not actually there himself: it is as if his mind, his conscience, had been transported far away to some other place.

I am thrilled by the scene, captivated by that angelic light, but Chloe seems to be bored, distracted. I point to an image and, as I ramble on about it, she keeps making a noise with her chewing gum. I'm growing nervous, frustrated. Finally, I just leave the chapel with the frescoes and with a fast stride walk through the dark church and emerge into the dazzling brightness of the square.

Half an hour later, as I am savouring a creamy espresso, my gaze alternating between a group of youngsters who are playing loudly and the pages of *La Repubblica*, I see Chloe crossing the square and coming towards me.

"Why did you walk out without saying a word? First you insist that I make the reservation for you and that we visit the chapel, and then—"

"I just realized that I had to check on something and couldn't…"

At that point I pick up a bag that I had placed behind my chair and hand it to her. At first she's not sure if she should stop her rebuke, which no doubt I deserve, but curiosity gets the better of her – or perhaps it's just courtesy – and she opens the bag and pulls out a lavishly illustrated monograph on the *Leggenda*. Chloe brightens up again. The murals of the chapel have been photographed inch by inch, allowing us to enjoy certain aspects of the painting that we could only see from a distance.

Chloe, however, doesn't fall for the trick. After flipping through the book with her long, careful photographer's fingers, she asks again about my inexplicable departure. Since I am in no mood for a discussion or a fight, and the heat is too strong, I call a truce and tell her I am going to go back to our hotel room while she completes her photographic session for *Fashion* magazine in Piazza Grande, the square in front of City Hall. It is a chance for me to return to the itinerant Aretine of two centuries ago as he continues his journey full of expectation – and now of misery – in Catherine the Great's Russia.

I became so engrossed in Roselli's tale that I didn't notice that the entire afternoon had gone. I look at my watch in alarm: I'd arranged to meet Chloe in the centre of Arezzo before sunset, but I'll be late. The hotel is nestled among vineyards and olive trees on the outskirts of the city: there's no way I can make it in time. Before I can come up with a solution, the phone in the room rings.

"We were supposed to meet at nine – how can you make it to Piazza Grande in two minutes?... I've taken some marvellous photos, the light's amazing!"

"You just caught me. I was leaving the hotel right now."

"Still buried in those papers you won't put aside for more than a couple of hours?"

"No, actually I went for a walk around the area. The countryside is like ours, I mean like that of our people, but better tended."

"I knew you'd be late. I'm actually pretty far from the square myself. I'm phoning because your friend" – and Chloe gives this last word an ironic intonation that she doesn't bother to conceal – "Sofia, is looking for you. Since you haven't checked your mobile for days, apparently she's finally managed to track down my number and—"

"Did she tell you what it's about?"

"No, but she sounded frightened or upset. She said she'd been trying to talk to you for the last couple of days. You'd better phone her."

I have a strange presentiment. Just when I was lying to Chloe about walking in the countryside, I had a sudden image of Jonàs and Sofia's house set in the brushwood among the Montsià Mountains. I rush to phone her.

When I get Sofia on the line, I have the impression she's about to reproach me, but then I realize she's dejected and only looking for comfort. I prepare myself as I glance through the window at the fading light that filters through the olive trees. I turn round and look at the almost blank walls of the room, fix my eyes on the memoirs. I find no words of comfort. I know the wave is about to crash over

me and sit down to brace myself. Sofia's voice is broken
– "Don't leave me alone, I need you. Jonàs hanged himself
in his cell in Tarragona. They told me in those words, just
like that. They don't know how it happened, but he hanged
himself. That was two days ago."

Jonàs dead. The Invisible City. The light from the days
when we were kids. The world turned upside down.

"Something else," Sofia adds when we are able to speak
again. "He left a sealed envelope with your name on it."

When I tell Chloe that I must return to Sant Carles,
she's furious, and rightly so: "All these years you paid no
attention to your friend, and now that he's dead you have
to hurry back to him." It's no use mentioning again the
envelope with my name on it and the tragic circumstances
in which it was found. That's not a good reason to spoil a
trip we've just begun. Judging by the tone in which she says
"Whatever. Do what you want," I feel she's been waiting for
this opportunity to pick a fight – the kind of thing I tend
to avoid.

Inevitably our dinner in a trattoria in the centre of Arezzo
is spoilt by arguing. Finally, I think I've found a way forward.
I make a phone call, then tell Chloe that I'll fly from Florence
to Barcelona, drive to Sant Carles to check the situation and
fly back to Florence, all in forty-eight hours. In the meantime
she can continue her work for the magazine, so that we can
start our trip again… That won't do. The idea shocks her
even more – she flies off the handle. But there's no turning
back now: I know I must meet with someone or something
– and I know I'll be accompanied again by Andrea Roselli,

now sitting disconsolate and bewildered in St Petersburg. I had hoped to find news of him in Arezzo, and I'm leaving empty-handed. But I'll be back.

I have enough headaches right now: I must put aside Roselli's misfortunes. Sofia's waiting for me with the note from Jonàs. Sometimes Roselli's vicissitudes have a calming effect on me, at other times they trouble me, but they always exert a magnetic attraction, one I can't escape. The reason for this must lie deeper than the encouraging but insufficient clues about Tiepolo or Sant Carles that he's given me before being thrown into the Fortress of Saints Peter and Paul.

I give Sofia a hug as she waits for me by the gate of her villa. She drily thanks me for my condolences and sets off up the path that leads to the terrace. The peak of summer has passed and the bright sun is now mitigated by the Montsià Mountains. Despite the grim look on Sofia's face this afternoon, it seems that the moment has come to keep the violent passions under control and discuss the many untold things. Wrong.

"I assume you didn't expect me to bring you up here when you turned your back on me at a time when..." Her voice breaks up.

"Please, Sofia. I'm sorry you think that I... that you had to go through this horrible mess on your own. But let's forget about it. I'm here now," I say as I take her hand, staring into her eyes.

"They're after me, Emili. They want the money."

"Who? What money?"

"The night of the party, when they arrested Jonàs, the Guardia Civil confiscated a huge amount of drugs on top of what was lost, and the suppliers – the ones who moored at Punta de la Banya – haven't stopped demanding money since then."

"What do you have to do with all of this?"

"Nothing at all! I don't even know what kind of associates Jonàs had, what kind of agreement."

"But he's dead! Why don't they collect from the others?"

"How the hell do I know! I only know that I'm up to my neck in shit. I suppose the other guys were a bunch of idiots and the Colombians figured they wouldn't get much from them—"

"How do you know they're Colombians?"

"I don't know. It's the accent. When they phone to threaten me. I don't know what to do."

"Listen, Jonàs is dead now, and you say you have nothing to do with this whole story, so why don't you report them to the police? You've got nothing to lose."

"Report who?

"Let them start an investigation! At least let them protect you."

"Look, Emili, one of the few things I learnt from the scrapes Jonàs got himself into is that the police won't be able to help me on this. This is not a game: they're threatening to kill me. Do you understand?"

"I'm trying to. So, if you are not planning to go to the police, the only alternative you have is to pay, right?"

"Yes! And that's the problem!" Sofia says, more and more agitated, and perhaps annoyed at seeing me so slow on the uptake.

"Do you know how much money it is? Did they give you an ultimatum?"

"They want to be paid, and the sooner the better. I may get up tomorrow morning and find them at my door…"

"Look, why don't you come to my place in Barcelona for a few days? They'll never find you there, and you'll have time to come up with the money."

"I really appreciate it, Emili, but you have no idea how much money we're talking about."

Now I'm the one who's annoyed. Sofia is a millionaire. This isn't something where I can be of any help. Without beating around the bush, I mention the family money, the real-estate company, the art gallery.

"I've been trying to tell you for some time. Jonàs's damned business washed it all down the drain. The real-estate company was going well, but the risks he was taking were getting higher, and required larger investments. From time to time he needed huge amounts of money, and he was getting deeper and deeper into debt. We turned to my family, but there came a point when they said they'd done enough. For a while it looked like sales were going so well that the financial problems were under control. I'd distanced myself from all of this, hiding out in the art gallery, but Jonàs had discovered a faster way to solve the cash-flow problem, and you can guess what that was."

"Trafficking."

"Yes. A great solution. Even if the money kept flowing in, the suppliers always wanted more, and Jonàs was forced to accept larger and larger quantities – sell it, pay for it…"

I listen to Sofia's explanation and it's like watching a movie. Everything follows a predictable, implacable logic, the dictates of a vulgarity thinly concealed behind the glamour, all because some idiots want their moment of brilliance, which lasts only as long as it takes to burn themselves out, like insects approaching a bright light. Perhaps I left the area where Sofia has settled because I didn't want to have my blood – or soul – sucked away at the sound of that old refrain that goes: "Things are the way they are and have always been" – or be part of that silent, century-old procession of people who laugh and obey. Every now and then, I feel a pang of nostalgia when I realize that I cannot recreate our circle of friends, that group now broken up and disbanded, but I know the dangers lurking in stagnant waters or the desperate cries of those who try to go against the flow when it's too late – Jonàs and the overreaction to what is immutable. But what does Sofia have to do with all this? When I first met her in Barcelona, I saw in her what I did not have and what I desired: art, books, travel, contacts, money. I can't believe that now...

"Here's the note Jonàs left you. Maybe the solution is there!" a distraught Sofia says as she hands me a slightly creased white envelope. I open it on the spot, convinced that if I don't do it now, it will only be more difficult later on.

The note is simple, unexpected. It contains one unsettling sentence: "Don't forget about Ariadna."

I remain speechless with the paper in my hands. My face turns into an expressionless mask as I look at the fast-disappearing clouds, all the while I am sinking, as if falling down a well – down, down. I weep with dry eyes as I am tossed about by a storm that I thought had been calmed.

Outside, far away, I see Sofia moving her lips, gesticulating, while I unconsciously crumple the paper into a ball, until it's hidden in my closed fist.

When I am again capable of understanding what Sofia is saying, I catch only the last of what must have been an interrogation or an explanation.

"We have to find the Tiepolo. That is the only solution. Five million euros."

"What are you talking about, Sofia? I'm in no mood for Tiepolos. I'm sorry, but I still haven't given my condolences to Valeriana or Ariadna. You'll have to forgive me. Come to my place in Barcelona for a few days if it's good for you. I have to go."

"Tell me one thing, Emili," Sofia says with a serious, persuasive tone of complicity, one that is suddenly very familiar. "Could anything the note says be of any help to me?"

"No, Sofia. Sorry. It's a personal matter, an old affair, something between Jonàs and me. Actually it's not even really between Jonàs and me. I must leave now, please understand."

"Emili, you must help me find the Tiepolo! I know it has to be somewhere. I know it exists! It would be the solution to all this!" Sofia pulls at my arm like a little girl as I walk towards the car in a daze. At some point she lets go of me and stands back, her arms crossed, only making a slight movement to wave goodbye when I'm in the car and to say: "Call me later."

I could only hear the words Jonàs had written in prison before his death: "Don't forget about Ariadna."

10

St Petersburg
From Memoirs of the Invisible City

At first, the insufferable damp and nauseous smells seemed worse than the loss of my freedom. But they were not, of course. Not even the rats that scurried from one cell to another, or the rotten food I was given on the second day of my imprisonment could be worse than being deprived of my liberty. A week passed with no news from anyone; I didn't know why I was kept in the fortress. The only information I received were the muffled groans and shrieks that reached me through walls and passages, making me fearful of the moment when I too would be led along them.

My eyes had grown accustomed to the dark. On the fourth day, I took courage and requested paper and pen, which were granted me on the fifth. In spite of the dreadful conditions, I set myself the task of drawing up a list of the studies I had undertaken in the city until then and the ones which still awaited my attention before I could consider my account finished. I realized that very little remained to be done, and I swore to myself that if I emerged from that living hell, I would hasten to finish the work so that my return to Madrid could be moved forwards by a few months. Drawing up the list required a couple of days, according to my plan, but then I fell prey to despair. How could it be that the Spanish ambassador, after all this time, had still not found me and come to my rescue, as was his duty? What if his intervention proved to be ineffective, or too late, and I ended up joining the ranks of prisoners who groaned or lay silenced for ever beyond those walls?

Perhaps the ambassador had given up all thought of me. I could not help thinking of what happened to the great Tiepolo when he arrived at the Spanish Court. So much effort had been put into securing his services in Venice, yet he was paid no attention when he set foot in the Kingdom of Spain. Ah, if only my Cecilia were here and could intercede for me before the Empress, I thought to myself mournfully, having received no letter from her in months.

Still more days passed, until finally a guard pushed me up the stairs and along passages that were as icy as my cell and left me in what seemed to be another, brighter prison chamber, where the light streamed from high windows beyond which I could glimpse people walking. I was given no explanation. Then a person appeared, announcing that he was from the Spanish Embassy, and begged me to accompany him. Together we emerged into glorious daylight, the steeple of Saints Peter and Paul Cathedral presiding like a torch over the St Petersburg twilight.

I did not fully trust the Russian man who muttered in poor French that he had come in the name of the Spanish ambassador, but I had no choice but to follow him, filthy as a pig, exhausted, rheumatic, my clothes all torn, frightened as a bird whose neck is about to be twisted. He was telling the truth: an hour later, at the Embassy, the Viscount bestowed every possible attention on me, including a warm bath and new clothes.

Only after I reappeared, refreshed in body and spirit, did he offer an explanation of what had occurred.

"The Minister of Justice himself has offered an apology for the mistake in connection with your arrest, Señor Roselli. I am very sorry that it took us so long to discover your whereabouts."

"I'd like to thank you, Viscount, for all you did to deliver me from the clutches of the law. The physical conditions were abominable – yet far greater was my fear of what might happen to me."

"You had nothing to fear, sir," the Viscount replied with apparent frankness.

"With all due respect, if you had heard the shrieks that filled the dungeon—"

"Russia is full of criminals, and justice has to run its course. The Tsarina has many enemies, and many friends who are sometimes too zealous."

"I am not following you, dear Viscount."

"Let's be frank, Señor Roselli. I gave you a warning that perhaps you ignored. The fact that the Minister himself has apologized and described your arrest as a mistake does not mean that there was ever any mistake. You can be certain that since the day of Her Imperial Highness's reception at Tsarskoe Selo your every move has been closely watched, so that if you were to – how shall I put it? – make any faux pas—"

"Well, I wanted to tell you of someone I met, but it was impossible for me..." I started, realizing that I couldn't conceal this from the ambassador any longer, but he interrupted me.

"Leave it be, dear friend. I know about it. You can be certain that this was intended as a warning. If something similar were to happen again I am not sure that my intervention would produce the same results."

We were approaching the saddest Christmas of my life. In a city that had grown more inhospitable than any other, when day after day one could not venture out of doors because of the raging snow storms, I took the opportunity to advance the study of my royal commission. By the beginning of the year – this was 1767 – my task was nearly finished, and I informed Viscount Herrería that I would set sail for Spain as soon as it was possible, not an easy undertaking in the middle of winter.

The lavish receptions, the dazzling architecture of the city's palaces, the boldness and rigour of its urban structure, its majestic scale, the insatiable social activity – all of this represented the brighter face of a capital that had likewise shown me its darker side: rat-infested dungeons, corpses of the poor who had died in the streets from the cold, serfs waiting in line for charity in the form of a bowl of soup.

Was Saint Petersburg the finest of the great European cities, as Peter the Great had hoped, or just a golden cage set in the middle of the icy white steppes? Was Catherine the patron of Enlightenment or a despot, worried about any move that might undermine her power? My invisible prison was something else entirely: for weeks now I had not written to Cecilia, tired of her humiliating silence.

When I arrived in St Petersburg the previous spring, I was excited by each new discovery in my research, each new idea for Charles's project, each conversation with a learned citizen – ah, the walks with the great Rastrelli, the wisest of all the wise men of this city! My heart was filled with the vivid, inspiring presence of Cecilia, though she was many thousands of miles away. The city smiled down on me, as did life itself. But then, surprised by Cecilia's silence and increasingly dispirited as it continued, I reached the point when I thought she was irredeemably lost to me, and even the memory of her face – in that icy prison where everything seemed hostile – had been erased. How then can reason triumph if a change of mood can transform your view of the world?

Fortunately my correspondence with Giambattista Tiepolo – always brief but affectionate – never stopped. The great Venetian led me to understand, if only indirectly, that his relationship with the court was not what he had anticipated. Once the glorious work on the Royal Palace was completed, he placed his services at His Majesty's disposal, which Charles accepted; yet, the painter's new projects were not so readily accepted.

The enigmatic Viscount Herrería managed at this time to assuage my melancholy by announcing that he had found a way for me to leave the Russian capital: I would travel by land to Riga, whence it would not be difficult to embark on a vessel for Amsterdam and from there to Cantabria.

I was preparing to embark from Riga to Amsterdam on another of those glacial Baltic winter days. The attentive official who had escorted me from the Embassy had placed my belongings in the cabin, and the commotion on deck reflected the crew's excitement as we were about to set sail. Then the official addressed me in a solemn voice: "Señor Roselli, someone at the Embassy has discreetly requested that I give you this parcel just before your departure. I have kept my word, and I must beg you never to reveal the circumstances in which this was delivered to you."

Some several hours later, now on the high seas bound for the Netherlands, when we were but a white dot on the grey and menacing sea, I carefully unwrapped the parcel and laid out its contents on the tiny table in my cabin. I braced myself: it was a bundle of letters tied together with a string – letters from Cecilia, more than twenty letters that had never reached their destination.

Her words were so wonderfully sweet – so passionate when no reply came from me, so powerful her show of affection, so hurtful her resentment when she thought I had forgotten her – so perceptive and moving when she began to suspect that I had not received her letters! This was my most shameful moment: she had shown hope and sympathy when confronted by my silence, whereas I had given up on her, believing she had stopped writing to me.

My regret at the way I had behaved was mixed with indignation and rage against the person who had held the letters from me. On my arrival in Madrid I would lodge a formal complaint against the Viscount. To whom should I address my complaint? Sabatini? The King? Once again I felt like a caged animal as I walked round and round in my cabin.

Only Cecilia's constancy of affection comforted me, but what future could we hope for if the delivery of these letters at the very moment of embarking could be seen as yet another warning, the confirmation that our relationship was no secret?

11
Imaginary Prisons

I walk through the lower streets of the village, the ones that more than two centuries ago invaded the pastures and clearings that had stood between the port – or the beach – and the Royal City, which was built on a strip of raised ground marked by a low precipice of coastal rock. In contrast to the grand squares, avenues and the quadrangular structure of the Royal City, the fishermen's district is a mass of narrow streets and alleys, low, modest houses – like the simple huts that had probably stood there before. This area lies between the land rejected by the royal architects and the beach, where the sand deposits from the delta continue to grow, driving the sea further out. It's the night of beginnings, perhaps of my own people: a bonfire blazes, you can hear the roar of the sea, a woman groans as she gives birth – the door of her house open – one of the royal labourers strolls deep into the fishermen's district, on the dirty beach a white sail is flapping, work on the nearby canal progresses, and there are rumours that a great port will be built.

I'm turning the page, however, because whether that happened or not in the eighteenth century, I am wandering through the streets of the twenty-first. Children are seated on their doorsteps playing with their Gameboys, from time to time you hear a television commercial, a seagull shrieks in the distance. Perhaps I've gone back so many centuries because I don't have the courage to enter the door of Jonàs's old house, where Valeriana sits in a wicker chair, the only woman in the entire district to be dressed in black.

She gives me a rather stern look, then her features soften into the shadow of a smile that doesn't quite materialize. When I embrace her to express my condolences, the silence she has kept until now is broken – she launches into a story that branches off into another and then another and then another. Everything becomes muddled in her head, as if past and present have no meaning: everything that has happened and everything she imagines are equally alive and follow their natural course. Nothing has come to an end, no one has died, we are all present. Jonàs and I are still running along the street towards the esplanade, where we'll play football, her husband is late from the fish auction, her mother has scolded her because she hasn't left for market yet, Ariadna... As she says her name, she becomes silent, searches for the buttons on her dress as if she is going to find the solution there, then adds in a lucid voice that startles me, as if she is again the Valeriana she used to be:

"She's upstairs. Go up."

I go up. Slowly. Each step sheds light on memories I had spent years trying to bury. I can almost recapture the smells coming from the ground floor, where they would be casting lead, that mixture of sea and petrol, the smells of the fishermen's houses when I was a child. Slowly I climb the worn-out steps with the grey wooden edges, the dark staircase I used to climb, whistling with joy, not knowing then that nothing lasts and yet nothing fades. If we were able to stop for a moment in the darkness, on the stairs we frequently climb – the cold metal of the handrail and the white pine cones at the end – we could see ourselves coming and going through the years, yielding to the night, embracing the full glow, descending or ascending. We would see what cannot be remedied – not when the events weigh on us and are past history, but before they happen, when we are free and not forced to act. But no one pauses in the troubling darkness of the stairs.

Pushing the half-open door of the tiny antechamber, I enter a small room that gives onto the narrow street. It is lit by a lonely computer screen and a gooseneck lamp shedding light on the pages of an open book and the hands and bare arms of the person reading it, her face profiled by the tremulous blue of the night coming through the window. On the street, the sound of a motorbike, squealing children and the damp cool of a September evening.

The woman who is sitting in the chair with the open book in her lap, and won't get up to greet me, is Ariadna. She won't get up. I was eighteen, she was seventeen. She won't get up. It was raining. I loved her.

Ariadna welcomes my visit with affected nonchalance, as if we saw each other from time to time. I'm uncomfortable, look for a chair so I can sit close to her. If anyone were to look in, they would see two bluish silhouettes in front of the window. Ariadna has her hair pulled to the back of her neck, her pupils are dilated by the close light, reinforcing the magnetic effect of her chestnut eyes, her cheeks are more hollow (she was only seventeen when I knew her before), her lips and her mouth, whose laughter used to brighten up her entire face, seem broader now. Her mouth is closed, enigmatic. It frightens me.

"Your brother loved you. Maybe more than you imagine," I say to break the silence and avoid the usual expressions of sympathy, remembering all the while the disturbing note that has brought me here.

"And what do you know about me?" Ariadna says, showing that her apparent lack of interest in seeing me is far from indifference, but she immediately seems to regret her words, as if realizing that she'd been too quick to draw her weapon. "It's a nice gesture for you to give your condolences to mother."

"And to you, Ariadna."

"A bit late for that, don't you think?

She was seventeen, I was eighteen, the purple-orange light of a summer evening was reflected on the wet asphalt, a strong smell of earth enveloped us after the downpour we had watched from the sheltered porch of a whitewashed hut set among carob and olive trees. We owned the world, we embraced the fresh air, the scent of grass, wide-eyed, our skin warm and sensitive.

"How's Sofia?" asks Ariadna, knowing that her question cannot be ignored.

"I've just come from seeing her… I was away on a trip. I'm not sure if you know, but Sofia's in a lot of trouble."

Ariadna shows her disdain with disarming ability. She looks out of the window, straightens her skirt, adjusts the lamp, and I realize that it was a mistake to come and see her, even if it was Jonàs's last wish. To hell with Jonàs! On the other hand, her silence and lack of reproach show an amazing dignity that shines through the beauty of her face, that beauty which captivates me and won't let me leave. As the light falls over her upper body, her breast, down to her waist, I see the same body that I loved when I was eighteen. Ariadna is wearing a yellow sweater that shows off her brown arms and shoulders and accentuates her small, full breasts.

We devoured each other on the whitewashed porch, the curtain of water isolating us from the world and showering over my motorbike. I can't remember how many summer afternoons I met her when the fish auction was over and she'd finished selling the day's catch. I would find her among the shouting crowd and the traffic of boxes filled with silvery, twitching snappers, crates of shiny prawns straining to move and a display of reddish baskets full of crabs and lobsters. I would find her among the excitement of docking boats, among blocks of broken ice, the chant of the auctioneer calling out prices. We would set off on my motorbike to a shriek-filled, deserted shore, up the solitary and fragrant hill to the hidden bay that smelt of moss. She was seventeen, I was eighteen.

One Saturday we walked to the Invisible City. We climbed down through the crack in the roof and amused ourselves by bouncing echoes off the huge empty space. Ariadna was no longer Jonàs's rowdy little sister, who

171

was a bit rude and spoke in fast, broken sentences: she
had become bright-eyed Ariadna of a few round words
– a natural force, a spontaneous charm – a girl I would
occasionally see when I returned from school to spend the
weekend in the village.

"You would have noticed me earlier if I hadn't been
Jonàs's sister," she said playfully in the half-light of the
Invisible City.

"What makes you think I've noticed you now?" I laughed
in reply.

"I know you have."

Her slender arm pulled me towards her and we stared
at each other for a moment. Her eyes were filled with
excitement and surprise, as if she'd just done something
she shouldn't have done, her lips trembling in an attempt
to smile. We embraced with tense arms at first, then more
relaxed – then our warm tongues met.

"It's time to leave, they're waiting for me at home."

That was the same clear limit that marked the end of
each summer evening before I would accompany her
to her door, to the house where I have now returned, to
the smell of fish and petrol and cast lead, beneath the
hard, threatening look of her father, who watched from
the terrace, seated in his wicker chair, before Jonàs had
stripped him of everything.

"Sofia's been obsessing about something for some time
now, and it has nothing to do with my brother," Ariadna
says, bringing me back to the present, while on the street I
hear a cat rummaging through rubbish.

"Really?" I say to encourage the conversation.

"Don't worry," Ariadna says almost absent-mindedly, but giving me an ironic look. "I'm not talking about the painter who lives on the delta—"

"Tarrés," I add, to keep things going.

"That's it. His paintings aren't bad at all." Now I'm the one who's surprised as I watch Ariadna's expression, which is not playful but one that says she's knowledgeable. "He's been able to give his work a conceptual element, like a giant installation – that's what he did with his house in L'Encanyissada—"

"But you say he's not what Sofia's obsessing about," I add to save time. Ariadna's comment has amazed me. What has happened during all these years?

"Not as much as the other thing. Most of Sofia's visits to me these last months were about this other thing."

"I don't understand."

"And it's been relentless since Jonàs died."

"I have no idea what you mean."

"Her obsession goes by the name of Tiepolo. Giambattista Tiepolo," Ariadna says as she scrutinizes me, waiting for a comment or perhaps a reply.

On that September evening, my motorbike skimmed over the purple-orange sheen on the wet road down the hill, Ariadna's body leaning against my back, her arms around me, until we skidded on a curve and swerved out of control. I made a few futile attempts to straighten the bike, and we crashed onto the edge of the road. We weren't going very fast, and landed in the ploughed earth beneath some olive trees, so I didn't think we could be badly hurt. I had scraped my right knee but got up

173

and limped over to Ariadna, a few metres away. She was stretched out, facing upwards; she looked like she was laughing, as was I, but her laughter turned to a frown. "I can't move my legs," she said. That is why she didn't get up when I came in today.

It couldn't possibly be true. But it was. I rushed for help, stayed by her side for the first hours and days in the hospital, hoping, praying it was just a temporary paralysis, the doctors not daring to say how serious the injury was. During the following weeks and months we went from one reputable Barcelona hospital to another. The clock had stopped at that moment, and I could not make it tick again. No one could.

At first Ariadna alternated between amazement – like a fish when it suddenly discovers it can be removed from water – and a rebellious instinct that took the form of denying or minimizing the problem. This was the most genuine Ariadna, responding with a sense of humour or brazenness to any manifestation of pity towards her. I was madly in love with her then, filled with such plentiful devotion. It was as if, in addition to being my girlfriend, she was also a sister and a daughter. But I could not set the clock in motion again: it had stopped that rainy, purple-orange afternoon.

It was the year I began my university studies in Barcelona, which allowed me to be with Ariadna during her frustrating stays in clinics and hospitals. Our roads, however, were already starting to divide. On my weekend visits to Sant Carles, she was more suspicious and critical, and our relationship grew exasperating, suffocating. Filled with a sense of guilt and helplessness, I went to see her less and less often. There was never an actual break – not an explicit one – yet there must have been one day that was the last, after which I never returned to the stairs with the cold metal handrail and the pine-cone knobs. Until today.

"Where was your trip?" Ariadna says, going back to the present.

"Tuscany. Arezzo. Actually I'm still staying there, I mean, I'm heading back as soon as I can," I say, realizing that I'm digging my own grave.

"Someone waiting for you?"

"Yes, Chloe. She's my... well, a friend."

"Your... or a friend?"

"It's all the same at this point, Ariadna."

"Did she take it quietly, knowing you were running off to console Sofia?"

"Ariadna! I don't have to listen to this!"

"Well then leave! You're good at that!"

"That's enough, Ariadna! Don't you think I'm doing just the opposite, coming to check on my friend's family?"

"Don't make me laugh. I'd love to know the real reason why you've come."

Something strange is happening. Ariadna's words are insidious, yet her face, gestures and manners aren't taut, angry or tetchy as would be logical. She knows more than she's saying.

"So, Emili, how's our friend Roselli doing?"

"What?" I ask, as if summoned from another world.

"Andrea Roselli," Ariadna replies confidently, her face brightening up.

"Roselli... How do you know about this?"

At that moment, Valeriana slips through the door at the top of the stairs, utters something incomprehensible and walks over to Ariadna's chair.

With a look that seems to suggest that she's annoyed at having to interrupt what promised to be a revelation, Ariadna says: "You'll have to excuse me. Mother needs me. Come and see me tomorrow, and we can talk about it."

"It'll have to be early: I'm heading back to Florence," I say, accepting her proposal.

When I leave Ariadna's house, the night is calm and silent. I walk beneath the jacaranda trees along the only street that crosses, top to bottom, the old district, the one that must have connected the elevated Royal City with the port. I head along the walkway that leads to the bay, trying to avoid the temptation of exorcizing all the demons of the last few hours: Chloe annoyed in Tuscany, Sofia threatened by drug-dealers, Ariadna tugging at Roselli's hand. Tiepolo.

I'm convinced that I'll only come out of this if I follow my instincts. I can't just start guessing, at least not until I've again spoken to Ariadna, seen Sofia, met with Chloe. I have a brief conversation with Chloe to confirm that I'm flying back to Florence the next day, but I don't mention the problems that have come up. Then I sit on the porch of my house on the beach, listening to the rhythmic, soothing sound of the night waves and bury myself in the Roselli memoirs.

* * *

Once again I can count the number of hours I've slept on the fingers of one hand. I was convinced that before meeting Sofia and Ariadna this morning I needed to know more about Andrea Roselli and those memoirs that consume my nights, almost as if they were the substance of my dreams, or my nightmares. Yet it looks like I'm in the same situation as yesterday, and I'm anxious to discover what Ariadna knows.

The sun-scorched lawn and the white limestones give the Mendizábals' mansion the look of an oasis. Sofia doesn't come out to greet me this time. I call out her name, but get no answer; I wander around the terraces with their view of the sea, my eyes drawn to the blue swimming pool. Finally, a large wooden door slides open and the slender figure of a tanned Sofia appears in a terrycloth robe. She's drying her hair with a towel.

"Sorry. I went to sleep late last night," she says, before looking away. She shakes her hair again, then stops. I remember her phone call, her persistent voice.

"I'm really sorry, Sofia. I told you that you can count on me," I say, feeling uncomfortable.

Sofia makes a face and tells me she'll be right back. I'm tempted to go downstairs to see if Tarrés's paintings are still there. What I really want to know is if the painter has been holding my friend in his arms. There are certain September mornings that are cool and dry, offering an escape from the boredom of summer, but the air today is heavy and the sun's glare worries me. Sofia worries me.

A little later the other large door to the patio by the swimming pool slides open, creating one big space. Sofia invites me in; breakfast is laid out on the table, making me fear that this is going to be a long affair.

"That's really nice of you, Sofia, but I'll have to be at the airport by around two."

"Well, let's get straight to the point. Eventually I'll find a solution to the real-estate mess Jonàs left. But I can't do anything about the Colombians. I can't possibly pay what they're asking."

"I've already told you that I—"

"Just wait. Don't say a word. You don't have much time – neither do I. I need you to listen and believe me. You're the one who holds the key to this."

As Sofia speaks, her face takes on a familiar expression, one that changed my way of looking at the world. It's a penetrating look, a mixture of determination, complicity and something else that's difficult to describe – something similar to sophistication.

"I hope so, Sofia. What key?"

"The Tiepolo."

"I have no idea what you're talking about."

"Maybe you don't, but Ariadna does, and she'll never tell me. Do you understand?"

I remain silent for a moment as I stare at her.

"Why don't you explain a little bit more?"

"She knows where the Tiepolo is, and she won't tell me!"

If Sofia had said this the day before yesterday, I would have burst out laughing, because Ariadna for me has always been the simple young girl who during our frantic, heated, cocooned relationship had sold fish at the port. But only yesterday she had asked me about Roselli. Sofia's nerves are on edge.

"All right, let's not lose our grip on things. Just what the hell are you talking about, Sofia?"

"I know it exists! There is one lost Tiepolo, hidden maybe, and Ariadna knows where it is. But I have to find it before she does!"

"Fine," I say, as if it were the most natural thing in the world.

"She's already gone to the trouble to hint at the secret. She did it to make fun of me, as a way of showing contempt. The little bitch thinks that because she's read a few books and taken a couple of online courses, she has the right to judge me. She thinks it's totally crass of me to buy and sell paintings, and that I can do it only because I've worked in construction and urban projects."

"Why? On what authority?" I say, startled by the news of Ariadna's recent life. I had heard practically nothing about her all these years, and I suppose all my efforts to erase her memory meant that, paradoxically, I imagined her as she had been, still the girl of seventeen with her naive sensuality – ruined at seventeen.

"She idealizes art because she's never had any artistic skills," Sofia continues. "Either that or she's a complete idiot. She doesn't understand how cruel she's been to me by not telling me where the painting is. My life depends on this! All because of her brother, that lying thief of a brother; it's her duty to help me out of this situation." Then she moves to another target: "Have you been to see her?"

"Yes. Yesterday afternoon."

"And?"

"And what, Sofia? Calm down, for Heaven's sake. I hadn't seen Ariadna in years. This whole story has been terribly unsettling…" If Sofia had shown me her vulnerable side, I could have shown her mine. "Let's just say that time and distance are the best healers. I thought it was all over, and now—"

"You're not going to tell me that now…" Even Sofia can show emotion. "You're not going to tell me that after everything that's happened you still think about her!"

"That's enough, Sofia," I say, beating a retreat. "Just leave it. It's all so recent, so fast!"

"As you wish. It's your business – but actually not just yours. She also hates me because she thinks it's my fault that you stopped seeing her."

"What?" I say, more upset at every turn of the conversation.

"Let's stop talking about all this nonsense, Emili. Listen to me: if I don't cough up the money, I'm dead, and I can only raise that amount of cash if I can find the Tiepolo. Only Ariadna knows where it is and, I'm telling you again, she'll never tell me – but she would tell *you*—"

"That doesn't make sense. A hidden painting."

"That was my first reaction too, but I was intrigued and searched through biographies and studies on Tiepolo to see if there were any unclear episodes, or a job that was never completed. As you know the painter spent his last years in Madrid, under the patronage of Charles III, who had this grandiose dream of building a city at the heart of the former kingdom of Catalunya and Aragon, a port at the mouth of the Ebro that would be allowed to trade with America. The King might have commissioned Tiepolo to paint a canvas – maybe more than one – for this new city. But no one's ever seen it. It's not included in any catalogue, but there's a rumour. Like I say, Ariadna has stirred my curiosity."

With so much information, I'm beginning to fear that Sofia has delved deeper into this than I have. I remember how clever she was when I first met her, how she moved between antique shops, galleries, private art collections in Barcelona, selling – or rather buying, mostly – family heirlooms, sometimes simply holding on to a canvas for a few months, then reselling it at a much higher price, without putting up any money at all.

"Let's be rational: I'm willing to talk to Ariadna about it – I'll do anything to help you. But I guess that when I bring up the subject she'll start imagining all sorts of things. Let's suppose for a moment that this doesn't happen and she gives me a clue, what are you planning to do then?"

"The important thing, Emili, is whether you want to help me or not. What we do after that, well, we'll discuss it later. You know there are all kinds of ways to—"

"To steal a painting?"

"No! To find it and sell it."

"OK. So let's suppose we find the painting. You know very well that to sell it discreetly and get the amount you want would take quite a long time, time you don't have."

"I know, Mr Rossell, I know that there are a lot of unknown variables here. For the time being, I'm only asking you for one favour, to sound out Ariadna, get all the information you can from her."

The tables are turned. Sofia's managed to get me involved in this – or at least I've agreed to discuss a matter which strikes me not only as improbable but foolish.

I look at my watch, then at my flight schedule, and promise to keep Sofia informed about Ariadna.

Half an hour later, having crossed the brushland and the village streets that are coming to life again after the sultry night, I find Ariadna at the top of the old stairs. She looks at me with an expectant smile, as if the last question of the previous night had been left suspended in the air. Our friend Roselli. I take a seat.

"I'm not the person you think I am," she says with a calm expression on her face. "I began to study from home, then to travel and read. In my own way I've created a world I didn't have before. Do you understand? At times it was out of spite, to show how far I could go without you. I decided to move on, as if you didn't exist. Yes, as if you didn't exist. But you did – you do. Right now you have the same frightened face as the afternoon of the accident. I saw your photos in the newspapers, even on television once, talking about a painter who had died. I thought you had learnt to hide, disguise yourself, escape. Don't pay any attention to me; Jonàs's death has affected me in an unexpected way: it's as if I've lost all sense of time, as if everything is happening in the present. Don't you have this feeling, that all those years were like a long, steady drizzle that has stopped now?"

"No, Ariadna. None of that was in vain," I say in an attempt to curb the poetic bent of the conversation. "I've changed too."

"Right. Of course," Ariadna says, suddenly alert after the involuntary abruptness of my comment. "Any idea what Cecilia's been doing while Roselli's in St Petersburg?"

"What?!"

"Cecilia Sabatini, or Vanvitelli, if you prefer."

"So, you've read Roselli's memoirs?"

"What do you think?"

"I'm really confused now. But to be honest, your sister-in-law has asked me to talk to you about something else, something we could help her with—"

"Tiepolo, of course!" Ariadna chips in. "But you can help her as much as I can with this, don't you think?"

"Judging by what I've read so far, I can't see how I could be of any help."

"And besides," Ariadna adds in an ironic tone, "you are in a hurry now, because someone's waiting for you in Italy. You're in a rush and you want to be on good terms with everybody. I don't know how you're going to pull this off..."

"It's true, I am in a hurry. My flight is leaving in four hours, but maybe I'd rather not catch it," I say, calculating the consequences of my words.

"I thought you'd turned into someone resilient, determined, and now it looks like you don't even know if Chloe is or isn't your girlfriend?"

"Cut the crap."

"That's what you said yesterday."

"Whatever – I'll need to work this out," I say, relenting, trying to open a door. "I can't go on any longer pretending that everything's great."

183

"Are you just pretending?"

"Let's drop it. I have to leave now."

"Well, that's a change!" she says as I get up and start walking towards the door. "But when you finish doing whatever it is you have to do, remember that Roselli holds the secret."

"What?" I say, stopping on the threshold.

"First things first. Then, if you want…"

Her goodbye is mixed with promise, maybe blackmail. In any case, I close the door and run down the stairs, towards the car, the plane, tomorrow, two centuries before.

From the sky the glowing Brunelleschi dome appears in the distance, announcing that we are about to land in Florence. Although I was dying to find out if the last pages of the Roselli memoirs held the secret Ariadna had alluded to, I hadn't even opened it. I was so overwhelmed by the events of the last twenty-four hours, so exhausted, that I fell asleep as soon as I was on the plane. In the taxi, driving through Chianti country to Arezzo for the last days of my holiday with Chloe, I tried to anticipate what sort of mood she'd be in, all the while recalling Sofia's desperate, intriguing words and Ariadna's startling comments. I'm strangely surprised, too, when I think about Armand Coll's silence: the newspaper I was given on the plane carried a long interview with him, presenting him as "The Hero of the Ebro" – all tanned, wearing Bermudas, on a ferry about to cross the river.

Any doubts about Chloe's mood are dispelled as soon as I set foot in the hotel. She has packed her bag, changed her flight and is returning to Barcelona early the next morning. She announces to me that "we need to talk". She is very tense as she says this, but once these crucial words are off her chest, she seems to relax. As if willing to grant one last wish, she asks me to tell her first how the trip went. In return, I will show interest in her photography.

After alluding to Sofia's anguish, I have no choice but talk about the Andrea Roselli papers and about his friend Giambattista Tiepolo. Contrary to what I expected – as I have only mentioned this to return her courtesy – Chloe seems intrigued by the possibility of an unknown or hidden Tiepolo. She asks me for more details and offers her own conjectures.

Until finally a heavy silence falls over us – a long, impenetrable silence. We look intently at each other, as we have not done for a long time, in an effort to avoid pronouncing the fatal words. But words aren't even necessary now. It's all over.

"I'll move back to my apartment. Fortunately I didn't stop paying the rent," she says laconically, even if she can't hold back the tear that rolls down her cheek.

"There's no hurry," I say, foolishly tempted to avoid the evidence. I'm familiar enough with this kind of scene not to be caught off guard. No one has ever lived with me long enough to give up their apartment for good.

A light breeze picks up in the hotel's rustic garden. I can tell that this is hostile territory for Chloe: we are city people, the two of us. That is, the part of me that loved her, that lived with her, the part I gave her. We should say more, but the last weeks have been a slow, unconscious farewell.

Despite the sudden melancholy of the moment, we have resisted the temptation of throwing accusations at each other: it's been a civilized, restrained affair. Yet, somehow I don't quite believe that it can be this civilized: I'm not the type who goes for all those social niceties, even if I have had a certain amount of experience in them.

Chloe brushes a wisp of hair from her forehead – an insignificant gesture that I've seen in other girls and women, but never in her – and I realize with a start that she's no longer mine and probably hasn't been for some time. I realize that I am alone, and I remember how I felt the afternoon I was left at the school door when I was twelve years old – the most intimate loneliness.

Through the years I have acquired many interconnecting layers that protect me or conceal me, that represent me or justify me, that replace me or project me. Each of us, simply by living in society, becomes an actor – or even a complete theatrical troupe, depending on the moment or the situation.

My tumultuous encounter with the person I was a decade ago – or even two – has created in me the unsettling feeling of being stripped of all I have acquired. Yet I am still capable of seeing, here and now, wrapped in night, as Chloe begins to fade, that some imaginary wall in an imaginary prison has just tumbled down.

12

Madrid

From Memoirs of the Invisible City

The welcome Giambattista Tiepolo was given by the Royal Court on his arrival in June 1762 was much the same as the one I received in March 1767. I returned to Madrid from the furthest ends of the continent after completing a project commissioned by His Majesty himself. One year before the King had proclaimed his dream, announcing the plan for a new city that would transform his kingdom. The monarch had even given it a name: St Charles. I had eagerly awaited the moment in which I would offer my Lord the fruits of the studies and observations I had carried out in the Russian capital, the model Charles wished to follow.

The city I returned to was not the one I had left the previous year, and most probably the King was no longer the same person. One of the three people present at the royal meeting that March day of the previous year no longer lived in the country. Esquilache, Charles III's minister, had been removed from office in order to calm those who had instigated the people of Madrid to revolt against the King's reforms. Charles's pleasure on first arriving from Naples had vanished with Esquilache. The King had discovered that it would not be easy to carry out his plans. Progress would have to be made slowly – more importantly, it could only be made if he was willing to enter into agreement with some of the country's century-old powers, the ones that had always held him back, preventing entire regions of wasteland from being cultivated, reaping benefits from the ignorance of the people, the ones that feared free trade.

I arrived at the port of Santander and reached the capital via Castile, travelling through silent wheat fields, with oak trees in the distance and herds of bleating sheep in front of the coach. I went straight to the Sabatinis' house, which had been my home before the Baltic expedition, both hoping and dreading to find there my former hosts.

Francesco and his wife were with the King in Aranjuez, the servants announced, informing me that orders had been given to offer me lodging. This was an ambiguous, uncomfortable situation.

As soon as I had settled in, I sent word to the King and Sabatini that I had arrived in Madrid, and requested permission to present my respects to the monarch and discuss the results of my mission. Days passed, and I received no response from Aranjuez. I grew more and more desperate at not being able to see Cecilia and fearful that the plan for the new city had been washed away by the torrent of involution that was sweeping over the country.

As I awaited an audience with the King, consumed by the desire to kiss my Neapolitan lady, I often visited my friend Tiepolo. During this period I also became acquainted with two illustrious gentlemen who were going to be involved in the project for the new city. One was a young Catalan, Antoni de Capmany, a former military man and lover of history and letters. The other was the extraordinary Peruvian, Pablo de Olavide, who was rumoured to have a tumultuous past and had lived in Paris before he came to embrace the Spanish capital.

Don Pablo had survived an earthquake in Lima, as well as the judiciary system in that remote colony. He had left the Indies and had come to the old continent in search of protection and sympathy; but the lawsuits he had fled followed him, and he was again imprisoned, this time in Madrid. When he was released, he had few high-ranking acquaintances, and all of his possessions had been confiscated. In spite of his precarious situation, the widow Isabel de los Ríos succumbed to his charms, married him and placed her entire fortune at his disposal. He travelled through Italy and France, where he had access to the latest currents of thought, and came into contact with thinkers such as Voltaire. Upon his return to Spain, he started a political career, trying to promote the reforms he judged necessary. When we met, at a reception held in his magnificent library, he was greatly thrilled, as he expected to be named Superintendent of the Nuevas Poblaciones de Sierra Morena, an agrarian and social experiment.

"In order to arrive at liberty," he said to me and Antoni, "one must have a choice, one must acquire knowledge and training – and training costs money, knowledge has a price, my dear friends. So the first thing a country must do if it wants its citizens to be free is to distribute resources, thus allowing wealth to be created, improving the knowledge and education of its citizens, who will eventually be in a position to choose. This way, they will be closer to liberty.

"Of course there are quicker ways, for example marrying a wealthy woman. But as this country has not enough wealthy women for everyone, you shouldn't be surprised if the enemies of liberty are precisely those who are against the distribution of resources. However, we must persuade them that free trade – as well as rotating the crops, cultivating new ones, breaking up large estates, limiting monopolies, building new towns, improving universities – is in their interest. Those in power must understand that this is the only way to ensure that hunger does not spur the poor to revolt, and that they can grow even richer."

I was disconcerted that the monarch was in no great hurry to know the results of my expedition to St Petersburg, worried about the shadows this cast on my future services to the King and the grand project he had envisioned, and troubled by the rumours that reached me concerning Señora Cecilia Sabatini – in spite of my efforts not to give any credit to them. I decided to put aside my natural reserve and enjoy every opportunity for social life in the warm climate of Madrid, which contrasted so greatly with the icy Baltic metropolis. Even if I knew that the rumours about Cecilia could not be true, something told me that I needed to brace myself for quite a different life from the one I had imagined.

I had been in the capital more than a month when Francesco Sabatini sent word through a servant that he had returned.

"My dear friend," he said, as we sat in one of his rooms, "we will need to examine with care your research in the

Tsarina's city. The new Spain could benefit greatly from this."

"Yes, Francesco, and I am anxious to have the opportunity to present my study and the possible applications for our projects."

"As you know, Andrea, the Count of Aranda is the most influential man in His Majesty's new government – and we should be pleased, because he supports the architectural and urban policies that Esquilache had begun to apply."

"Splendid! If you will allow me to speak frankly, I must say that I had begun to have my doubts."

"How is that possible, Andrea?"

"Forgive me, Francesco, for interpreting in this way the King's delay in granting me an audience."

"Don't worry. The plan for the new city is not urgent, that is true, but His Majesty has not forgotten it. I can assure you."

"Then, how do you explain—"

"There have been many changes in the government, Andrea. If you want my opinion, I don't think that building a new city is a priority for the Count of Aranda. It does remain, however, in the King's mind. Therefore, be not discouraged."

"I am sure you realize that I am in a very strange position," I say, referring to more than one essential aspect.

"As far as I am concerned, you can resume your previous activity while all this is resolved." His words cut into me like knives. "Better still, take your choice of the works I am supervising, and direct it yourself."

"I'm deeply moved by your kindness, but I'd rather not continue abusing your generosity. With your permission, I will seek a new lodging and free the rooms you have so kindly offered me again."

"I see, my dear friend – you wish to enjoy greater freedom."

I felt my heart racing as I said farewell to Sabatini. What was this man made of? How could he say not a single word about my relationship with Cecilia? He must know, yet he did not even blink. The person who intercepted the letters must know about our liaison, and news must surely have reached Francesco – assuming that it was not Sabatini himself who had us spied upon. If he has the proof he was looking for, why does he continue with this game of courtesies? I can think of only one explanation: he does not want to oppose the royal decision to have a project carried out under my supervision. If this is the case, then Sabatini will probably try to obstruct the project in order to gain time. It frightens me to see him so strong, so controlled. What might a man like this be capable of?

The moment I saw Cecilia crossing the garden, all my fears and doubts disappeared as if someone had drawn the curtain in a darkened room. The look in her eyes reflected the determination I witnessed on our last encounter, her body still had the fullness I knew. She stretched out a hand and I kissed it. Her eyes were aflame.

"Your letters were kept from me, Cecilia. They were delivered to me when I was about to sail for Spain. Someone was spying on us."

"You, on the other hand, made a few friends in St Petersburg, I have heard."

"This is so unfair, Cecilia! I thought of you every day, anxiously awaiting your letters, and wrote to you in spite of all. I was thrilled when I read the ones you wrote me, the ones which were delivered to my ship. I was deeply moved."

"I have no doubt, but time does not pass in vain. It would be ridiculous if we were to maintain a situation that can lead us nowhere. On the contrary, we must change our strategy: remain friends but grant each other full freedom. This would be more beneficial to us both, and keep us both happy, don't you agree?"

I was so astonished by her words that I could not respond. Cecilia kissed me on the cheek and caressed my shoulders as if I were a child, then continued:

"My dearest Andrea, don't be sad – and do not judge me. Put aside your worries. You were right when you tried to convince me to marry Francesco. He has been very generous with me: he is tolerant, and Madrid is a magnificent city if you attend the balls and join the general merriment. You should do the same as I do: accept invitations, go to receptions, enjoy the gatherings, be a little daring, laugh, tell a few lies! I am sure you must have heard things about me during these past weeks—"

"Yes, but I placed no credit in them. I refused to listen."

"Some of the gossip you have heard may be true, Andrea, but accept the friendship I am offering you now."

"Cecilia, this is not what I expected – this is not what we had. Your letters were filled with passion!"

"Then forget about me! But I don't want to forget you, and I can be useful to you. I hear people talk, I ask questions – and people listen to me. The Count of Aranda wants to have nothing to do with the St Charles project: he believes that if it becomes known that the King wants a new court or a new capital, this will provoke the resentment of the people of Madrid and part of the nobility, which could lead to another revolt, like last year. Aranda cannot openly go against the King's plans: he is now putting together a proposal whose only purpose is to delay the project as much as possible. He will recommend to His Majesty the creation of a high commission to study and finalize every aspect of the project. It is a way to gain time and see if the King tires of the idea. The commission will include you and Francesco, Aranda himself and a man in his confidence, Pablo de Olavide, and another politician who is gaining influence, possibly a rival of the Count, José Moñino."

"This is good news, Cecilia. And I am grateful to you for telling me, but…"

It is better not to dwell on the bitter hours. Cecilia disappeared among the scent of lemon trees, her presence more splendid and cruel than that of any woman in the whole of Madrid.

A few days later His Majesty received me and listened with great interest to my report on the architecture and town planning of St Petersburg, and on Tsarina Catherine's patronage of the arts. Again he showed enthusiasm for the new city and announced that a commission had been created to draw up the definitive project. He then gave orders to prepare for his afternoon hunt.

As soon as we left the audience, Minister Aranda, who had been at the meeting, confirmed the names that Cecilia had already provided me and added:

"Please do not think that this committee will interfere with your work, but rather the opposite. You are aware of His Majesty's regard for Señor Sabatini, and I have full confidence in Don Pablo de Olavide. Therefore you can begin to work in all freedom. As to Señor José Moñino, for the moment you need not worry about him. Devote all the time you need to a detailed description of the site of the new city, the glory it would bring to the Crown and the benefits the entire country would derive by building it. Do your best. Once Señor Sabatini has finished examining the study, the only role that Señor Moñino and I reserve for ourselves will be to judge if it is worthy of His Majesty's consideration."

From the ambiguous information provided by the Count, I concluded that my best chance of support would come from Pablo de Olavide, who had now moved to Seville to direct the Nuevas Poblaciones de Sierra Morena. My friend Antoni de Capmany, who was in close contact with Olavide and had good connections with José Moñino, agreed with me, and said he was happy to accompany me to Andalucía to talk to Olavide. After the meeting, Capmany would provide the advice I needed about Iberian geography and political history, so that the site for the city could be chosen.

Months passed: Olavide was too busy with his Andalusian Arcadia, and Capmany and I found it difficult to make time to travel beyond Despeñaperros. Madrid was again buzzing with balls and receptions, and the management of the country was conducted in the afternoon salons. Sabatini's urban planning advanced, with or without Aranda's tutelage, for Francesco had an audience with the King whenever he wanted. In short, no one in Madrid bothered to think whether a new city should be founded or not. Cecilia, in the meantime, was like a little bird that fluttered from branch to branch with Sabatini's benevolent consent, far removed from my quiet grief. I frequented the various salons to take my mind off the exasperating slowness of the project, and attended the receptions to ease the bitterness of Cecilia's distance. I talked and chatted and danced to disguise the silence of my lonely, sad soul.

At times my feet would wander through the streets without any direction, often finding their way to the study of the old Giambattista Tiepolo, who was pleased to be working on a new royal commission: seven canvases for the altars of the convent of St Pascal Baylon in Aranjuez. The serene Giambattista was glad to lend me his ear, and recommended patience, advising me never to let a day pass without trying to perfect my project, no matter if the likelihood of the actual undertaking was great or small. Tiepolo would have preferred to paint the new rooms of the Aranjuez Palace that Sabatini was building, but the King's influential confessor, Father Eleta, was opposed to this, judging the painter's profane compositions immoral, their bodies reflecting ecstasy and lust. In the end Tiepolo agreed to paint the saints for the Franciscan convent. The one of St Pascal for the high altar was finished, and he was working on the sketches for the other six chapels devoted to St Joseph, the Immaculate Conception, St Francis, St Charles Borromeo, St Anthony of Padua and St Peter of Alcántara.

Giambattista's eyes would sometimes fill with tears when his home country was mentioned, but despite that – and the fact that part of his family was far away – he made no complaints. He was pleased to see how his sons Giandomenico and Lorenzo prospered in their art. He looked like one of the saints he was painting: he had given himself up to the priesthood of art and was convinced that his work had continued to follow the path towards improvement. On one occasion he ended a heated discussion about the appreciation of painting in different historical periods with a phrase I often recall: "Beauty will save the world".

Early in the spring of 1768, following a frequent corre-spondence, Antoni de Capmany and I finally visited Don Pablo de Olavide and unrolled a detailed map of the Kingdom of Spain in his office in Seville. It was clear that St Charles should be built on the Mediterranean; for one, the King continued to pine for the Bay of Naples, but he also wished to strengthen his power on the sea, where the English presence was growing.

Cadiz was already renowned for its trade with America; the South did not require another city. On the other hand, the bellicose welcome given to the Bourbons by Valencians and Catalans made it advisable to build a new royal city in their region. Antoni de Capmany pointed to the Ebro as it passed through Saragossa, then his finger slowly followed the course of the river until it reached the delta. Here he stopped and tapped his finger several times on that muddled area of estuaries, bays and lagoons.

As the three of us looked at the map, the illustrious
Catalan, Antoni de Capmany, seemed to have the same air
of solemnity with which our sovereign had proclaimed,
two years before, the birth of his St Petersburg. "A bay for
Charles, a city for the arts, a port for trade, a maritime
canal for the navigable Ebro. Here, my friends, we will
build the city of St Charles!"

Capmany continued to explain his reasons for the
choice of the Bay of Alfacs, the largest natural port in the
Mediterranean. "It is the central point between Barcelona,
Valencia, Saragossa and Mallorca" – and was therefore close
to Menorca, which the English claimed – "and is located at
the end of the most important Spanish river, the Ebro, which
crosses Aragon and is used for commercial navigation, but
requires a safer artificial outlet to the open sea, a canal" –
which had actually been designed some time before – "linking
the river to the port on the bay." My own reasoning did not
contradict Capmany's: the city of St Charles would help
develop trade with the interior of Spain, whilst increasing
its maritime strength, much as St Petersburg had done for
Russia. It would be built near the mouth of an important
river, similar to the city of the tsars on the Neva. It would
be conceived as an ideal city, well proportioned, beautiful,
like the dazzling Baltic capital. But the city of Peter the
Great had been erected on a symbolic site, filled with the
significance of the victory over the Swedes. What was the
historical importance of the Bay of Alfacs?

No sooner had I expressed this doubt than I noticed a
condescending smile on the face of Don Pablo, which
seemed to suggest that a history lesson by Capmany would

follow. "Despite certain inconveniences which we will try
to look at as advantages, we could not possibly choose a
better location, my friend. As the bay is near Tortosa, the
second city in Catalunya, this means that important pages
of history have been written on its shores. In the eleventh
century, Ramon Berenguer III reconquered this spot where
the Arabs had erected their convent-fortress of Ràpita,
and handed it over to Benedictine monks. Half a century
later, Ramon Berenguer IV placed the city of Tortosa and
the rest of the region under Catalan rule; with time the
convent passed into the hands of the Knights Hospitaller.
The monastery of Santa Maria de la Ràpita was a favourite
retreat of the kings, some of whom sojourned here before
setting off on epic expeditions. This was the case of Jaume
II in the year 1323, according to the *Crónica* written by Peter
the Ceremonious, as well as Alfonso the Magnanimous
in 1420. From the beaches of the port of Alfacs, Jaume
II's troops set sail for Sicily and Sardinia. Alfonso's fleet
began their first Neapolitan campaign from this site. This
last event is bound to inspire Charles III, who will see it
as a good omen. There's one final remarkable occurrence,
although it's a slightly unpleasant one. In the year 1610, all
the Moriscos that remained in the kingdom were gathered
on the beaches of Alfacs before being expelled: they were
loaded onto ships and transported to the opposite shore
of the Mediterranean – or to death. It is true that this was
not an honourable episode, but considering that our King
personally expelled the Jesuits... who knows?"

Pablo de Olavide laughed at the joke, and I was filled
with emotion at the thought of the undertaking. Antoni

de Capmany would be charged with transforming the
Ràpita convent and the port of Alfacs – formerly known
as El Fangós – into the symbol of that patriotic, artistic
and Mediterranean spirit that best suited Charles. Alfonso
the Magnanimous had, after all, created on his arrival in
Naples the court that would become the first humanist
centre in Italy. I thought of the white marble of Alfonso's
Triumphal Arch at the Castel Nuovo, which was like an
elegant window opened to knowledge and the world
beyond the massive earth-coloured walls that enclosed and
confined the medieval castle. Our city would be comparable:
the new city would rise – elegant, well-proportioned and
agreeable – above the century-old wilderness of the delta.
A new Pompeii.

Yet another year passed before the Count of Aranda would
authorize me to lead an expedition to the site to study the
plants and animals of the area, the crops, the climate, the
resources of the land, the transportation routes and the
distribution of settlements. I was to make observations
and measurements, and produce a plan for the project.
I managed to gather ten men of the greatest technical
knowledge available at that time, and we left for the Ebro
delta in June 1769. I thought that this would be the final
step: at the end of the year we would present the definitive
project to the King, approved by the Commission for the
New City of St Charles.

My farewell visit to Giambattista was not a pleasant one
this time. The canvases for Aranjuez were virtually finished.
He had worked hard in his efforts to attain purity, something

well suited to his disposition, but also conforming to the austere tone approved by Father Joaquín de Eleta, Charles III's confessor, who had become – Tiepolo lamented – the artistic authority of the Court. Giambattista knew that if the priest were to object to his paintings, no one from the Royal Academy of San Fernando, which was led by Mengs, would do anything to defend his artistic worth. Tiepolo had decided to show the monarch each canvas separately, as soon as it was finished, so that any grievance might be made known to the painter – though in reality this was a deft move in order to receive the priest's blessing. Tiepolo's courteous offer had received no response from the Palace, and now he was beset by severe doubts, fearing that he would never see his paintings hang at the altars of St Pascal Baylon.

I could not hide my joy at setting off, but at the same time I did not want to seem insensible to the artist's sadness. I found it disgraceful that the Spanish Court could treat the finest painter of our century with such disrespect, at a time when we were about to launch the project for a city conceived to welcome beauty and exalt it.

As I was leaving for this decisive journey, I embraced Giambattista, who had recently turned seventy-three. I wished with all my heart that he would live long enough to see the new city and walk with me down the main road of the Ràpita. I hoped one day to see his paintings cover the domes of St Charles, reflecting the orange light of its skies and the clouds mottled with cobalt, a hand emerging from a golden cloak, its strong finger pointing towards glory, ecstatic riders galloping on their wild horses through the waves of the Sea of Alfacs.

13

Does the Mystery End or Begin?

Perhaps it shouldn't be like this. Perhaps I should feel dejected, or at least sad or melancholy. Chloe has left for good, and I am staying on another three days, alone in the hotel in Arezzo. Perhaps I should think about the twelve-year-old boy who stood in front of the school door in the unsettling twilight on that endless afternoon a long time ago. I have thought about that boy, as always, but in a different, new way, as if I could see that today's loneliness would draw me closer to the home that was wrenched from me that day, the one I briefly regained during the months spent with Ariadna, before the blow fell again on another afternoon. Our souls take certain paths that should simply be followed, without any effort to understand them.

Chloe left yesterday and, rather than thinking about our breakup, which we had rehearsed half a dozen times, I sat in the hotel garden, beneath the dense foliage of olive trees and the swaying vigilance of a cypress, staring into the abyss of the Roselli papers. Late at night, numb from the cool, damp air, I was overwhelmed by what I could deduce from the Aretine's notes on Tiepolo and the founding of Sant Carles, and disillusioned by what will never be known.

The memoirs have come to an end – there's no other page – just as Roselli is about to embark on his expedition to the site where the new city will be built. What remains are mere promises and mysteries.

When Ariadna said that Roselli held the secret, is she talking about this? The memoirs cover ten years, from the time the Tuscan arrives in Naples in 1759 to work under Vanvitelli at the Caserta Palace and meets Charles, King of the Two Sicilies, who would soon be named the King of Spain, until 1769, when he is about to leave Madrid. During this time he has accompanied Tiepolo from Venice to Madrid, travelled to St Petersburg to study how that city was built and returned to Spain to carry out – with the help of the illustrious Olavide and Capmany – the Sant Carles project. But Aranda's political intrigues or perhaps the bureaucratic red tape suffocating the project seem to have drained Roselli of his initial drive, and the annotations have become sparse. Who knows? Maybe the change in Cecilia left him so dejected he had no wish to continue his memoirs.

The great infrastructural works preceding the building of the actual city have been documented. We know that the construction of the canal between the Ebro and the Bay of Alfacs was begun in 1770; the port was granted the right to engage in trade with America in 1778 and work began on the city itself in 1780. The great mystery is why the construction of the city slowed and finally halted around 1786, even before the King's death, and why this enormous project fell to ruin before it had even come to fruition. These are ruins that two centuries later still remain and raise questions, that challenge and perhaps elude understanding. The Invisible City where we played as children, the cracked vaults and the dark echoing space where I kissed bright-eyed Ariadna. Or was it she who kissed me?

Despite all this, Roselli tells us a lot – perhaps that's all we need. As he was saying goodbye to his friend Tiepolo, the Venetian expressed his fear that the canvases he had painted for the Franciscan convent of St Pascal might not be hung. Could some of these paintings meant for Aranjuez have ended up in Roselli's hands, even as he hoped that the old painter would live long enough to paint the domes of Sant Carles? Or maybe Tiepolo prepared sketches for future frescoes? Or perhaps, even better, the Venetian artist actually produced a painting for a palace in the new city, or for his friend Roselli?

I walk towards the centre of Arezzo, filled with impatience and excitement. Roselli holds the secret, Ariadna said, and I'm sure she drew that conclusion from the parting scene. Yet this was enough for Ariadna to stir Sofia's imagination – and Sofia, relying on this remote possibility, has embraced it as her only means of salvation. The tragic thing is that, even if the painting exists, it has to be found soon, because I doubt that the Mafiosi who are blackmailing her will show much patience.

The Biblioteca della Città is right in the middle of old Arezzo, among winding stone streets and beautiful squares, near Petrarch's house. I immediately discover that they have an extensive archive devoted to local history and the city's most famous sons: Petrarch, Piero della Francesca, Michelangelo, Pietro Aretino, Vasari... At first I find no trace of my Andrea Roselli, although the surname is fairly common in the region. There is a Cosimo Rosselli, a painter from the fifteenth century, listed by Vasari in his *Vite*, as well as philologists and scientists from a much later date.

Hours go by unnoticed as I frantically jump from an encyclopedia to a dictionary, from a treatise on painting to a collection of historical chronicles. It is summer, and it is off-season from an academic point of view, which means that I am almost the only one in the library this afternoon and the material I request is quickly delivered to me. By the time the library is about to close, we (the solicitous archivist who has helped me and I have formed an efficient research team) have lost practically all hope of finding any reference to the globe-trotting Andrea. Having checked the catalogue of titles and authors, studied various lists of names, reviewed the most exhaustive reference works and completed the research online, my Roselli seems to be fading away, turning into a mere ghost, feeding a suspicion that I don't dare commit to words.

What if this was all a huge hoax? What if someone, prompted by some mysterious reason, had invented the memoirs? And what if Andrea Roselli was merely a pseudonym for the real author and protagonist? There is of course a third possibility, probably too remote and too implausible: that the news of Roselli's activities at the court of Charles III never reached Arezzo.

The librarian is beginning to rearrange the large amount of material I've used and has told me that it's almost closing time. I'm trying to come to terms with the prospect that

no documents exist in Arezzo about Andrea Roselli, when
the woman stops what she's doing for a moment and says:
"Maybe we won't find anything in there, but there is a *Storia
del commercio e dei commercianti d'Arezzo* published in
1963 that we haven't consulted, because it was catalogued
in a strange way. But we might discover something, you
never know." She leaves the reading room and returns five
minutes later, past the library closing time. I eagerly flick
through the pages till I find the first third of the eighteenth
century – and there it is! The note is brief but bright as an
explosion at night.

Alessandro Roselli, distinguished Aretine silversmith
and goldsmith, was born in 1720 and died in 1787.
His workshop received such acclaim that it became
distinguished not only within the rich tradition of silver
and gold work in Arezzo but was highly regarded by
important families in Florence and Rome, who gave him
many commissions. Alessandro Roselli married twice,
but had no children, for which reason it is believed that
his workshop ceased its activity at the time of his death
or shortly thereafter. It has been established, however,
that the wealthy Alessandro funded the studies for his
nephew, Andrea Roselli, who had lost both parents while
quite young. Andrea, architect and engineer, born in
Arezzo in 1739, worked for Charles of Bourbon, first in
Naples and later in Madrid.

Hallelujah!

* * *

Last night, after my research at the library, I wandered aimlessly for a long time through the streets of Arezzo. The reference to Roselli was brief, a mere verification of his existence, but it had left me in a strange state of grace. I had to share the news with someone – yet, every time I considered doing so, something inside me immediately rebelled against the idea, inviting me to remain silent and take pleasure in the solitary joy of the discovery – or the mystery – and the emotions evoked by it.

I was tempted to talk to Ariadna; I knew she'd be excited, and maybe she'd tell me if Roselli's secret was something she had deduced from the comments about Tiepolo's projects. I was also tempted to phone Sofia to learn more of her situation and give her a glimmer of hope, even if I couldn't offer anything concrete. But I did neither. The result of my discovery the day before was nothing more than a confirmation of what was already known – if we exclude presentiments and opinions. I know now that research should be focused only on Tiepolo, on the canvases he painted for the convent in Aranjuez.

For that reason this morning, after working out the best place for my research, I didn't head for the centre of Arezzo, as I would have liked to, but for the Aretine branch of the Università di Siena, for its Facoltà di Lettere e Filosofia, which houses an amazing library. A stack of books have reached my desk: two extensive biographies of Giambattista Tiepolo, three large catalogues of recent retrospectives and a couple of short books devoted exclusively to the Spanish years of the painter, the last years of his life.

Thanks to all these volumes, I have been able to ascertain that by 28th August 1769 Tiepolo had in fact finished the seven oil paintings for St Pascal. Tiepolo himself provides this information in a letter to Charles III's Secretary of State, Miguel Múzquiz, where he requests the approval of the powerful royal confessor, Father Joaquín de Eleta, who oversaw the decoration of the convent – despite the fact that Sabatini was the architect. Weeks and months passed. The Venetian master indicated that he was willing to alter the paintings if necessary, but Eleta didn't even deign to look at them. Half a year later, on 27 March 1770, Giambattista Tiepolo suddenly died in his home in Madrid, suffering no serious illness – he was almost seventy-four. He never saw his paintings hang in Aranjuez. An unworthy end for a Titan.

The King, who was in El Pardo, learnt about his death the following day, ordered Sabatini to gather the paintings from Tiepolo's study and show them to him as soon as he was back in Madrid. Apparently, that was when Charles III decided to honour the painter as he deserved. The appreciation that Tiepolo was denied when alive must have been enjoyed by his sons Giandomenico and Lorenzo – and perhaps by our Roselli – two months later, on 17th May: when the new church was consecrated, his paintings adorned the altars for which they were conceived. But only six of them: the one dedicated to St Charles Borromeo was replaced by a crucifix.

The journey of the Aranjuez canvases begins here. Before the end of 1770, Joaquín de Eleta announced that the oil paintings by Tiepolo would be soon replaced with others by Mengs, Maella and Bayeu – and in fact they were. What happened to Tiepolo's *St Pascal Baylon*, *St Joseph*, *The Immaculate Conception*, *St Francis*, *St Charles Borromeo*, *St Anthony of Padua* and *St Peter of Alcántara*? Is Sofia Mendizábal dreaming about finding one of these?

Various travellers and observers of that period claim that the Tiepolo works were carelessly stored away in some corner of the convent and finally disposed of after the paintings by the members of the Royal Academy of San Fernando were hung (Mengs controlled the Academy and the other painters were his favourite disciples). Eventually five of the seven were recovered as part of the royal patrimony. The one of St Pascal Baylon for the high altar was damaged: it split into two halves that do not fit together perfectly. It can be viewed in the Prado, along with *The Immaculate Conception*, *St Francis* and *St Anthony of Padua*. *St Peter of Alcántara*, on the other hand, hangs in the Royal Palace of Madrid.

Going through the list, I notice that two paintings in the series aren't accounted for in the books I've consulted. But I can easily fill the gap: I track down on the Internet the *St Joseph* and the *St Charles Borromeo*. Both paintings are damaged, but have a clearly established location and owner: the most important part of the first painting has ended up at the Detroit Institute of Arts, the central part of the other at the Cincinnati Art Museum.

I start to realize that I will have to admit defeat. If there is a Tiepolo waiting in some dark corner somewhere, it isn't one of the controversial canvases painted for St Pascal Baylon. Once this becomes clear to me, I feel like I've run out of steam, as if I had found the painting and it had been stolen from me. A swarm of titles, dates, paintings, owners and other details runs through my head, leaving me more dazed than dejected. I ask the librarian to hold the books for me – after lunch I want to check on a few details I overlooked when I was focusing on the most important points.

My phone never stops ringing during lunch. Sofia checks on me and asks a lot of questions, pressuring me about her situation, and finally announces that the opening of the Barcelona gallery has been moved to the end of September – a big event. After disappearing for some time, Armand Coll also calls, urging me to meet him as soon as I'm back to discuss something extremely important which he can't reveal right now. Summer is almost over: it's time to return to Barcelona.

But first I want to return to the series of paintings that Tiepolo did for the St Pascal convent. It's surprising how tight a rein Eleta kept on the painter. The Venetian was asked to submit *modelli*, or sketches, of the seven paintings to the King before the project could be approved. These sketches often differ from the final, huge canvases, but show the same high quality, even surpassing them at times. It was clear that Tiepolo's commission depended on them: he had to submit the very best of his artistic efforts, knowing that he had the priest against him.

Ironically, the sketches ended up in the hands of one of Tiepolo's rivals – Meng's close friend Francisco Bayeu – who was the father-in-law of the great Goya, an artist who was about to make his grand entrance. Goya was actually one of the few contemporaries who is known to have been influenced by Tiepolo. Bayeu held on to the sketches for a while, but fortunately they can be seen today at the Court-auld Institute Gallery in London. The works at the Court-auld (*St Pascal*, *St Joseph*, *St Francis* and *St Charles*) are the best examples of late Tiepolo: vivid colours alongside the sober expression of saintly mysticism, heightening the sense of devotion Tiepolo wished to represent. These sketches form one of the most valuable collections of Tiepolo's work. But three are missing: *The Immaculate Conception*, *St Anthony of Padua* and *St Peter of Alcántara*. This time however, before counting my chickens, I look for all the available references, both in the books I have and on the Internet. After hours of frantic research and controlled enthusiasm, I arrive at a certainty: the sketches for these three paintings that Charles III and Joaquín de Eleta examined in 1767, prior to accepting and commissioning the work – sketches that perhaps passed through Bayeu's hands (and maybe Goya's) – are the missing Tiepolos!

I remember seeing the luminous *Immaculate Conception* of the Aranjuez series in the Prado, and now I've seen the *St Anthony of Padua* and the *St Peter of Alcántara* in a variety of catalogues. The *Immaculate Conception* is probably the most moving of the series; the other two are the most personal, very innovative in the way they portray asceticism. But artistically speaking, they are tame. However, considering the differences between the other sketches and the final altarpieces, these three *modelli*, if discovered – and possibly brought together with the other four – would be extremely valuable. Have we reached the heart of the enigma? Are these sketches the ones Ariadna appears to have more information about, the ones Sofia so desperately wants?

I returned from Arezzo two weeks ago. Since then, I've been carrying out further investigations – discreet in a convoluted way – on Tiepolo, on the itinerary the three sketches might have followed and on their potential value. It is still uncharted territory, and maybe just an illusion, but in any case their improbable sale could come nowhere close to solving Sofia's problems if it's true that she needs five million euros.

All of these things are running through my head as I see Armand Coll approach my table with a firm stride – like a campaigning politician – at a restaurant on Carrer Enric Granados in Barcelona.

Armand starts the conversation with his favourite subject, the give and take surrounding the national hydrological plan. He seems incredibly relieved that no notice has been taken of his presence at the Mendizábal house the night Jonàs was arrested. It wasn't easy, he tells me, pretending it's all very confidential:

"A matter of striking a deal with the two main Barcelona newspapers: silence in exchange for information."

"What kind of information?" I ask, trying to conjure up some interest.

"Oh, you know, positions within political parties aren't always uniform. I hinted that there are factions in our party that are against a head-on confrontation over the interbasin water transfer."

"But that goes against your interests, doesn't it?"

"Information in exchange for silence? Of course. Don't be naive, Emili. In the long run we won't be able to maintain our radical policy against the water transfer – which is only a tactical position – so in order to avoid a complete volte-face when the time comes, we need to make clear that not all of us from the progressive parties view this issue in the same way. Besides, this demonstrates the plurality of opinions within the party. With regional elections coming up next spring, if we stick to our radical opposition to the hydrological plan, our party will stand no chance with the communities that need water."

"Which means that in your case it's better if this in-formation gets out," I say, appealing to his ego, friend to friend.

"Most of the those from our party who hold a public position in the Barcelona area are really alarmed that all these politics might leave them without any water, from the Ebro or the Rhône."

"It's a huge mess, Armand."

"But a pretty common one. Don't you know that the Catalanists and the conservatives often feed contradictory information to the press? It's a game of nuances and countermoves. First they ask journalists not to interview anyone from the Ebro area, then they send them to the Rhône, then they let them speak as much as they wish with their politicians from the Ebro, then they provide them with scientific reports... What's the matter with you? You don't seem to care about any of this?"

"Maybe."

I smile, and Armand pretends to be angry; then he realizes there are no microphones or cameras around, so he relaxes and looks up at me.

"You know what, Emili? I need your help."

"I can't see how I can be of help, you're good at what you do," I say, without any resentment.

"No, no. I'm not talking about politics. I'm talking about Sofia. She's desperate. She needs us. Do you realize the danger she's in?"

This time I'm caught completely off guard, confused. Perhaps it's my guilty conscience that makes me react in self-defence.

"I do realize, and I've offered her my help – she knows she can stay with me. And besides, I'm no longer—" Armand cuts me off:

"I have no doubts about your good intentions, Emili, but I must be totally frank with you. There is a solution that I know you don't want to consider, maybe out of scruples, or perhaps fear, but you can count on me, because I—"

"What the hell are you talking about?"

"About the Tiepolo!"

"What Tiepolo? There *is* no Tiepolo."

"I understand you are reluctant, but you have to decide between a human life – Sofia's – and your principles."

"What principles, Armand?"

"Let's stop fooling around, Emili. I know you have a document that's led you to the Tiepolo."

My mind goes blank. It's impossible for Ariadna to have told them: she despises Sofia. I observe Armand's impassive expression. He must be accustomed to putting people under pressure, backing them into a corner, laying siege. What's going on? We have Armand Coll here, a politician, chasing Tiepolos to pay the drug Mafia!

"Where did you hear that, Armand? You know this doesn't make sense."

"Don't force me to hurt you, Emili."

"Just what I needed to hear! Who told you that?"

"So it's true? There's some hope then?" he says, suddenly very happy.

"Tell me where you heard it."

"You asked for it: Chloe told Sofia, let it slip out, I suppose."

"I don't know what Chloe might have told you, but I can assure you that she has never read the document. I've done some research, but unfortunately didn't get very far. In any case, first we'd have to find this damned painting; second, sell it for an amount that could never be enough for Sofia's needs. And third – a very small detail – how many laws would we have to break along the way?"

Armand's expression has changed. I realize he's not listening, but looking for another way to convince me.

"It's time to stop pretending, Emili. Sofia and I have been seeing each other for some time."

"You're seeing each other?" I say, not really following him.

"In Sant Carles, Barcelona and Madrid.

"Everywhere," I mutter.

"I love her. I've learnt what it is to be happy, and I'll do whatever I can for her. You understand? I can't bear the idea that a bunch of thugs might hurt her because she didn't get rid of that vile man, Jonàs, in time."

I'm trying to digest the news, but Armand won't give me a break.

"Sofia was convinced that Ariadna knew more than she said about the Tiepolo, and then, after speaking to Chloe, she thought that you had figured everything out or were about to do so."

"I can assure you that—"

"Just wait, Emili, I'm asking you to listen to me carefully now. Tonight, at the opening of the gallery, Sofia will introduce you to three people who have already shown an interest in the Tiepolo."

"Have you all gone mad? Leave me out of this!"

"Please, Emili, for the sake of our old friendship. This is a question of life or death; we have very little time, so we have to think ahead. These people have heard that a great Tiepolo might be sold – a new and unique Tiepolo – and want to be quick off the line. They don't want to miss the opportunity. One of them has even presented a bank guarantee of up to five million."

"How did Sofia manage to create such expectation? How far are you willing to go?"

"However far you tell us. We need you, Emili, and your prestige as specialist and gallery owner – we want you to talk to them, give them technical details and any explanation they want about the painting. Your support is essential in order to inspire confidence. And don't tell me now that you've never seen it! You have four hours to move heaven and earth! Or would you prefer to see Sofia dead?"

* * *

Not a bad idea – but let's forget that one. In the heat of the scene, Armand has "warned" me that, because of Tarrés's international reputation, several foreign television channels will be reporting on the opening this evening, so my dealings will have to be very discreet. He must think that this is all fine, and will help create the feeling of a great event. The potential Tiepolo buyers need to know how important the new gallery is. What does he know about Malaquies Tarrés's international reputation? What does he know about managing an event of this magnitude? He has clearly been converted to a new faith, that of Sofia Mendizábal.

I'm thinking about all this as I walk back to my gallery along the sticky pavements of the Eixample, the entire city lost to the hysteria of traffic, suffocating in the sultry heat, every Barcelonese wearing an expression of haste and tension. Only a group of young girls seem to be exempt, as they leave their secondary school squealing and showing their navels.

Then I hear Armand's troubled voice screaming to me over the phone: "They've set the car on fire, Sofia's! You see? No, not here. They just called from Sant Carles. Jonàs's SUV, which was parked at the house. You have to help us!"

I try to calm him down. "Nothing's changed," I tell him. "We said bye to each other half an hour ago – I'll think of something, I'll come up with something between now and eight o'clock," I say, ending the conversation, as I realize that I've now been completely drawn into Sofia's world.

I dial Ariadna's number – no answer. No answer an hour later. No answer just before eight, when I phone from the taxi that's driving me to the converted warehouse in the Poblenou area of Barcelona, where Sofia is inaugurating Amphora, an antique dealer's name applied to a modern-art gallery which is opening with the return onto the world stage of Malaquies Tarrés.

Half a dozen European newspapers have devoted part of their Sunday supplement to Tarrés and have commented on the ambitious new Barcelona gallery showcasing his art, which they consider as bold as any in Manhattan or Munich. Sofia has managed to attract the *mundillo*, the crème de la crème of Barcelona. High ceilings with huge skylights filtering the last rays of the day hover above a swarm of cultural and political figures. The Mayor and the Catalan Minister of Culture greet the glittering hostess almost simultaneously, uttering kind, witty phrases, after which they are immediately surrounded by their respective retinues. Once they have paid their compliments, the politicians seek out actors or writers so they can demonstrate their knowledge of the field, but they keep bumping into more politicians and journalists.

Rescue comes in the form of waiters who, in their attempt to serve cava, slice through circles or create new ones. People make about-turns chasing a glass, others suddenly lose their interlocutors and end up talking to themselves. Amidst all the bustle, I run into Sofia, who hugs me in order to whisper in a hollow voice, "I'm counting on you." Then I spot Armand, who gives me a look that says "Any news?"

Then, above the general clamour, a phrase is repeated: "Where's the artist?"

There's a flash of lights and cameras as Tarrés strides forward, towards the spot where, presumably, the dignitaries are gathered. This movement creates a space on the side of the room closest to the office, the area where the painter has been giving a string of television interviews. At that point Armand seizes me by the arm and leads me away.

Seated at the austere desk in the gallery office, the sound of the crowd more distanced, I wait for the representative of a British collector interested in the Tiepolo. The huge exhibition room is the whitest of all whites, both ceiling and walls, so that lights and paintings can take centre stage. The office, leading to a small Japanese garden, goes very well with it: everything is uncontaminated, geometric, cold. The British gentleman does not show up right away, and I keep drinking from the bottle of cava.

Finally, a small bald man sits before me, asking brief questions in a high-pitched voice and taking notes in a tiny notebook. I start talking, giving away too much information. At first I probably sound convincing: the painting is one metre eighty by one metre ten, almost certainly from 1763, the master probably did it while painting the frescoes for the palace, because the mythological motif it presents can be associated with one of the figures. The gentleman seems pleased until we come to more concrete information: who has it? Where? When can he see it? Why isn't there a photo of it? Something in his brain lights up, like a slow halogen bulb, until he politely interrupts my series of absurd remarks and leaves the office in a huff, convinced that someone is trying to swindle him as if he were a novice.

I know the next visit will be from Sofia. I don't even try to leave the office, but down the last drop of cava. Lady Mendizábal storms in, ready for the kill. She blames me for everything, insults me, threatens me, weeps as she reminds me of the danger she's in, alludes to her guests with pride. I apologize, tell her I understand, and again offer her my place to hide while we look for another solution, because the one we have does not exist and will not work, and in any case would be illegal. When she hears this, she loses her temper and starts shouting:

"Illegal? Are you telling me that you're going to turn over the Tiepolo to the Museu Nacional d'Art de Catalunya or to the Reina Sofia!"

"Sofia, you are totally mad. The problem is quite simple: there is no Tiepolo. It doesn't exist."

"Of course it exists, you idiot! The problem is you're a bloody fool who's incapable of finishing anything! You're a coward, that's what you are. What would you do to get a painting you like? Or to get the money the painting is worth? Nothing. Listen to what I've done – you still think that wretch, Jonàs, left you the note so you'd keep his sister company! You didn't even stop to check whose handwriting it was!"

"What do you mean, Sofia?"

"Just what I'm telling you. Start learning! I wrote the note because I knew you were the only person that numbskull Ariadna would confide in. To hell with both of you!"

"I'd strangle you right here, you bitch, if I didn't know that someone else might do it for me!"

"What are you saying! I thought maybe I could get you to react with the bit about the Mafia's threats, that you'd try to save me. But no, not even that! You're a worthless bastard."

Sofia puts her hand over her mouth. This last part wasn't in the script. She realizes the game's over now. After her slip-up, I straighten up, catch my breath and walk to the door with a reasonable amount of pride. Lady Mendizábal is totally undone and full of self-pity now, but she still has the strength to yell:

"You still haven't learnt that this isn't a game with a bunch of stupid rules: the only real rule is that you have to win! Go out there and look at people's faces. Everyone here is out to win."

14
Unknown Paths

I was lucky that I could cross the gallery without running into anyone I needed to speak to – a couple of times I actually pretended not to hear a voice calling to me from a distance – and made it outside without having to look anyone in the eye.

All the official cars have left. If it weren't for the television and radio vans, the street would be deserted. The Barcelona night lights up, and I hear the distant sounds of a storm, can smell it as the damp air brushes my face through the open window of the taxi. I shift my mobile phone from one hand to the other, but manage to resist the temptation.

I'm home when I finally dial her number, standing in front of the balcony amidst the fading rumbles and sharp thunderclaps, one step from the comforting downpour that is engulfing the entire city.

"Ariadna! I couldn't track you down all afternoon."

"I know."

"What do you mean?"

"I knew you were trying to call, knew it was you, so I didn't answer."

"Well, thanks very much!"

"I can explain. But first, tell me: how did the launch party go?"

"Great. A huge success. Tons of people."

"And?"

"Let's just leave it! The important news is I had a fight with Sofia. She's taken off her mask and I told her to go to hell. The story about the Tiepolo is over."

I give her the details, skipping the bit about being tricked by Jonàs's note. When she sees that the situation is irreparable, she says in a mischievous voice:

"You see, I was right not to answer the phone!"

"I don't understand."

"I mean, if I had told you, you would never have been able to resist the pressure from Sofia."

"If you'd told me what, Ariadna?"

"That I actually do know more about Roselli, and about Tiepolo of course…"

I take one step forward, then another, and stand on the balcony by the railing. The rain leaves me drenched: hair, eyes, mouth, water dripping down my neck, soaking my shirt, trousers and shoes.

"Say that again?" I'm shouting.

"I have the second part of the memoirs, you fool. But if you want to know what it says, you'll have to come here to read it!"

"Will you still be up for a couple of hours?" If necessary, I'd walk the two hundred kilometres that separate us.

I leave the Diagonal behind as the radio announces that the lower part of the city is starting to flood. The lights on the motorway show the downpour on the pavement, and I hold tightly to the steering wheel, my eyes as wide as saucers while I replay everything that has happened these last weeks, from the moment Sofia invited me to the party in the Montsià until tonight's showdown in Poblenou.

Sometimes all we need is a slight, accidental shove at a particular moment in our life to make us see that everything that we thought was packed tightly away, wrapped in slumber – perhaps something we had not paid attention to – has suddenly woken up and taken shape, acquiring the force of a hurricane.

The Invisible City can only be approached by unknown paths, I repeat to myself as I park in Sant Carles de la Ràpita and walk towards Ariadna's street. It's after midnight, and the lights have gone out during the storm. I feel my way up the stairs in the dark, the cold iron of the handrail with the white pine cone at the end, my feet touching the worn edges of the steps. I slowly push open the door at the top and glimpse Ariadna in her chair, reading by candlelight.

She sees me and crosses her arms with an imploringly look. The flame's orange tongue flickers across her face, making her eyes seem bigger, unavoidable, her white teeth, her lips tightened into a smile, her high-boned cheeks at once fine and sculpted. She's wearing a white, almost transparent linen blouse that slyly clings to her tight brown skin, like snow on a greenish bronze statue.

She hands me a pile of papers and says gently:

"Enjoy! Come back tomorrow and we'll talk about it. Right now, I'm going to bed. I'm dead."

And then something extraordinary happens, or rather it simply shows how long I have been without news of Ariadna, how long since I covered my eyes and ears pretending she didn't exist. Ariadna slowly gets up from her chair, takes the crutches she has on either side of her and heads to her room. When she notices my amazement, she stops and says:

"What are you looking at?"

"I thought—"

"Don't be an ass! I only use the wheelchair for long-haul journeys and the crutches if I'm taking the bus. Goodnight!"

I have tears in my eyes as I start down the stairs, but I don't stop. There's no time to lose. When I reach my house on the bay I begin to search for the Invisible City along unknown paths.

St Charles

From Memoirs of the Invisible City

I returned to Madrid, my eyes filled with the light of the Ebro delta. It is a vibrant light, almost corrosive. The sea is like the cloudy, light-green-and-blue waters of the Venetian lagoon or the Pozzuoli marshes on the Bay of Naples. The expanse of wasteland, plains, deserts extending all the way to the horizon reminded me of the Tsar's grandiose idea of building a city in the middle of nowhere. I suddenly realized that in that world devoid of human footprints, any civilizing gesture became a heroic deed, any line drawn on the ground could become a path, any markings an avenue, any word a speech. It was as if I were contemplating the earth on the very day of its creation, when merely to name something meant that it came into existence.

Once the Ebro River is connected to the bay through a canal, the site for the city will form part of the municipality of Tortosa, the second most important city in Catalunya. Choosing this location would help develop the large area between Valencia and Tortosa. The Bishop of Tortosa commands great authority here because his diocese straddles both administrative districts. Also, the region is sufficiently removed from Barcelona and Valencia – or from Saragossa, to which it is connected by the river – to preserve its independent character. The merchants of Tortosa enthusiastically received news of the construction of the canal and the port, as the transport difficulties and the wild currents of the Ebro have always affected their trade. The building of the new city, however, soon divided public opinion, a situation that may grow more tense when the scope of the royal project is revealed.

After the course of the canal was traced, the location of the new city near Alfacs could be more easily outlined. The mouth of the canal and the port needed to be sheltered by the splendid bay, but away from the shallow waters further into the large natural harbour. The Montsià is not particularly high, nor does it cover a large area; nevertheless, as it rises abruptly near the beaches on the bay, it is always there, like the sudden shadow of a giant. The Guardiola hill – the last ridge of the Montsià (like the Neapolitan Capodimonte) – seems to have been destined since the beginning of time to create a similar effect of protection and beauty above the city – the new city – Charles's – mine!

This is, of course, a vain comment on our part, as others had made the same remark centuries before: someone had realized long before us that this was a suitable, agreeable place. The Ràpita sanctuary or fortress was built under Moorish rule and stood on the precise spot where the canal would empty into the bay and the new city would be erected. When the Catalans conquered this area, as Antoni de Capmany has informed us, they transformed the sanctuary into the Monastery of Santa Maria de la Ràpita, which became the site of pilgrimages made by the devout – including kings.

Only a few ruins remain of the monastery; some two centuries ago the monks who lived there were removed to Tortosa. The place – abandoned, uninhabited – has perhaps become again what it was in the full and innocent days of ancient times: the gentle sea lapping against the low rock, the flat bay like a Dutch painting, the blue, silent Montsià guarding the site. I told myself: no matter who you will be obliged to obey, you must build a city worthy of the beauty that nature has bestowed on this area.

During the first few months, in which we surveyed and calculated the positions of the two extremities of the canal – the river at one end, the sea at the other – I would often leave the men carrying out their tasks and ride my horse to the place where one day St Charles would stand. I observed it from the top of the hill, from a boat in the bay, from the wilderness of the alluvial lands towards the east, from the dry lands towards the west. The image of the new city began to take shape in my mind. I imagined it, dreamt it, and drew the first sketches of it.

The slight slope of the terrain from the foot of the hill down to the beach would permit terracing along the elevated land, which would draw attention to the city when approached from the sea, while at the same time providing the houses with a fine view of the bay and delta. The city boundaries would be marked not only by the Guardiola and the sea, but also by two ravines that run on either side of the hill.

In reality, however, Minister Aranda had only given his approval to the canal, whilst the city continued to be a illusion.

Nevertheless, I began my survey of the area and soon gathered sufficient data to allow me to determine that the city's plan would stem from two great axes or perspectives: one running from the port to the foot of the hill, which would be crowned by a chapel; the other, perpendicular to the first, would be parallel to the coast. The road to Barcelona (to the north) and to Valencia (to the south) would start from this point. Where the two avenues met, we would create a large square, similar in size to Piazza Navona, which I remembered so vividly from my years in Rome. Here we would erect palaces, administrative and military buildings and a church. The central part of the square would open like a large balcony over the port and the bay. The entire city would be built within the rocky area, leaving the sandy parts for the development of the port; we would likewise need a shipyard and an area devoted to the defence of the city.

I spent the summer and autumn of 1769 in frantic activities, in the company of the workers assigned to me, each of whom shared my faith in the canal and city. It was a blind faith that refused to see legal impediments, bureaucratic setbacks and the deplorable want of all manner of things necessary for our undertaking.

When I rose each morning, I was filled with joy and a youthful spirit, my eyes glistening, as I directed the improbable, complex but worthwhile task that lay before us. It was as if the world began anew each day, the sea so still that any route seemed possible, the olive-coloured waters of the Bay of Alfacs like a bed sheet pulled tight. As I recall those blissful hours, I again reflect on the tortuous ways of fortune. My happiness was not the result of certain things that I might have desired and then obtained, but on the contrary it corresponded to a state of mind that was not altogether logical. My joy seemed to be born from what I did not possess, something that did not take on a physical form: a mere idea; and while I desired and coveted it, the idea took hold of me, excited me. How long can our joy last, if we are like a fragile leaf, constantly changing, like passing clouds?

The seasons pass. Black- and pink-winged flamingoes camp in the marshes and then fly away; almond trees bear their fruit, then blossom again; rivers grow from a weak trickle to rumbling thoroughfares; large heaps of salt crystals form, then slowly disappear; women cover themselves, then show their wrists and arms, their necks and throbbing breasts in the discreet salons of Tortosa; olive trees are stripped of their fruit, which is then pressed to produce oil. Nothing could take from me the sense of enchantment in which I lived. Not that year, not in that land where everything existed because nothing existed or had decayed yet.

The post was unpredictable, but I was kept loosely in touch with the world. I received official communications from the Count of Aranda and Francesco Sabatini – increasingly cold and distant; letters from Antoni de Capmany describing the progress he was making with his history of commerce in Barcelona, the city which had once been a major Mediterranean trading centre; missives from Pablo de Olavide concerning the forthcoming report of the country's great agrarian reform. Giambattista's anxious letters asked repeatedly when I would return to Madrid; Cecilia's seemed to offer covert messages, thinly disguised admonitions, open taunts and a friendship that was at times detached, at others licentious.

Her letters spoke of frequent visits to Tiepolo. What interest could she have in the Venetian painter, so far removed from courtly intrigue, so little interested in social life?

The seasons passed, and the fatal hour of the scythe arrived. A letter from Cecilia dispatched by messenger caused me to regret that I had ignored Giambattista's anxiety and had postponed a journey to Madrid that would have allowed me to embrace him one last time and witness the sadness of his last days. Tiepolo had died.

I exhausted one horse after another in my mad rush to reach Madrid, as if I were racing against time, against my own devastation at ignoring my dear friend's request to return, against each day that had separated me – for ever – from him. By the time I arrived in the city, my fury had softened, and I found myself tired and dejected as I realized that my gesture had been useless.

Giandomenico and Lorenzo greatly appreciated my three-day gallop and showed sympathy for my dismay. They told me about the bitterness that had slowly consumed their father as the court continued to withhold its opinion about the paintings for the Aranjuez convent. Giambattista had spoken with enthusiasm to his sons of me and my obsession for the new city on the Mediterranean. I can imagine the figure of the vexed Giambattista, anxiously pacing about his studio, his unmistakeable profile with its aquiline nose, its ironic eyes grown nostalgic and the scattered works he had painted and would never see again – and I am saddened rather than angered by the ignorance of the odious Father Eleta, who had allowed Tiepolo to die without seeing his paintings displayed at St Pascal.

I offered to speak to Sabatini immediately to request that he intercede with the King so that Tiepolo might receive at least the posthumous honours he deserved. The Crown would be tarnished by disgrace if Tiepolo's paintings were ignored, I told them. Giambattista's sons informed me, however, that as soon as His Majesty learnt of the painter's death, he had ordered the canvases to be shown to him, demonstrating the insidious role the accursed royal manipulator and confessor had played in this affair.

Giandomenico must have noticed that I did not look well, for he insisted that I rest a few hours before pursuing our conversation. From his comment I was able to infer that he had some important revelation for me, but my exhaustion from the journey outweighed my curiosity, and I withdrew to rest.

The following day I found the liveliness of the streets offensive. My grief clashed with the greasy sky, the clouds swollen with the April light of Castile. Giandomenico was visibly nervous as he waited for me, and began to ramble about trivial matters before suddenly announcing:

"Señora Cecilia came to see my father many times in the last months."

"Did he request her visits? Señora Cecilia could have interceded with the King through her husband, because…" I began, not confessing that I was aware of the visits, but Giandomenico stopped me.

"No. Yes. Actually, I do not know why she started coming, but my father was painting a portrait of Señora Cecilia."

I remained silent for a moment as a succession of images of Cecilia flashed through my mind. "Perhaps Señor Sabatini commissioned a portrait of the lady. She is very distinguished, very beautiful – do you not agree, Giandomenico?"

"You must allow me to finish, Andrea. Señora Cecilia arranged to come here during her husband's audiences with His Majesty. Sabatini knew nothing of the portrait, and still doesn't."

"Perhaps it was a surprise, a gift for Señor Francesco from your father or from the lady herself."

"No, Andrea, no! My father painted her for you. She posed for you, but this has become a very awkward affair now – I am sure you understand. I cannot keep the painting in this house any longer. I managed, with difficulty, to hide it when the King sent Sabatini's men to collect my father's last works, the oil paintings for Aranjuez! You can imagine the scandal! The portrait is yours, Andrea – my father wished it so. You may take it."

"You are a true friend, Giandomenico. I will be for ever grateful to you for concealing the painting and for your honesty in giving it to me."

I was filled with emotion as I rushed to Tiepolo's study without waiting for Giandomenico. He allowed me to do so, and witnessed my dismay on seeing the state of the room, which seemed to have been purposely thrown into disarray – a jumble of paintbrushes, easels, strips of canvas, paint residues, all sorts of things scattered around the room.

"If I had left the portrait of Señora Cecilia here, we would never have seen it again. Sabatini's men turned everything upside down," the young painter said with a sarcastic laugh.

I waited until night, and with great care and discretion removed the rolled-up painting that Tiepolo's son had put aside for me. Fortunately I had kept my agreeable lodgings near the Plaza de San Martín, and once I was in the drawing room and had assured myself that no servant was nearby, I unveiled the canvas and adjusted the lamps so as to view it properly.

I seated myself before the large canvas, taller than me and broader than the length of my outstretched arms, and gazed at the portrait for a long time as I tried to control the flood of emotions. It was without question a portrait of Cecilia Vanvitelli, but Tiepolo had painted her with the attributes of a goddess – with the demeanour, look and character of the Cleopatra I had seen at the Palazzo Labia in Venice, though here there was no Antony or other companion. Cecilia is wearing a reddish-purple garment similar to a Roman tunic, like the girl collecting flowers in the fresco in Pompeii. The cloth is gathered at one shoulder and falls like wondrous silk across one breast, but leaves the other one gloriously exposed. Her chin is raised to denote defiance, provocation; she smiles joyfully – shamelessly perhaps – her lips are the colour of pomegranate, almost the same as her dress. Her hair is pulled to the left, highlighting the youthful, elegant sensuality of her neck, freeing her forehead and giving it a determined expression. Her eyes, however, are disconcerting. They do not convey the lascivious joy or the boldness of the rest of the painting, but rather reflect a light that seems to spring from an old offence which has finally been righted, a look of lament and rancour, as if yearning for victory.

I marvelled. Giambattista Tiepolo had not painted images with such lack of restraint for many years. What had happened since the sober, austere sketches for the Aranjuez paintings that I had seen before leaving for the Ebro delta? How could this explosion of light, this sumptuousness which surpasses the masterpiece in the Palazzo Labia be interpreted? How could this be explained, when no one was expecting more than a prudent final gesture from Tiepolo? Could this really be the work of an old man, dejected and exhausted?

In the background of the painting can be observed the faint suggestion of the bluish domes and noble façades of a coastal city, like the one I had described to Tiepolo in our nostalgic conversations in Madrid and in the handful of letters I had written him from the Ebro. I was deeply shaken – exhilarated at first, captivated by the entrancing music of the painting, and then moved when I recognized the allusions to St Charles, the finishing touch of my old friend.

I paced around the house, unable to sleep, contemplating the portrait again and again. As the painter's son had rightly predicted, the portrait could create a scandal. Especially for me. But fortunately Giandomenico had saved it from the hands of the King. It is true that Charles III had a certain right to the work and also had a habit of confiscating things: when he left Parma and Piacenza for Naples, he was followed by a caravan of coaches filled with jewels and works of art. Strangely, the longer I observed the painting the less I saw of Cecilia; what struck me was the lesson the Master wanted to impart, a much bolder lesson than the triumphant body and the forceful gesture of the person portrayed.

Many years have passed since I first set eyes on the painting, yet I still recall how disturbing that moment was, how effectively Tiepolo opened my eyes, to the point of setting in motion a revolt within myself that would transform me and lead me to view the world in a new light.

Tiepolo was held in little esteem by those who for half a century had financed his works, making him a fairly wealthy man. Nevertheless, these same people who were incapable of appreciating the greatness of his art owned his works, could make demands on them and do whatever they liked with them. Tiepolo realized that this situation – of which he was partly responsible – was terribly unjust. He was old, noble and gifted, yet he had conferred greatness, beauty and glory in return for very little. More than that, he had limited or adapted his works to the intentions, orientations and dictates of patrons according to how generous they were.

He had had enough now. This time it would be different. Here we have Tiepolo's Cecilia, who is both wise and provocative, a woman who stimulates one's senses and moves one's spirit. Through her figure we see the artist struggling to liberate himself from his own fetters, announcing the birth of a free city.

How greatly I regretted not arriving in time to share with Giambattista this painful yet exultant moment, the lucidity of the last stage of his life! I could only commemorate this embrace from beyond the grave by toasting him with a glass of wine the same colour as the tunic of his new sun goddess.

＊　＊　＊

How many years had passed since he first contemplated the painting in amazement? Roselli is referring to events in 1770, but when did he write this – when is he recalling these details? Where? I've been wide awake for many hours, absorbed in reading these memoirs, excited and disturbed, but I put the papers aside in the end. I hadn't even realized that my body was aching, that there had been a continuous downpour and that it was almost dawn. On the other side of the Bay of Alfacs, eastward, a slow, reddish wave, as if rising from the white salt mountains, is about to conquer night and the cloudy, fleecy sky. I put on a pot of coffee, but before it begins to hiss I notice a deeper, persistent sound coming from the bay. I go out onto the terrace and observe the long procession of fishing boats heading towards the Punta de la Banya and listen to the combined rumble of their engines. I watch them for a while, entranced, then, as I'm returning to Andrea Roselli, the telephone rings.

"How did you know I'd be awake?" I ask rather awkwardly with a hoarse voice.

"I didn't, but you've just confirmed it," Ariadna says in a mocking tone. "Don't tell me you've been up all night looking at the stars!"

"I spent it watching Venus, Tiepolo's indomitable Venus. But I didn't get any further."

"Well, that's enough for one night!"

"So, now at least we know which painting…" I say with enthusiasm. "But actually I have more questions since yesterday. Some need to be answered by Andrea Roselli, some by you."

"Me? If you say so! And what else? You have the memoirs, read them!… Anyway, is that the sound of your coffee pot? Because if you invite me to breakfast, I might just accept."

"I'll come and get you right away!"

"Hey, hang on. No need to rush. You fix breakfast and I'll be over in a moment."

I'm left holding the receiver. Five minutes later I watch in disbelief as Ariadna drives her car down the road to the bay and into my front yard, flashing the lights and waving to me through the window. I remember her words of a few days ago – "I'm not the person you think I am" – and the nonchalance with which last night she brushed off my amazement that she could walk.

"In July 1936, the day before they began to burn down the churches, some kindly soul brought the parish archives to my grandfather's house. He was very young at the time – it was mother who told me the story. My grandfather's friend must have thought that it was worth saving and figured that no one would look for the archives in some poor person's house. As you can imagine, once the war was over and the man who'd saved the papers was dead, my grandfather probably had no interest in returning them, or keeping them for that matter. I'm guessing he didn't give a damn, as long as it didn't cause him any problems of course!

"Apparently, the papers stayed in the attic for a long time, and then one day, when the village was preparing to celebrate the newly rebuilt church, dear old grandfather remembered them. He calmly explained the story to the rector, who was so overjoyed he almost kissed him. And so the documents went back across town to the parish...

"All except one folder, either because it was forgotten or because it looked different from the rest and the family thought it wasn't part of it – as you can imagine, they weren't much into books – and the papers lay for decades in my grandfather's attic, totally forgotten. The house could have been torn down, the attic cleaned out, the papers dumped in the canal or used to feed the bonfires on the eve of Sant John, and we would have been left without our Andrea Roselli!"

"But you found it in time!" I say with impatience.

"When Jonàs went to live with Sofia, we fixed up the house a little: painted it, made a few little repairs, redid the bathroom. The girl who was cleaning in the attic discovered the folder full of dust and cobwebs. The only thing I did at the time was clean it off, give it a quick glance and put it with my books, never thinking it was anything of interest.

"Some time later I had a look at it. I had come across Tiepolo in one of my online art courses and, curiously, I remembered seeing his name in those papers."

Ariadna talks and I'm enthralled, engrossed by what she is saying. I realize that my passion for Ariadna has remained unchanged. It's been dormant for a long time, and now it's waking up again with all the force of the years that were turned upside down on that distant afternoon.

"Why did you decide to send me the memoirs?" I ask hopefully.

"For two reasons. That witch Sofia has always imagined that the story about Tiepolo and Sant Carles was more than a simple legend; she'd heard you and Jonàs talk about the Invisible City. She managed to get some information from me and came to the conclusion that I knew more than I was saying. After that I was besieged by Sofia, and needed help. You can't imagine what she's capable of – or maybe you can now—"

"And the other reason?"

"What do you mean?"

"You sent me the copy of the memoirs for two reasons—"

"Ah, the other reason..." Ariadna's eyes brighten up, her supple lips forming a smile. "Tonight I'll need your help. You don't have much longer before saying goodbye to Roselli. I suggest you get some sleep, you should see how awful you look!"

"Thanks a lot!"

"You'll pick me up at nine?"

St Charles
From Memoirs of the Invisible City

Sabatini, gracious and polite as always, showed both that he was unaware of the existence of the painting and that St Charles was too far from Madrid for him to be interested in my report. The Count of Aranda continued with his strategy of slow reforms, which kept the monarch pleased without displeasing the landowners – or perhaps it was the opposite. My friends Olavide and Capmany continued with their studies, their discussions and their lives as best they could, especially the Peruvian, around whom dark rumours were spreading, fuelled of course by those who opposed his ideas.

His Majesty received me a few weeks later and listened attentively to my account of the advantages of the Ebro canal, the site chosen for St Charles, and the glorious future of the city. The Count was present at the audience, vigilant and suspicious; he was clearly unhappy and tried to change the course of the conversation when he saw the King's enthusiasm and heard him announce his plan to visit the delta personally to inspect the location of his new city. I had of course been careful to inform the King that the stay would offer him marvellous opportunities for hunting.

I knew that Aranda would do everything in his power to prevent Charles III from ever setting foot on the Bay of Alfacs. I was also aware that, as Cecilia had predicted that same year, Aranda's influence was on the wane, whilst José Moñino's was on the rise. The latter had now become the

Count of Floridablanca; he had played a significant role in Rome in convincing the Pope to promote the suppression of the Jesuits which the King had initiated.

Cecilia was involved in the various charades of the capital, which I found increasingly difficult to understand, caught in the web she herself had created to survive in the hostile atmosphere she encountered on her arrival. She continued to move from ball to ball, from intrigue to intrigue, and was granted complete freedom by her husband in return for procuring him an ever greater number of official positions. Francesco Sabatini was now one of the most powerful men at court, more powerful than any minister.

How much did this Cecilia resemble Tiepolo's painting? Very little. Her manner had changed; she was no longer the fearful, determined Cecilia who had driven me mad before I left for St Petersburg. She had traded her natural seductiveness for an affected sophistication. Her body was as desirable as before, but her constant striving for pre-eminence in court – which pervaded all her gestures, looks, tone of voice – had robbed her of the sensual attraction she possessed on first arriving in Madrid. Her wild cry was now domesticated – she lived in a golden cage.

During the following years all of her predictions about the court turned out to be correct. The Count of Floridablanca, following his policy of transportation improvements, favoured the seemingly interminable construction of the canal from the Ebro River to the Bay of Alfacs. With the canal it became more evident that we would need a well-defended port and a city on the site of the Ràpita convent.

In 1778 the King signed the *Regulations and Royal Tariffs Governing Free Trade Between Spain and the Indies*, which also authorized the construction of the port of Alfacs. This was essential, as two years later, when navigation through the canal began, the port of St Charles acquired the importance that we were expecting.

By this time I was no longer the ingenuous young man who had stood on the Bay of Naples in 1759 and enthusiastically witnessed the festive farewell offered to the Good King. I was almost forty years old, and I realized that it was not too late to avoid the dead end of Giambattista Tiepolo's last years. I could even now follow his final advice...

I had spent over a decade with commissions and meetings, ministers and secretaries, audiences and reports, dividing my time between the works on the Ebro delta – real or imaginary – and my errands in the capital. The King expressed his wishes less and less forcefully, yet clearly: I was to devote myself exclusively to the project of the new city. Sabatini never dared to oppose His Majesty, but still he gave me minor projects all around the kingdom – which, following the example of the royal architect, I supervised without visiting them even once.

When the canal and the buildings required for the port to operate were completed, the first small community could be established, following the urban plan I had designed. In order to supervise the work more closely, I would sometimes leave my lodgings in the little palace in Tortosa provided by the ministry and settle for several days in one of the rooms in the new Customs House, at the point where the canal joined the bay.

Between the seashore and the low cliff where the rocky mountain began – the spot where I had planned the avenues and squares for the new city – lay an undefined area of beach, shrubs and muddy land, where a few precarious dwellings had been set up for workers or the fishermen who worked in the bay. One morning, a barefoot girl emerged from one of the huts, her large eyes dark, her hair tangled, her face dirty but friendly, her stride purposeful, perhaps a nice figure concealed beneath her tattered garments. She was holding an oval-shaped fish by its tail.

"It's a *muixarra*," she said when I showed my surprise. "Papa told me to give it to you."

"Thank you, but I don't think I know him. Why does he want to give it to me?"

"Because he does. Because he says you are a friend of the King – but I don't want to give it to you."

"Why is that?"

"Because I don't, not if you are a friend of the King!"

"Ah! If you don't want to give it to me, I can't take it. What do you have against the King?"

"It's obvious! If they finish the city, we will have to leave – and this is all we have."

I looked at her dirty feet, her rags, her bold attitude, her nimble hands, the shiny fish dripping with water.

"I cannot take it."

"If you don't, my father will kill me."

"I cannot take it – I don't know how to cook," I said absurdly, since the men from the Customs House would have prepared it for me. "But you probably do – would you cook it for me?"

I came to an arrangement with Maria's father, who in spite of his kind gesture did not seem to trust me, and she became my cook when I stayed in Ràpita, as she proudly called the place.

Maria was sixteen years old, and with the first wage she received from me she asked that I buy her some proper clothes in Tortosa. She would only wear them when she was with me in the Customs House; she said her parents did not want to see her so well dressed. I begged her to make use of my toiletries, and when she reappeared with a clean face and combed hair, her clothes tidy, I saw a very beautiful girl in front of me.

When she finished serving my table, she would withdraw to the kitchen, but when her work was done, she would ask permission to come in again. I remember the devotion with which she turned the pages of a book for the first time: she was fascinated, asked questions, her eyes following the lines of the maps and drawings. She was so anxious to discover new things that I finally agreed to teach her to read. She wanted to see more books, more drawings, wanted to hear the details of all my travels.

I spent many hours in the Customs House in the company of this young girl who waited on me. She had unexpectedly become my disciple, and I was filled with an inexplicable sense of well-being from living in that area. I began to feel a bond with that world, far removed from the whimsical decisions of a bitter king or a favour-seeking minister.

So distant seemed the days of my youth when I would wake up at night, afraid I would die without anyone realizing or caring, frightened at the thought of not knowing who

I was, where I was, who I belonged to – afraid that when the voices from the salons had vanished, the pleasure of the balls faded, I would be besieged by solitude and darkness, and the many faces I had seen and greeted would mean nothing to me.

The nightmares vanished. Almost without realizing it, I exchanged them for the colours of a crushed pomegranate on a sunny day, for the scent of a juicy peach, for the heady wine from the nearby vineyards, for the murmur of a ship's prow on the still waters of the Alfacs, for the blue shadows that swathed the Montsià as night fell, for the nocturnal song of crickets all round the lighted house – for Maria's smile.

It was May 1780, and the time had come for the King to decide whether he still wanted to build the new capital that he had dreamt about – St Charles, the meeting place of trade and art – or if it was enough that the navigable Ebro River now had a proper opening to the sea and a small settlement of people.

Together with Floridablanca and Sabatini I had prepared my latest proposal, which covered the architectural, legal and political aspects of the project. All we had to do was to submit it to His Majesty, who would need to take the helm in order to make of St Charles the great work of his kingdom. We were at Aranjuez, and the hustle and bustle of people was intense. Many of the dignitaries who had heard of the project followed the events with great interest: some had even sent emissaries to the region so that the discussions would not take them by surprise. Merchants and landowners from Tortosa examined the situation to learn if their businesses would prosper or the price of their land increase.

Francesco Sabatini had settled in Aranjuez with his wife. Cecilia's salon was more animated than ever these days, as she was one of the best sources of information about the Court and government. Despite all her engagements, Cecilia was generous with her time. Our years of correspondence had kept our friendship alive, and on my annual trips to Madrid I had always paid her a visit. But now, in a few hours, the project for the new city would be approved, the greatest undertaking in all the kingdom of Charles III, and I would become the important man of the moment. All the more reason for her to be seen arm in arm with me.

I could never have suspected what had happened a few days before between Cecilia and her husband, the consequences of which would soon become apparent. With the natural frankness allowed by our friendship, I had spoken of Maria in my correspondence with Cecilia, and had told her how the girl had gained my affection, how she had helped me to settle in the area. Something dark from our former relationship must have re-emerged in Cecilia's heart, some unextinguished flame, perhaps a premonition motivated by a simple word from me. She responded to my confidences with humour and condescension, yet some fit of pride or jealousy led her – prompted, I hope, more by vanity or the heat of conversation than by a will to harm me – to boast to her husband that Tiepolo had made a portrait of her.

For all those years I had tried to conceal the existence of the painting; it had never left Madrid as I awaited a more appropriate, definitive home for the compromising portrait. In the meantime I had entrusted my good and truthful friend, Antoni de Capmany, to hide the cumbersome piece. He didn't know what lay behind the wrapping.

In a wild show of vindictiveness towards her husband, Cecilia convinced the poor Capmany that she must see that piece – it was a question of life or death. Faced with the impossibility of obtaining my permission quickly enough, she assured Capmany that she could be trusted. Knowing Cecilia's gift for persuasion and dissimulation, it's not difficult for me to understand why even the illustrious Capmany chose to console the lady rather than keep the word he had given his friend. Not only did she get access to Tiepolo's painting, but she also showed it to her furious husband, Francesco Sabatini. Capmany knew nothing of all this.

The architect grew dejected and melancholy, and remained so for several days, never speaking to his wife, shut away in his rooms. He could dismiss the rumours about his wife or turn a blind eye to her behaviour, pretend he was not aware of her frivolousness. For him it was enough to have her at his side, show her off from time to time, stroll with her through Madrid, be treated by her with respect. He could not, however, accept or consent to have this situation illustrated in such a blatant, humiliating manner, or allow the painter to raise this proof of his failure to the level of art. Francesco immediately recognized the outline of the city in the background, the same as in my plans, and found evidence in the painting of Cecilia's first mistake, the one that had hurt him most deeply and troubled him the longest.

But Sabatini knew how to remain calm. He waited several weeks, until the day of the meeting at Aranjuez. Even then he greeted me as always, and we worked together in the meetings preceding the decisive audience with the King. One hour before we were supposed to see the King, he sent for me. I found him at his desk in his darkened office. He asked me to sit in front of him, and I stared into his tearful eyes. He stood up slowly, walked about the room, and in a rising voice addressed these words to me:

"I trusted you as one trusts a friend. Not only did I speak highly of your work to His Majesty when you were still unknown, but I showed you the greatest confidence by placing myself in your hands at the delicate moment of my wife's arrival. I have always believed you a man of talent, one for whom the greatest work should be reserved. I always believed that you were destined for glory... but I have never understood the folly of some of your actions, the ingratitude with which you repaid my generosity, the vanity that has led you to believe that nothing could stop you on your road to success.

"But everything has a limit, my friend – we all have our limits. I know mine: I know when to yield, when to close my eyes. You, on the other hand, have not been able to appreciate my sacrifices or my warnings. How could you not understand? Was it not enough to have the King send you to that cold and remote city? Could you not see what this meant, not even when your correspondence was kept from you for a year? Was this all in vain? Can you not see how many bitter pills I have had to swallow? It was one thing to ignore where Cecilia ventured during certain hours of her day, quite another to know beyond a doubt that she spent her time with my assistant, my protégé, my friend!

"All of this has given me pain, has made me grow old before my time, but I've endured it, knowing that one day it would end, that either the royal will to build the new city or Cecilia's whim would separate the two of you. And so it was. I thought that the years would cure my anger, my fury, but I was mistaken again. I could never have imagined that you would be so foolish as to transform your folly into something lasting. I have seen the painting by Tiepolo – another miserable soul – and I can assure you that I will never forgive you for this. As long as the painting exists, so too will my curse upon you.

"No, wretched Andrea, no. It doesn't matter if this happened some ten years ago. I was prepared to bear all except this – to be portrayed by that painting in this manner. Rest assured I know how to punish you, how to fill you with bitterness. I can promise you that the city that Tiepolo painted will never exist, and the privileges you have enjoyed so far will be taken from you. Farewell, Señor Roselli, when we gather before the King in half an hour we will both be different people."

Sabatini kept his word. Contrary to everything that he, Minister Floridablanca and I had discussed, Francesco Sabatini now delivered an elaborate speech to the King in which he argued that instead of the plan for the great city, we should have a simple village carrying out the necessary port activities. José Moñino listened in astonishment, unable to defend the original plan – perhaps sensitive to the fact that he would be liberated from the huge expense

of building the city and could invest the capital in roads
and other transportation projects throughout the country,
especially in Madrid and around the royal residences. I
refrained as much as possible from speaking, knowing that
for once I had to show prudence – a quality Francesco had
found wanting in me. The King did not have the strength
to go against three of his advisers who, through their
actions, consent or silence, seemed to agree on the policy
to be followed. Naturally, Sabatini knew how to dress the
declaration with the necessary pomp, so that it seemed the
best choice rather than the end of a dream.

I left the Court of Aranjuez that same evening and hurried
to Madrid, to Capmany's house, where I was able to verify
that the painting was still there in one piece. Here I also
learned about Cecilia's visit a few days before. Early the
following day I left Madrid, bringing the canvas with me.

I knew that Sabatini would have the means to persuade the
King. Work on the city of St Charles was brought to a halt,
and soon after a messenger made his solemn appearance at
the palace in Tortosa to inform me of the suspension of my
employment, salary and benefits, including the lodgings
where I was receiving him. The Crown declared me "free"
of any obligation, and Floridablanca informed me that he
had named his own representative to supervise "the pending
works" and the completion of those "in progress".

I could have tried to fight the decision and prove to the
monarch that the decision was unwise. I could have decided
to return to my country – in Florence or Rome I would
have found projects of interest – or even offer my services

to a different monarch, another lord. Perhaps Catherine of Russia would have remembered the young architect who had seen the frescoes in Pompeii. But, instead, I came to an agreement with Floridablanca's representative – a considerate, pragmatic man – and rented the part of the Customs House I had used on many occasions. I settled there in the wing that was not needed for official matters.

I waited for time to be the judge of my decision; I had, after all, sufficient income to allow me to live for the rest of my days. Maria continued to grow: not only did she look after the house, but she spent more and more time in the library I had put together at the Customs House. Her natural intelligence grew with the encouragement of culture.

"So, the King's city will not be built?"

"Not now."

"Not now?"

"No, it will never be built."

"And will you leave?"

"I don't know. Not at the moment."

"Not at the moment?"

"Never."

I thought to myself: "I will stay to see the ships sail through the canal into the open sea. I will stay because I have known too many cities that have never been mine. I will stay so that you will come in the afternoons and open these books and the pale light will illuminate your sun-browned face. I will stay because I am nobody, and in the service of nobody, and there will never be a king who can take from me what is mine!"

In the end, the minister's representative was more occupied in supervising the departure of officials than in assuring that the essential buildings were actually finished. Of the thousands of men who had worked on the construction of the canal, a few hundred remained to build the first edifices of the village. More workers would join them as the urban centre grew. None of them were willing to leave, even though fewer and fewer buildings were commissioned as the days and months passed. Some devoted themselves to agriculture, others to the sea; a few tradesmen stayed, as more people arrived needing houses, clothes and food.

A new town was growing without the King's or his minister's knowledge. On the site where palaces should have stood, modest houses were raised. Simple fishing boats occupied more space in the port than the merchant ships crossing the Atlantic. Instead of magistrates and courtly people, peasants made their way through the great avenues and squares we had planned. Rather than the grand church that had been envisioned, religious ceremonies were held in the remains of the ancient monastery.

I knew that the government would not leave this budding town to itself, as they needed to secure a permanent settlement at the mouth of the canal and near the port, which had been built with such enormous effort. But this was put in doubt when a frightening rise of the Ebro covered part of the canal with slime, making it unusable for large boats. I watched as the ministry stopped all maintenance work on the canal, much to the dismay of the supervisor, who gave up for good after a quartan epidemic spread through the community.

253

Now that the canal was rarely used, almost the entire Customs House was ours, and Maria had been using part of the building to teach ten of the village children how to read and write. Three of them died in the outbreak, and a shadow was cast on our lives. I realized then that I could not afford to lose the most valuable thing I had encountered during the whole of my strange life of travels and hard work. With a mischievous look, she asked:

"You will not leave?"

"No."

"Not now?"

"Never."

"Why?"

"Because I love you."

We were married in the ruins of the old convent – the most precarious church in the Mediterranean. I don't know when the new church will be completed: it's being built slowly, with patience, outside the village, with the approval of the bishop, and consequently the passive acceptance of the ministerial representative. With its white limestone columns and its sienna tiles on the walls, the church stands among olive groves as an invitation to hope, a human-scale homage to beauty, a jewel from the nephew of the Aretine goldsmith dedicated to the disinherited who have remained in St Charles. It will be the monument to a city dreamt by a king – a city that we will make real as we begin to awaken from the long slumber of our servitude.

But it is in the humble chapel of Ràpita that tomorrow we will christen our first child; and Maria will wear the ring made by the great Alessandro Roselli of Arezzo.

When I am troubled by doubts that perhaps this was not the port where I should have anchored, renouncing all courtly honours and contact with people of high rank, I only need to climb to the garret of our Custom House and let my eyes grow accustomed to the half-light. There I unveil Tiepolo's painting and I am filled with his spirit of life and liberty.

* * *

With no time to fully grasp the discovery of the last page of Andrea Roselli's memoirs, inebriated, filled with his spirit and aspirations, I let myself be guided by Ariadna. Night has fallen over the town, over the bay and the fields of the delta.

Outside the town, we follow a road that is still muddy from yesterday's downpour, and in the shadow of night I glimpse a vague shape, like a dismasted ship: the Palau del Canal – Roselli's Customs House. The building was the last remnant of the Invisible City and had not only suffered the ravages of time and neglect, but had been used as a municipal warehouse before turning into the ruinous, sad structure of today, its doors and windows haphazardly boarded up. The surrounding area is covered with discarded building material, and the shrubs have grown so thick that it's difficult to find the shattered roof of the silo where we used to enter as children.

Ariadna won't let me help her as she walks with her crutches from the car to the only serviceable door that remains. After several shoves it gives way and we enter. Using Ariadna's flashlight we look around, but it is no better inside than it is out: it's impossible to make our way through parts of the ground floor, because the ceiling has collapsed. We see some stairs in the section of the building that has remained intact, and go up them. Once we're on the first floor, Ariadna consults a rough diagram she made based on Roselli's comments.

Using some old pieces of wood strewn about the floor, I improvise a rather dangerous scaffold, and I manage to climb into the garret. My first sensation is relief. From the outside, the sloping roof seems to be in ruins, but the interior of this triangular room is in reasonably good condition. I crouch as I move forward, across joists and beams, using the light to help me find my way along the full length of the garret. I step carefully, for the floor has given way in places and I could go straight down. Ariadna yells up to me, checking that I'm all right, wanting to know if I'm making any progress, but the results are so far very disappointing. She calls out to me, insisting that I start over at the first area I examined. The memoirs – the part full of technical data and routine annotations that I didn't bother to translate – seemed to suggest that this was the spot.

I continued to search for another hour. It made no sense: it couldn't have been hidden here. As I was about to give up, manoeuvring myself to start back down to where Ariadna was impatiently waiting for me, my body hanging half out of the opening through which I had gained access to the garret, my eyes at the level of the garret floor, I make an important discovery: directly beside me, the space between two of the joists is not the same as elsewhere. But it's too late, I'm already down.

"I want to go up!" the shadow of Ariadna says when we're together and I explain what I had just noticed.

"Are you crazy? You could kill yourself, and besides I don't know how—"

"You can help me climb up there. Do you think I could miss this chance? There's an old ladder outside, among the rubbish – go get it."

As we both lie face down on the timber floor of the garret, we hear a creak, close and far away, as if the entire building were howling. The sound is the only thing that gives us an idea of how big this place is, for the flashlight is pointing at the spot we are interested in, while the rest lies in noisy darkness.

"What was the other reason?" I ask in a low voice as we tap the beam that has caught our attention.

"It's a hollow beam! Like a long compartment, large enough for..." Ariadna says, not daring to complete the sentence and ignoring my question. "I've got it! There's some kind of cover that we have to lift..."

Hidden inside the beam we discover a long leather sack; we carefully remove it and place it on what seems to be the soundest spot on the wooden floor. I tremble to think that this might be the canvas that Antoni de Capmany kept in his house for his friend Andrea – until Cecilia's indiscretion provoked Sabatini's vengeance, which eventually meant that this city would remain invisible for ever...

"Let's go down – we can open it at home," I propose, mainly because the building seems so unstable, but also to give this treasure the attentions it deserves.

"No. We have to open it here to make sure it contains what we think it does. And then I'll tell you the other reason I sent you the memoir."

Ariadna flashes the light on the sack, and I undo it, uncovering a roll of dusty canvas. A few moments later – both of us on our knees, Ariadna leaning against me to keep her balance with her arm around my back – the burgundy dress, the pomegranate lips, the gesture that invites you to rebel and to live, the wise and determined look, the blue domes of the Invisible City are finally revealed to us.

"Now put the light down and listen to me."

But what I feel is the fragrance of her skin against mine, her moist lips biting my neck, kissing my eyes, her body overcoming mine, drawing me towards that encounter too long postponed, the struggle to recover that moment before the tragedy.

15
Epilogue

In the few surviving pictures of her, my mother is always standing next to me and my grandfather, as if she had never had a life before the one filled with bitterness and denial that followed my arrival in the world. I wouldn't have thought more about that had it not been for Father Patrici's insistence and the magazine from the summer of 1966 – the one that was missing part of a page, as Daniel the Tiger told me.

My mother used to keep those photos in a tin cookie box. When I closed down the family home in town and moved the few remaining things to the house on the bay, I remember carrying the tin box and not daring to look inside. It has remained closed all these years, but now Ariadna – who seems to shrink from nothing – has given me the courage to open it. I've discovered that mother kept a few other things in addition to the pictures of my grandfather and me. Not many, but they are very revealing.

I had never seen any of the other photos. They are all newspaper or magazine clippings from 21st June 1966, the day when General Franco visited the region before embarking on the *Azor*, the yacht that was docked at the port of Sant Carles de la Ràpita, heading for Barcelona. In all the pictures – even the one that was cut from the magazine I had lent Daniel – my mother is standing in front of her house, surrounded by a crowd of people who are waving to the haughty general and his retinue. Among the dignitaries accompanying him stands out the provincial Member of Parliament from Tortosa, Juan Coll, and – surprisingly – his son who, as far as I know, didn't hold any official position in the town, but was clearly pleased to form part of the entourage.

José Antonio Coll is the man my mother is waving to in all of the photos. Although I've never seen him, I recognize him because he looks very much like his son, Armand Coll, today: bald with one surviving tuft of hair.

The pictures were taken the month before my mother danced one night on the beach with a French or Belgian man – according to the ambiguous and always discouraging accounts I was given. Two months later she fainted in the wine shop. Ten months after the photos were taken, I was born. A bit more than twelve years passed until the fraternal Armand Coll came to rescue me from loneliness in front of a deserted school door. Would he have known at that time? Did he ever know? Do I want to know?

If history is a just a predetermined sequence from one point or another in the past, then it's not for me. I like history if it's filled with a passion that excites me, stimulates me and nourishes me. If it makes me what I am. If I can make myself what I am. Otherwise, it would only be the acceptance of tragedy.

This is why I repudiate the Colls and run to embrace Andrea Roselli. This is why I have spent time examining the earliest annotations in the parish archives in Sant Carles de la Ràpita, which miraculously survived the fire of 1936. They date from the 1790s, not from the 1780s, so they do not record the marriage of Andrea and Maria and the birth of their child, which is mentioned in the memoirs.

In the registry, however, I discover my forefather, under the name and trade adapted to his new life. On Easter Sunday 1791 their son, born two days before, is christened, the third child of Maria Pipop and *Andreu Rossell, mestre d'obres – master of the works*. My benighted people on their path towards light.